Bias Cut

A NOVEL

Morgan Richter

Luft
Books

Published in the United States by Luft Books, New York
www.luftbooks.com

Cover design by Morgan Dodge

Library of Congress Control Number 2012915264

ISBN 978-0-9859768-0-4

*To my parents,
Erich & Verna Richter*

In remembrance

WHEN NASH CALLED to ask for a favor, it took Nicola a moment to consider the request. Nash was a good friend, dating all the way back to their undergrad days at Berkeley, and she was a pretty decent person, and perhaps most apropos to Nicola's present situation, she ran her own business and thus might be a possible source of future employment. Everything considered, it wouldn't be a bad thing to have Nash owe her one.

Still, the forced cheer in Nash's tone made her wary.

"Maybe. I don't know. What's up?"

"I've got an interview set for noon today, but this other thing just came up. I've already rescheduled once, and I don't want to seem like a flake by postponing it again, so . . . Could you do it? It'll be fun, I promise."

"Let me think. Who are you interviewing?"

"Laurie Sparks? From *NYC Elite*? It's on MTV, I don't know if you've seen it."

NYC Elite. A reality show, Nicola knew, though she hadn't watched anything on MTV in years. Decades, maybe. She'd seen glossy advertisements plastered on subway walls and adorning the tops of cabs, some nonsense about a gaggle of nubile young creative types making their way in the big city. Actors, or artists, or an assortment of both.

It looked annoying as all hell. The title alone set her teeth on edge. "Never heard of her."

On the other end of the line, Nash giggled. "Him. Laurie Sparks. He's a boy. LSD."

"Huh?" Somewhere along the line, Nicola had lost track of the conversation. She picked up a slim gold pencil and scrawled "Laurie Sparks" onto a tablet by the phone. The tablet had gold-bordered pink sheets patterned with fancy hats and stiletto-heeled shoes, drawn in a spindly Gorey-esque style that made them look like squashed spiders. Spiders would be an improvement.

The tablet was Donya's, the pencil was Donya's, the glass-topped slim-legged console table it rested upon was Donya's as well. Everything in the apartment, the rose-colored throw rugs and the plush amethyst sofa and the pink crystal chandelier, it all belonged to Donya. The bulk of Nicola's worldly goods, twelve boxes filled with pots and pans and paperbacks, were stacked in a storage locker on the west end of Pico back in Los Angeles. Until she found a job, it didn't seem right to clutter up this dainty jewel box of an apartment with her unfussy, utilitarian things.

Alex had kept all the furniture, back in L.A. He'd offered to divide it up, but she hadn't had much use for it.

"LSD. Laurie Sparks Designs. Adorable little shop on Prince. Those coats with the hoods attached with loops that all the skinny hipster chicks are wearing, you've seen those, right? They were huge last year. Those are his, he designed those. He's kind of a big deal."

Nicola glanced at the clock. Almost eleven. "Look, I'd love to help, but I can't interview someone I've never heard of before. It'd be a disaster. I wouldn't know what to ask him."

"No sweat, I threw together a bunch of questions already. I'm emailing them to you right now. Please? This month has been crazy. Normally I've got Heather to help with the site, but she's visiting her folks in Buffalo, and I'm *slammed*."

"What's your conflict? A better interview?"

"No. Well, yeah. Paula Abdul." Nash giggled. "She's holding a group interview with a bunch of bloggers this afternoon, I just now wrangled myself an invite, and . . . I mean, I can't pass it up. It's *Paula*."

"Laurie Sparks will be crushed to hear he rates lower than Paula Abdul."

"Does that mean you'll do it?"

Nicola closed her eyes and overrode her knee-jerk impulse to refuse. "What do I have to do?"

"Thanks, Nick." A rush of gratitude flooded through the phone, an almost tangible warmth, and Nicola immediately felt better about the decision. "I'll let his people know about the change. You're going to meet him at noon in the tearoom at the Shire-Kinsey. On Eighth, near . . . 46th or something, I don't know. Midtown. You'll have to tape it, obviously. Do I need to loan you a recorder?"

"I can borrow one from Donya."

"Great. Pick up the tab for whatever he orders; I can reimburse you tonight, if you want to meet for drinks later. Just ask him my questions, try to engage him in conversation, flatter his ego. Don't make me look bad."

"Don't mention Paula, in other words?"

"That, yeah. But bluff your way through it the best you can. Maybe you shouldn't mention that you don't know anything about him."

"Why not? Does he have an ego problem I should know about?"

"No, nothing like that. I haven't met him, but he's adorable on his show. You'll love him. He's this huge drama queen. Totally over the top," Nash said. "Hey, I've got to run. Check your email. And thanks again."

"Give my best to Paula," Nicola said, but Nash had already clicked off, before she could point out that "huge drama queen" didn't sound like much fun at all.

She pulled on her gray suit, the one she kept pressed and ready for interviews. Black loafers without heels, good for navigating the subway. No jewelry. A quick dash of lipstick, just to be fancy. Then she plopped down in a chair (tiny, dainty, gold-painted) in front of Donya's laptop (sleek and high-tech, with a lavender protective cover featuring a silk-screened print of swallows in flight) and prepared to do some lickety-split research on Laurie Sparks.

A rustle of keys at the front door. Nicola looked up as Donya entered. "Hi. I thought you were going to Arizona?"

"Change of plans." Donya dropped her oversized satchel with a thud. "The Cold War retrospective got scrapped. So, no Titan Missile Museum." She slipped out of her shoes, four-inch crocodile pumps. "Ouch. These have been destroying my feet all morning."

She padded across the living room, bare feet on the gleaming wood floors, then flopped into an overstuffed armchair and tucked her legs beneath her. She looked like an urban Scheherazade, all face-framing wings of black hair and large dark eyes.

"Sorry about that," Nicola said, most of her attention still on the laptop screen. Laurie Sparks. The first search result was his company site, LSD. Women's clothes, young and flashy. Dark wool coats and short satin dresses. Wasn't too helpful, so she moved on to his Wikipedia page.

"No biggie. We're going in another direction. Less newsy, more breezy. More gossip and entertainment pieces, in other words. The Cold War didn't cut it." Donya was a correspondent for a prospective reboot of *PM Magazine*. It was set to launch next month, though the focus seemed to shift daily. "They're sending me to L.A. tonight, so I have to repack. Need to bring my glamorous Hollywood clothes instead of my I'm-a-serious-journalist wardrobe. I'm doing a new segment. *The Facts of Life: Where Are They Now?*"

"High concept," Nicola said. She scanned the Wikipedia article. Laurie—Laurent, actually—Sparks was all of twenty-two. His clothing line had shown a profit of close to fifty million dollars the previous year. Egad.

"Totally." Donya smiled. "You want me to bring anything back from L.A. for you?"

"My self-respect, if you should happen to find it. I think I left it somewhere on the Sony lot."

"Will do." Donya looked at Nicola as if seeing her for the first time. "Hey, you're wearing your interview outfit."

"I am indeed."

"Is this a good thing? Do you, in fact, have an interview?"

"Yeah, but I'm on the wrong side of it." Nicola printed out the Wikipedia page and checked her email. Yes, there was a message from Nash already, containing a short list of questions and directions to the Shire-Kinsey Hotel. She printed that as well. "You know my friend Nash?"

"The *HyperReality* girl? Sure."

"I'm interviewing some reality star for her site this afternoon. Is it okay if I borrow a recorder?"

"Knock yourself out. That's cool. Which reality star?"

"Laurie Sparks? *NYC Elite?*"

Donya snorted. "Oh, boy. Nash hates you."

Nicola turned to look at her. "She assured me I'll love him."

"She lied. He's a mouthy little fameball. Mind you, I only watched that damn show once, so I might not be the best judge, and honestly, he's probably no worse than anyone else on there, but..." Donya rolled her eyes. "At a guess, he's going to drive you crazy. Oil and water."

Nicola looked at the tiny snapshot on Laurie Sparks's Wikipedia page. It was cropped from some larger photo; the caption indicated it was taken at a press conference for the launch of *NYC Elite*. A puff of bleached hair, dark smudgy eyes. Could be Laurie Sparks, could be Debbie Harry, or Madonna circa *Who's That Girl?* She skimmed the article. "Hey, his mom is Maggie Sparks."

"Who?"

"Former Senator from Pennsylvania. She was a big deal in the eighties. Sort of a bad-ass. She pushed for unilateral nuclear disarmament, not that it went over very well at that time."

"Huh. Too bad the Cold War got scrapped. I could've interviewed Laurie's mom," Donya said. "Is Nash paying you for this?"

"I'm getting a free lunch out of it, I think. Maybe post-interview drinks, too. This is just a favor for a friend. No big deal."

"Sure." Donya smoothed the hem of her skirt over her bare knees. "You going to be able to cover your share of rent next month?" Casual, so casual.

"Yeah, no worries." She could cover it, probably. "I'm good."

"Great." Donya glanced at her and frowned. "Do you want to borrow something to wear?"

Nicola looked down at her outfit. "Is this okay?"

"Sure. But he's a designer, you know, and that jacket is, what, Gap?"

"Old Navy, I believe. For me, Gap is aspirational." Nicola retrieved Nash's questions and the Wikipedia article from the printer tray. She'd take a crash course in Laurie Sparks on the train. "He's a designer, I'm not. If he doesn't like what I'm wearing, then screw him."

"You're interviewing him, Nicola. You're trying to establish rapport. It should be *friendly*." Donya looked at her. "You're going to be nice to him, right?"

"I'm always nice."

"You're a pussycat. But you've got to admit, you've been a little raw since moving here."

Nicola felt a quick stab of irritation. "Not without reason," she said.

"No, but there's no sense taking it out on little Laurie Sparks. Don't bite his head off, okay?"

"Good advice. I'll take it under consideration." Nicola picked up her messenger bag.

"Let me get you that recorder." Donya disappeared into her bedroom. She was gone a suspiciously long time. Nicola heard the jangling of coat hangers and winced.

Donya came back with the recorder, plus a handful of colorful silk, an ornately patterned square of blue and gold and black and violet. "Here. It's vintage Hermès." She draped the scarf around Nicola's neck, tucked it beneath the lapel of her jacket, and tied it into a loose knot. She stepped back and scrutinized her handiwork. "Check it out. See the difference?"

Nicola glanced in the mirror that rested atop the brick mantel. The scarf made the gray of her suit look richer, brought out a hint of blue in her muddy eyes. She looked wealthy and glamorous. She felt silly and affected. "I can't borrow this. I don't want to lose it."

"I don't want you to lose it, either." Donya smiled. "You're meeting Laurie on his own terms, see? You're putting him at ease by showing him you're a stylish woman who can work an Hermès scarf, right?"

"If you say so." She glanced in the mirror again. Damn it, the scarf really was an improvement. "Thanks, Donya. It looks great."

"Good." Donya gave her a quick hug and an airless kiss on each cheek. She smelled like jasmine tea and tuberose. "Have a blast. You can tell me all about it when I get back in town."

And Nicola was off, striding toward the subway entrance. It was a sticky late summer morning, the last gasp of heat before the cooler days of September, and it was much too warm for her jacket. She'd be sweaty and gross by the time she arrived at the hotel.

As soon as she was a safe distance from their apartment, Nicola whipped off the scarf. She folded it into a tiny triangle and stuffed it into a zippered pocket in her messenger bag.

CHAPTER TWO

THE EXTERIOR OF the Shire-Kinsey Hotel had no identifying features, save for a small plaque engraved with an ornate "S-K" mounted on the wall beside the bronze revolving door. Nicola strode right past it, then had to double back after checking the address on the email from Nash. At ten minutes to noon, she entered the lobby.

Dark, confusingly so after the brightness of outside. She hovered near the door and tried to orient herself.

The entrance to the tearoom was located to the right of the concierge desk. Nicola glanced into it. At the hostess stand, a pretty woman with very straight hair gave her a welcoming smile.

A pair of women in flowery sundresses sat at a table in the front window, sipping tea and nibbling tiny cakes, but the tearoom was otherwise empty. No sign of anyone who looked like Debbie Harry. Nicola considered asking the hostess for a table, then decided against it. Laurie would have to pass through the lobby anyway, so she sat down on a leather loveseat with a view of the front door and waited.

She discreetly reviewed Nash's questions for Laurie: *Are you coming back for a second season? How has being on television changed your life? What do you have to say to critics of the show?* Soft lobs. Due to the nature of Nash's site, the questions focused on Laurie's reality-show career instead of his fashion-designer career. Nothing too intrusive or obscure. With a bit of luck and a dose of moxie, she should be able to muddle her way through this.

Twelve o'clock. Twelve-fifteen. No sign of Laurie. The hotel lobby was small and tasteful, all muted grays and mossy greens. Tinkling piano music played, piped in through unseen speakers overhead. Not a luxury hotel, just a cute boutique, but still plenty nice.

Twelve-thirty, twelve-forty. Nicola walked around, used the ladies' room, peered into the tearoom again to make sure she hadn't missed her tardy interview subject. Menu in hand, the pretty hostess gave her another optimistic smile. Nicola hastily withdrew.

It was ten minutes after one, and Nicola was giving serious thought to leaving, when Laurie Sparks came gliding in through the revolving door.

A magical fairy creature. A puff of white-gold hair darkening to copper at the roots, a face covered with well-applied makeup. Glossy peach lips, eyes lined in bronze and shaded with gleaming gold above a velvety black fringe of lashes. His skin was pale and creamy and flawless. He was tiny, maybe all of five-four in his black leather boots, which, Nicola noted, had bronze kitten heels. He wore a ruffled violet blouse underneath a shimmering silver-gray suit, which was meticulously tailored to fit his pixielike form.

Her hips were bigger than his. Her shoulders were broader than his. Her waist was wider than his. When Nicola got to her feet and waved a hand for his attention, she felt like something lumbering and clumsy and enormous. A water buffalo, maybe. "Laurie Sparks?"

Huge eyes blinked in her direction. They were light green, almost yellow, like sunlight on a budding plant. She'd had a cat with eyes that color, long ago. "Yes. You're Nashville?"

Nicola paused. "No. Sorry. Nash couldn't make it. I thought she'd explained—"

"No, she did. I just got confused." The small peach mouth drew into a tight line, as though the switch wasn't entirely to his satisfaction. "I don't know your name."

"Nicola Strozyk. Nice to meet you." She held out her hand. After the slightest hesitation, Laurie took it. His hand, like the rest of him, was tiny and fragile. Nicola shook it gently. Bird bones. She might crush him by accident.

He looked up at her. His gaze was frankly assessing, and Nicola felt a flush of self-consciousness. He was noting the disparity in their sizes, noting her cheap suit and her sensible shoes.

He raised his pointed chin and jutted it in the direction of the tearoom. "Well. Should we have tea?" he asked. A flutter of lashes, flirty and mischievous. "And by 'tea' I mean 'champagne.'"

"Fantastic," she said. Champagne. Well, Nash *was* reimbursing her, right?

The pretty hostess with the straight hair gave Nicola a pleasant smile and Laurie a dazzling one and led them to a quiet back corner. She lingered a bit after they were seated, her attention fixed on Laurie, her smile still cranked up to maximum wattage. Did she recognize him, or did she just instinctively realize he was somebody to be fussed over, someone worthy of special treatment and secret smiles, someone several notches above the plain-Jane Nicolas of the world?

When the hostess tried to hand them menus, Laurie waved them off. "We're having the full champagne tea," he told her.

"Of course." A flash of teeth. "What kind of tea do you want?"

"I don't care. Something without caffeine. Ginger."

She smiled and turned to Nicola. With no menu to consult, Nicola was lost. "Ah . . . same."

The hostess smiled and withdrew. Laurie settled back in his chair and crossed his legs at the knee. Pale fingers drummed on the pale wood table. His manicured nails looked like chips of mother-of-pearl. "I live for caffeine in the morning, but later in the day it

10

makes me twitchy," he said. "I have a lot of work to get done today."

Then maybe champagne wouldn't be the smartest move. Nicola smiled in a neutral way and glanced around. Brass fixtures and olive green walls, with leafy plant fronds dangling down from hanging bronze pots. Watercolors on the wall, muted washes of pastels depicting teacups and high-heeled shoes. Shoes were having a big moment as a popular artistic motif. Nicola hoped the moment passed soon.

"I've never been here before," she said. "It's nice."

The pretty mouth twisted into a quick grimace. The tiny hand gave a dismissive flick. "It's okay. They only use the cheap champagne here. Not the real stuff. The Italian kind. What's it called, prosecco?"

"Prosecco, yeah." Good news. Less pricey.

The cat eyes met hers. "So why couldn't the other girl make it?"

"Nash? I'm not sure. Something came up."

"I see." Nicola thought she'd sounded trustworthy and convincing, but something about his expression—somewhat irritated, somewhat bemused, somewhat challenging—made her think maybe Laurie Sparks had a little more on the ball than his frothy appearance would suggest. "Something more important than this?"

It was that expression, in fact, that made her reflexively switch tactics, change the subject, go on the offensive. "Did you have trouble finding the place?" she asked.

Now disdain crept in, blending with the bemused irritation on that pretty face. "It's just *midtown*," he said. He was quiet for a moment. "Oh. Was that because I was late? I'm always late. Most people don't mind." Wholly unapologetic, mildly incredulous that Nicola would even bring up such a trifling thing.

Yeah, this would be fun. "We should probably get started," she said. She brought Donya's recorder out of her messenger bag and set it on the table. She clicked it on. It was one of those tiny digital ones, about the size of her palm, both sleek and functional. "I'm recording this, is that okay?"

"It's fine. Obviously." Another assessing look from those cat eyes. "You're monstrously tall, aren't you? Six feet?"

"Just about."

"You'd look taller in heels."

It was such a spectacularly inane comment that Nicola revised her previous assessment of Laurie being maybe less fluffy and featherbrained than he looked. "I'm plenty tall enough."

"Were you a model?" he asked.

Under other circumstances, Nicola would suspect anyone suggesting this of trying to plump her ego. But Laurie seemed earnest, like he thought this was a real possibility, and in any case, he probably never gave much consideration to any ego outside his own. "Ha. No way. No."

"You could have been, though," he said. "Models used to be a whole lot heavier, back when you would have been young enough."

Still radiating sincerity and, at a guess, entirely unaware there was anything in that statement that might be viewed as tactless. "Nope, no modeling. I played volleyball at Cal. The height was kind of a plus for that."

A shrug, a small twitch of narrow shoulders. "Oh, sports. Sports are dull."

"Ditto for modeling."

For a second, she thought he was going to argue the point, which would have been a fascinating conversation. Then their server returned, bearing two trumpet flutes of fizzing prosecco, and Laurie found something more important to focus on. "Opinions vary," he said grandly. He accepted his glass from the server and hoisted it. "Cheers."

Nicola clinked in reply. "To a painless interview," she said. She hadn't meant it to sound sarcastic, she didn't think, but Laurie's beautiful eyes narrowed into beautiful slits, and the corner of his pretty mouth twitched.

Tea arrived immediately thereafter, served in a china pot patterned with nesting doves. Conversation ceased as Nicola poured it out into matching cups. Laurie drizzled honey into his, transferring copious amounts into his cup from a tiny crock.

Her phone buzzed. Laurie was still involved with doctoring his tea, so it didn't seem like it would be too impolite to ignore him for a second. She eased it out of her bag, flipped it open beneath the table, glanced down at the screen. Text from Nash: *Everything OK with Laurie?*

She texted back discreetly. *Yup. All good.*

Laurie looked up from his tea as she slipped it back into her messenger bag. "Is that a flip phone? I didn't know they still made those."

"Yeah. Jealous?"

He almost smiled at that. "Terribly," he said. He held out his hand. She passed it over. He flipped it open, stared at the dinky and inadequate display screen. "No internet access?"

"Decidedly not," Nicola said.

He passed it back and reached for his prosecco. "You're really behind the times, aren't you? How old are you?"

"Fifty-seven."

Laurie gaped at her, his glass frozen halfway to his mouth. "What?"

"Kidding. I turned forty last month."

"Wow. I can't imagine being forty," Laurie said cheerfully. "It seems so old."

"Naah, it's awesome. Already got my room in this kick-ass retirement home picked out. I'm looking forward to a lot of shuffleboard."

Laurie looked blank, as though he didn't find her especially amusing. Or maybe he wasn't sure she was joking, and wasn't that a lovely thought?

Sandwiches and cakes arrived next, served on a four-tiered china tray. Whole chocolate-dipped strawberries and glacéed orange slices, dainty sandwiches and savory tarts, and a glorious assortment of petit-fours and cream puffs with pastel fillings. Laurie perked up at the sight of these. He headed straight for the petit-fours and dove in. Prosecco and cake. Yeah, he was looking for a productive afternoon back at the . . . office?

He wouldn't have an office, would he? He was a designer, so it'd be a studio or something, right? She picked up a sandwich. Lox and crème fraiche on dark pumpernickel. Yum. "Where do you work? Do you have a design studio?"

Laurie bit into his cake. He chewed delicately, head tilted to the side, assessing the flavor. He'd already drained his glass; the server appeared at his side and wordlessly refilled it.

They probably charged a fixed price for the champagne tea. Nicola hoped they did, at least. If they charged by the glass, her bank account might be in trouble.

"Yes," Laurie said. More than a hint of acid in his tone. "I have a design studio. You know, the one that's featured on every single episode of my very popular television show? The show you're here interviewing me about?"

Well, crap. Nicola felt color rise in her cheeks. First question, and she'd already blown Nash's very reasonable request that she bluff her way through it. Laurie's reaction pissed her off, though, the arrogance and entitlement, the palpable disgust aimed at her for not being an expert on his life. She picked up her glass and drained it to give her some time to formulate a response. Nice stuff, this prosecco.

"Sorry," she said. "Haven't watched your show. Never heard of you until about two hours ago." She smiled once, brisk and impersonal, then returned her attention to the trays of treats. She picked up a miniature quiche and bit into the flaky crust. "Ooo. Crab. You should try this."

Laurie stared at her, his expression lethal. She smiled again. "I'm just the fill-in, remember?"

"Sure, but I assumed you'd be a qualified fill-in. That you'd be familiar with my show or, failing that, that you'd at least do some research," he said. "What kind of journalist are you?"

"Not any kind, actually. Not my line of work." She shrugged. "I'm just doing a favor for a friend in a pinch. Honestly, I'm not all that interested in you or your show. Everything I know about you, I gleaned from your Wikipedia article."

Laurie blinked his long, long lashes. "Wikipedia? Really?" he asked. "You're not kidding about not being a journalist, are you?"

"Cut me some slack, kiddo. I only had a few minutes to learn everything I could about you. No sense working yourself into a snit about it."

Laurie snorted. He drained his prosecco, and the server was at his elbow again for a refill, as noiseless and unobtrusive as before. She refilled Nicola's glass for good measure and withdrew.

"Yeah, okay." A shrug. "I'm sort of cranky today, I guess. Sorry."

As an apology, it seemed sincere enough, if a touch surly. He seemed very, very young, and almost human. She exhaled. "I wish I were better prepared for this. But I'm not, so we should probably try to make the best of it." She held up the list of questions. "Nash sent me these to ask you. Why don't we get through them as best we can and give her a salvageable interview?"

Laurie considered, then held out his hand. "Pass them over and I'll try to burn through them."

Nicola handed him Nash's email. He glanced down at the questions, the stem of his glass held between two slender fingers in his other hand. He was a gorgeous creature, really. His painted face was a work of art. Nicola doubted she'd worn that much makeup when she'd gone to her high school prom; she knew it hadn't been applied nearly as well. He was lovely and dainty and glamorous, and she wasn't immune to the appeal of that. Shame he was such a little snot.

"Here we go. Number one: Am I coming back for a second season of *NYC Elite*? Answer: If they renew it, probably. Maybe. I'll find out if we've been picked up in January, I guess. Number two: How has television changed my life? Answer: I was already famous for my clothing line before the show even started, so not so much. I guess my fans are getting younger. The MTV crowd, you know, tweens and high school kids." A quick glance at Nicola. "Old people tend to hate me, I've found."

It was a dig, but it wasn't worth calling him on it. Nicola sat back and let him ramble on. He went down the list, rattling off pat answers to the questions. Hopefully Nash wouldn't be too upset about this. It was an unsatisfying interview on pretty much all levels.

When he had finished, Laurie set down his now-empty glass and looked at Nicola with something approaching triumph. "There. Will that do?"

"Hell, why not?" As Nicola could have predicted, the server materialized at his side to refill his glass. Their glasses; she'd drained hers, too, without realizing it. Was that three now, or four? Maybe even five? Her tolerance wasn't bad, but the prosecco was starting to hit her. She was feeling a little reckless, a little expansive, simultaneously fonder and more disdainful of the snippy ball of fluff seated in front of her. She probably had a good thirty pounds on Laurie, maybe more, and the alcohol must be hitting him even harder. "Thanks for that. It makes it easier for us both."

"I quite agree." Yep, Laurie was tipsy. No slurred words, no visible signs of intoxication, but his speech was a little grander, the elegant arch of his brow a little more exaggerated. "What do you do,

Nicola?" he asked. "Since we've established that you are, in fact, not a journalist."

"Not even close." She giggled. Goddamn. She never giggled. "I am presently amongst the august and populous ranks of the unemployed. Which is why I had my afternoon free to botch this interview."

"Aren't I lucky?" Laurie looked over the trays, a hand hovering in the air. He picked up one of the strawberries and bit into the tip. A tiny kitten tongue shot out and licked a trace of chocolate off his upper lip.

"Before this, I was in Los Angeles. I was a researcher in the story department of Sony Entertainment for twelve years," she said. "I moved out here four months ago."

"Why? I mean, I get why you'd want to live in New York, but if you didn't have a job—"

"I had a job." It came out sharp. She dialed back the reflexive anger. "I was all set to work for a production company here, same sort of work, research." She shrugged. "They offered me a position when I was still in Los Angeles, they moved me out here, and the slump hit them hard. They downsized. My job was gone before I ever started it."

"You should sue them," Laurie proclaimed, all worldly experience at twenty-two.

"I should get a new job, that's what I should do."

"At least you get to live in Manhattan. It's better than L.A. anyway."

She shrugged. "Well, Queens, actually, but I get your point."

"I've never been to Queens," Laurie said. "Is it awful? It seems like it'd be awful."

Nicola laughed. A little loud, maybe, for this demure room. From her podium at the front, the hostess glanced over at them. Nicola lowered her voice. "No, Laurie, it's not awful. It's nice. It's not all that different from Manhattan. You should visit it sometime. Broaden your horizons."

"Thank you, no," Laurie said. "I've spent my life adding beauty to the world and avoiding tackiness. Queens is synonymous with tacky." He added an extra syllable and a superfluous "h" to "synonymous." "I mean, I've seen *Working Girl.*"

Nicola laughed again, involuntarily. "That was Staten Island, you—" She almost said "nitwit" and stopped herself just in time. Slinging insults at her tiny, drunken interview subject was probably not the correct approach. "*Working Girl?* Really? You need to update your pop culture references."

"Nonsense," he said with great dignity. "Anything that was worth happening in pop culture happened in the eighties." He leaned across the table, very earnest. "I grew up in the nineties. Isn't that the saddest thing you've ever heard?"

"Because . . . ?"

"Because I missed the most awesome decade ever entirely. My pop-culture reference points all start in the grunge era. All that flannel and unwashed hair, ugh."

"It's entirely possible you're a snob, kiddo."

"I should certainly hope so." A smile, the first real one of the afternoon. His bottom teeth were crooked in front. A rare flaw in all that immaculate prettiness, and probably the reason he didn't smile more. "You don't like me much, do you?"

Nicola considered. "I like your mom."

Whatever he was expecting her to say, it wasn't that. "Really?"

"We learned about her in school. She was great. I always thought 'Senator Sparks' sounded like the civilian alter-ego of a superhero."

"My mom is a superhero." Said without a trace of sarcasm or embarrassment. Laurie Sparks was an unapologetic mama's boy, and Nicola liked him for that.

The cakes were eaten, their teacups were drained, and the server seemed disinclined to bring them more prosecco, not that Nicola could blame her. The check arrived. Fixed price. Whew. She could pay it without wincing.

They left the hotel, Laurie wobbling on his kitten heels. The revolving door seemed to flummox him, but he figured it out eventually.

Tall buildings and crowded sidewalks, a cacophony of traffic noises, Eighth Avenue a stagnant river of stalled yellow cabs and delivery trucks. A traffic jam, or just the usual afternoon chaos of midtown? Was there any difference?

Laurie stood on the sidewalk and looked around. He seemed befuddled and helpless, or maybe just sort of drunk.

"I guess this is it," Nicola said. "Nice talking with you, Laurie."

"Okay." Laurie nodded without looking at her, his attention fixed on the street. He looked up and down the block in both directions, his tiny mouth drawn into a frown.

"I'm going to head to my stop now," she said. She paused. "Is someone picking you up, or . . . ?"

"I don't know," he said. Genuine wonder in his tone.

"How'd you get here?" she asked.

He looked at her, uncertain and blurry. "The girl at the desk in my studio called a car. I had an assistant," he said. "Jonathan. Jonathan was amazing. He always handled this sort of thing. And he left me last week." His face crumpled, and Nicola had the sudden panicked thought that he was about to burst into tears.

Nicola's sympathies were instantly with Jonathan, whoever he might be. "Call your studio and see if they're going to pick you up," she said.

"I left my phone there."

"Use mine." She handed it to him. "It's crappy and outdated, but it does, in fact, place calls."

"I don't know the number," he said.

His own studio. Jesus. He was useless and pathetic, but she had a civic responsibility to make sure he got wherever he needed to go without getting lost or murdered. "Just take a cab."

"My wallet's back in the studio, too," he said. "I was in a hurry to get here. I didn't want to be late," he added piously, and it was so patently untrue that Nicola wanted to laugh.

She stepped to the curb, hailed a cab, opened the back door, bundled the drunken magical fairy creature into the backseat, and handed the driver a twenty through the sliding partition, all in one seamless string of actions. "Take him wherever he needs to go," she said to the cabbie. "Goodbye, Laurie."

He didn't answer. He was already leaning forward, talking to the cabbie. Hopefully he was giving him an address, and hopefully it would be the correct one. She closed the door after him, then stepped back to the sidewalk and watched the cab pull out into traffic.

CHAPTER THREE

"SOUNDS LIKE YOU had an interesting time with Laurie," Nash said.

Nicola stirred the swizzle stick in her sangria, mixing up the chunks of apples and peaches. The stick was bamboo, topped with a little plastic bird. She didn't want the sangria, was still feeling dehydrated and bloated from all the prosecco, but it was nice to be here with Nash anyway. They sat at a picnic table in the tiny backyard of an East Village watering hole—in the "beer garden," as it was optimistically described on the sandwich board out front—while Nicola filled Nash in on her adventure with Laurie.

"It wasn't magical," she said. "Have you listened to the recording yet?" She'd emailed the digital file to Nash as soon as she'd returned to her apartment along with a few general notes about the interview: what Laurie wore, what he ate.

Nash smiled. She had a great smile, huge white teeth in a smooth brown face. Her generous frizz of hair was tied back in a silk scarf. Cropped pants, sleeveless cotton blouse, easy and breezy on a late-summer evening. "Oh, yeah," she said. "Like I said, interesting."

"Sorry for mangling things. Did I give you enough information to work with? Can you get an article out of that?"

"I had a bad moment right before leaving here. Laurie's publicist called me, asked for the correct spelling of your name. I thought Laurie might've complained to her about your, ah, unconventional interviewing style, but she seemed totally chill. Probably going to send you a thank-you note or whatever. I gave her your phone number."

"Crap. I hope I didn't get you into trouble."

Nash shook her head. "You did okay. I put you into a tough spot, I know, so that's on me. And it sounds like he was being a dick about it."

"He wasn't that bad, just bratty. Spoiled, but I guess you'd expect that. He's sort of a mess. He said his assistant just quit, and it seemed like that was enough to throw him off his game."

"Wait. His *assistant* quit? You mean Jonathan?" Nash was suddenly alert, and Nicola had no idea why. "You're kidding. When did he say this? It wasn't on the recording."

Jonathan. That was the name Laurie had mentioned, right? "It was after the interview was over and he was getting into a cab. No one had arranged for a car to pick him up, because Jonathan had just quit. I think that's what he said."

"Nicola, that's major. Jonathan's a huge part of his show. Like, he's everybody's favorite character." Weird the way people talked about reality-show participants as characters, like they surrendered their real-life identities in exchange for camera time. "Is Jonathan even going to be on the next season? Did he say anything about that?"

"He didn't say much at all. He seemed upset about it, but I think that was just because there wasn't a car. Our boy Laurie likes his creature comforts." Nicola sipped her sangria. Fruity goodness. "What's so special about Jonathan?"

"He's just a cool guy, you know? Smart, calm, grounded. He and Laurie were tight, which is funny, considering how Laurie's pretty much his polar opposite."

"Were they a couple, you think?"

Nash shrugged. "I doubt it. It would have come up on the show, because that's not an angle the producers would try to hide. Sex sells, right? Though I think they were friends before the show even started." She took a swig of her drink. An Old Fashioned, cherries and a long strip of lemon rind bobbing in whiskey.

"So Davey has this friend, Mike," Nash said. Davey was Nash's husband, a freelance studio percussionist. When Nicola first moved to New York, they'd invited her over for dinner in the cluttered shoebox they called an apartment, with the beanbag chairs and the handmade jute rugs and the omnipresent hash smell. They'd served a casserole made from orzo and organic broccoli rabe. "And we were hanging out with Mike the other night, and it dawned on me that you two might have a lot in common."

Nicola looked at her. "Oh. No. Thank you, but no."

"Not yet?" Nash looked a little disappointed, but not surprised.

"Not yet." *Not ever.*

"You sure? Doesn't have to be anything serious. Maybe you and Mike just want to get a drink sometime, hang out. He's a mellow guy. Zero pressure. Works at the Strand. The *Voice* did a piece on his personal collection of 1950s pulp novels." Nash considered her, her expression filled with earnest goodwill. "You haven't been yourself since you moved out here, Nick. You're a little . . . sour or something. Meeting new people might be good for you."

"Sour" wasn't good. Nicola had been rough lately, like her nerve endings were close enough to the surface that even a slight ruffle would trigger a reaction, but "sour" was worrisome. She looked down at the picnic table. Someone had scratched "Benji loves George" into the painted wood. Well, hooray for Benji.

"Thanks. It's nice of you to think of it, but it's not the right time for me," she said at last.

"No worries. Just thought I'd try." Nicola didn't look up from the table, but she could feel Nash staring at her, boring down on her with the full brunt of her concern and good intentions, and it felt like it might crush her.

HOME. A QUIET, dark apartment. Donya would be en route to Los Angeles by now. In a few hours she'd land at LAX, where she'd pick up a rental car and drive through the melancholy oil fields lining La Cienega, the still pumps standing like silent soldiers, before continuing on to the palm tree-dotted streets of West Hollywood on the way to her hotel. She'd probably stay on the Sunset Strip, someplace with a view of the posh hills to the north or the low sprawl of the city to the south.

Was this homesickness? She didn't want to be back in Los Angeles, she didn't think. Maybe she didn't want to be here, either.

Online. Check email.

One hundred and twelve new messages.

That couldn't be right. Nicola felt a spike of panic. Something bad had happened, a spammer had gone plumb loco with her address, or her account had been hacked.

Checked her inbox. Twitter followers, new ones, a series of unfamiliar screen names.

Well, huh. She scrolled through them, baffled. She had a Twitter account, mostly neglected, never put to any important use. She posted updates occasionally to her handful of followers: Donya, Nash, old classmates, former coworkers. Nothing in it to attract new followers in droves.

And there, at the very bottom of the never-ending list of emails, the Twitter message that started it off.

Twitter handle: HiLaurieSparks. Nicola clicked on the message. *You should follow @nicolastrozyk because I was a twat to her today.*

Nicola laughed out loud. And indeed, Laurie's Twitter followers—well, one hundred and eleven of them, anyway—had taken him up on his suggestion.

She checked out his Twitter page. It featured a professional portrait, in which he sported bright copper hair and the same exquisite makeup job and pouted sexily for the camera. He tweeted drivel, off-the-cuff observations about his life, where he'd been, what he'd eaten, what he felt: *The fall clothes in the windows at macys make me want to kill myself. Chocolate croissants are the greatest invention of our time. Pop music pretty much peaked with Kajagoogoo. Why do taxis always smell like ass?*

He had almost half a million followers. Damn.

She was charmed by the message about her, she had to admit, charmed he went to the effort to offer up this public mea culpa. She tweeted back at him:

@HiLaurieSparks Thanks. Nice meeting you. You were fine; sorry I was grouchy.

She hung around online for the rest of the evening, cleaning up her inbox, idly surfing a few favorite sites. Hoping to hear back from Laurie, her hopes riding far too high on it, not that she wanted to admit that to herself. Just hanging out online on a Friday night in a silent apartment in New York City, hoping for a spark of human connection from someone whom she hadn't liked all that much. Nothing pathetic about that.

No reply. After a while, after far too long, she gave up hoping and went to bed.

NASH'S ARTICLE WAS up on the *HyperReality* website by noon the next day:

A HyperReality Exclusive: Laurie Sparks speaks! The NYC Elite cutie weighs in on his runaway success and the future of his hit series. Reporting by Nashville Cabot.

When Laurie Sparks walks into the tearoom of the Shire-Kinsey Hotel, an exclusive Manhattan hotspot, you can feel the electric charge in the air. People stare openly. Our waitress appears to be in love. Laurie Sparks is Someone, and you can be sure everyone knows it.

The 22-year-old fashion wunderkind and breakout star of MTV's hit reality show NYC Elite sat down with HyperReality for a highly entertaining luncheon. He's ostensibly here to promote the DVD release of Season One, which comes out on Tuesday, but for this opinionated and ever-stylish pixie, no subject is off limits.

When we meet, he's resplendent in silver satin. He's wearing his trademark makeup, of course; he wouldn't be caught dead without it. "It's kind of part of who I am," he says thoughtfully over a lunch of strawberries and champagne (très glamorous and decadent, of course, but we'd expect no less from our Laurie). "I mean, it's become this huge part of my image, and what's fashion without image?"

In person, Laurie is more serious and less frivolous than you might think from watching him on the small screen, whether he's fretting about his collection for Fashion Week, or feuding with buyers, or getting into tiffs with his long-suffering loyal assistant, Jonathan. He's surprisingly grounded, in fact, especially when he speaks about the show that made him a star. "I have nothing bad to say about NYC Elite. The show's been good to me. I think it's quality television, really, and anyone who thinks reality programming is a waste just needs to watch an episode to be proven wrong. It's all about people, young people, who are good at what they do and are making a success at it. I think it's one of the more positive shows out there." His catlike green eyes twinkle with amusement when he adds, "And it's been pretty great for my clothing sales, too!"

Laurie is mum about the future of NYC Elite—he won't find out if it'll be back for a second season until January—but after the enthusiastic viewer response, it seems likely the lovely and talented Laurie Sparks will be on our screens for some time to come. We can't wait.

Oh, God. Nicola didn't know if she wanted to giggle or hang her head in shame at the train-wrecky aspect of the article. At least her name appeared nowhere on the piece. Which, come to think of it, was maybe a little unfair, but she'd be damned if she was going to complain about it. The article was awful.

She had to be fair to Nash, though—she and Laurie hadn't given her much usable material to work with.

Her phone rang. Unfamiliar number, 212 area code. "Hello?"

"Nicola? It's Laurie. Laurie Sparks."

"Oh. Hey." A brief surge of confusion. "Ah. Did you see the interview?"

"Just read it." His tone was dry, dryer than the prosecco they'd overindulged in yesterday. "If you could see me right now, you'd know that my catlike green eyes are twinkling in amusement."

"Oh, crap." Nicola cleared her throat. "Not to pass the buck too much here, but I didn't actually write that."

"I could tell. If you had, it would have included a comprehensive assessment of my failings." Laurie definitely sounded amused, and that was good, because Nicola didn't think she was up to dealing with a pissed-off reality-show diva today. "I'm pretty sure it would have included the word 'snob' at least once. Maybe even 'fame-whore.'"

"I wouldn't go that far. Though my roommate did refer to you as a 'mouthy little fameball' yesterday."

"Ouch. Unkind. Made all the worse by being sort of accurate." Laurie fell silent for a moment. "Hey, I wanted to thank you for yesterday. Putting up with me and all. I was in kind of a bad mood."

"No problem."

"I had something I wanted to ask you, actually. Are you free? I'm at the studio. If you could come by, that would be great."

She wasn't expecting that. "Ah . . . right now?"

"Whenever. I'll be here all day. Probably all night, too. I'm chained to this place until Fashion Week. Metaphorically, at least."

"Where are you?"

He recited an address on Prince Street. "It's just off Bowery. Upstairs from my shop. I'll leave your name with the security guy, and he'll send you up."

She glanced at the clock. Just after noon. "I'll probably be there around two, will that work?"

"Fine. Like I said, whenever. Seriously, I'm here all day. Not going anywhere."

He clicked off. Nicola was mystified. And intrigued. It was probably something dumb, like he wanted to return the twenty she gave him for the cab ride. Still, she found herself looking forward to seeing him again.

She might like Laurie Sparks, kind of a lot. That surprised her.

LAURIE SPARKS DESIGNS took up the eighth and ninth floors of a squat stone building in a cluttered SoHo neighborhood. As Laurie had mentioned, the LSD shop was on the ground floor. A small storefront space with a black awning with the LSD logo in ornate gold script above the door. Gold featureless mannequins, zombielike in their blankness, modeled belted wool coats in the windows. Clothes for cooler weather, a sign of autumn, which still seemed years away. Nicola glanced through the glass doors and saw throngs of stylish teen girls and hipster twentysomethings, all with artfully ragged haircuts and expensive shoes. Maybe the shop attracted tourists, too, fans of *NYC Elite* hoping to catch a glimpse of the dainty star, or maybe out-of-towners were scared off by the intimidating man with the wide shoulders and the expensive black suit who stood at the door—more menacing than a doorman, less thuggish than a bouncer, but undoubtedly encompassing both functions at once.

The shop and the building had separate entrances, so Nicola entered the lobby. Old, maybe from the turn of the century. Somewhat shabby, in the way even nice places in New York were often shabby, at least compared to the glossy newness of Los Angeles. Dirty cracks in the marble floor, dust dulling the chrome gleam of the fixtures.

There was a high reception desk here, and a uniformed security guard, who nodded once when Nicola told him her name and who she was here to see, then pointed to the elevator. "Get off on eight. Someone will take you up to nine," he said.

Eighth floor. No shabbiness here. The elevators opened with a muted whoosh into a silent sanctum of taupe. Taupe was, she'd always felt, a singularly unremarkable color, but here it *sang*. Taupe walls, matte stone floors in a lighter shade of the same, suede armchairs and a low marble table, all clumped in the same general area on the color spectrum, and yet it seemed rich and sophisticated and even somewhat exciting when it should be the visual equivalent of staring at one of those paint sample strips given out in hardware stores.

The receptionist looked up from her computer as Nicola approached. She was young, Laurie's age or younger, blonde hair cropped close to her scalp in a way that looked both hard-edged and chic. "Can I help you?"

"Nicola Strozyk. I'm here to see Laurie. He should be expecting me."

The young receptionist pulled her mouth into a quick grimace. "Laurie's out. He's not back from lunch yet."

"Ah." So much for being chained to his studio. Still, the kid needed to eat. Couldn't hold that against him. "Is he expected back soon, do you know?"

"I'm not sure. He left before one."

It was two-fifteen now. "So he should be returning around now, probably?"

The receptionist looked skeptical. "I really couldn't say." Something in her tone, some note of resignation, gave Nicola a glimpse into what keeping track of Laurie's daily schedule was like. It was almost certainly a nonstop stretch of missed appointments and delays of every possible definition, of soothing bruised feelings and making apologies for Laurie without admitting to his faults. It would, in a word, suck.

"You know what, I have errands to run in this area," Nicola said. Grabbing coffee and a sticky bun at the cute bakery she'd passed along the way qualified as an errand, surely. "I'll come back in half an hour or so."

"That sounds good." The receptionist didn't look like she thought it sounded good. She looked like she doubted, highly doubted, the situation would change in half an hour. "Sorry about this."

Her and Nicola both. Nicola got back on the elevator, feeling a little steamed.

The cute bakery sold turnovers as well as sticky buns. Nicola had an extraordinary one, tart cherries oozing through gaps in the flaky, buttery pastry, the dusting of raw sugar on top forming a crunchy, caramelized layer of awesomeness. She perched on a high, fixed stool at the counter by the front windows. The counter was one of those super-narrow ones, just a three-inch strip of wood fastened to the wall, barely wide enough to accommodate her coffee cup as she ate. She looked out the windows in the hope of spotting Laurie's telltale puff of gold hair, but saw nothing.

A teenager loitered in the bakery, waiting while the barista prepared her order, some kind of coffee drink involving a mountain of whipped cream and a river of drizzled butterscotch. She leaned forward, elbows propped on the counter, standing up on tiptoe in her unlaced ripped Converse sneakers. She wore a tunic-length sleeveless sweatshirt in a rich dark blue with a long fabric belt and a draped hood. The hood was attached with dozens of wide fabric loops; when the hood was down, the loops overlapped onto each other in a cool woven effect. Nicola had seen that same style before, common over the past year, both here and in Los Angeles, and it clicked in her brain: That was what Nash had been talking about. This sweatshirt was a Laurie Sparks original.

As if aware of Nicola's scrutiny, the teen turned and glared at her. Nicola shifted her stare to make it look like she'd been examining the laminated CPR poster on the wall above the espresso machine.

There was a limit to how long she could loiter here. At ten minutes to three, she returned to the eighth floor and tried her luck again.

The receptionist's face told the story. "Sorry. I haven't heard from him." A pause, then a reluctant offer. "If it's important or something, I could try calling him."

"It's not. Thanks anyway."

She considered her options. Laurie might not be returning at all today. It wasn't like Nicola's time was all that valuable these days, but still, she didn't care for being jerked around, which was what this felt like. Then again . . . "Okay if I wait here?"

"Sure, no problem. There's magazines and stuff there." The receptionist gestured toward the coffee table.

Nicola sat. And read. At three-thirty, Laurie waltzed off the elevator, arm in arm with a middle-aged woman in a red pantsuit. She wore understated makeup; her unfussy brown hair was anchored behind her ears. Nicola recognized her on sight: Maggie Sparks, former United States Senator. Nicola set down her magazine and got to her feet.

The receptionist silently pointed in Nicola's direction. Laurie glanced over at her and beamed. "Nicola, hey! I'm glad you could make it. That's so cool." He took Maggie Sparks by the hand and led her over to Nicola. "Nicola, this is my mom. Mom, this is Nicola. She interviewed me yesterday. She says she likes you."

"Senator Sparks, it's an honor to meet you." Maggie Sparks had given up her office years ago, but Nicola thought that still might be an appropriate way to address her.

Maggie Sparks shook her hand. Strong grip, warm smile. Even in her pumps, she wasn't much taller than her itty bitty son, but she had a great deal of presence. "Maggie, please. Nice to meet you, Nicola."

"You haven't been waiting long, have you?" Laurie asked.

Nothing to be gained by embarrassing the kid in front of his mother. Nicola shrugged. "No big deal."

"Laurie . . ." Maggie turned to him. "Did you have an appointment with Nicola?"

"Yeah, sort of. It slipped my mind. Sorry, Nicola." Laurie looked abashed, though Nicola suspected he'd be significantly less embarrassed without the presence of his mom.

This was a more casual version of Laurie today. Same full face of makeup, same crazy fluff of hair, but he was wearing a simple black stretch satin t-shirt paired with tight white pants. A wide silver belt, positioned well beneath the belt loops, encircled his slim hips. Silver moccasins with flat soles. Must be his work clothes.

Maggie made a noise of exasperated disapproval. To Nicola, she said, "I apologize for this little stinker. As you've probably noticed, his internal clock isn't synchronized with the rest of humanity's."

"That's always been the case," Laurie said. "I almost got expelled from boarding school for chronic lateness. True story." He seemed proud of this.

Maggie placed her arm around Laurie's narrow shoulders and hugged him against her. With her free hand, she ruffled his hair. "Terrible habit. I'm not sure how he gets away with it."

Probably because he was beautiful and rich and, at a guess, fairly comprehensively spoiled. "No harm done. I didn't have much planned for the afternoon anyway," Nicola said.

"It's partly my fault. I stopped by without warning and dragged him away for lunch to cheer him up."

Not sure why Laurie was in need of cheering, but it seemed to have worked. He looked bright-eyed and bouncy. "I feel perfectly comfortable blaming it on you, mom," he said.

Maggie shook her head in resignation. "I should go. I've left my driver in traffic." An outstretched hand, another firm handshake. "Nice meeting you, Nicola. Don't let this one boss you around." She kissed her son on the top of his head. "Goodbye, sweet prince. I'll call you this weekend, all right? Keep those spirits up." A final hug, a buss on each cheek, and she retreated for the elevators.

Laurie looked embarrassed but pleased by his mother's physical demonstration of affection. His cheeks were bright pink. Then again, that could have been the blusher. He grinned at Nicola. "So this is the place," he said with a grand sweep of his arms. "If you'd ever watched my show, this would all look very familiar to you."

"Very nice. Why am I here?" she asked.

"Come upstairs. I want to show you where I work." He beckoned for her to follow him up a wrought-iron staircase that twisted like a DNA strand from behind the reception area.

It opened into a wide space, an expanse of unfinished wood floors, the entire level interrupted only by wide white support pillars. Rolling chrome racks laden with hanging garments lined the walls. One wall was occupied in total by open shelves, which were overflowing with bolts of fabric stacked high, crammed into every available nook, a riot of colors and patterns and textures. Long work tables cluttered with scraps of fabric and pattern pieces, standing dressmaker forms draped in half-finished garments. A half-dozen stylish young women, whom Nicola guessed were members of Laurie's design staff, buzzed around the room and leaned over the tables, fussing with fabrics. It all seemed industrious and organized. Which was funny, because "organized" was not a word Nicola was likely to associate with Laurie.

"This is what I'm working on right now," he said. He took her arm and half-pulled her over to one of the racks along the wall. "This is Spring. It's sort of an homage to Stephen Sprouse. Eighties punk and graffiti, only in an upscale feminine interpretation."

Nicola wasn't entirely sure she knew who Stephen Sprouse was, nor was she sure the garment Laurie showed her made her think of either punk or graffiti. It was a sleeveless jersey dress, mostly black but with narrow patches across the abdomen in a frenetic hot pink print that looked like a toddler had gone hog-wild with a highlighter pen. She wasn't sure what reaction Laurie was expecting from her, so she just nodded.

"It looks good, Laurie. It all looks nice." She glanced over the rest of the rack. Short dresses, mostly. Some blouses and what looked like either Capri pants or tailored knee-length shorts, most of it done on a black base with neon-bright print patches. She wasn't at all sure it looked good—she sure wouldn't wear any of it—but she wasn't Laurie's target customer, and her opinion in sartorial matters didn't count for much.

He laughed. "You're lying. I can see it in your face. But it's totally cool if it's not your thing."

"I'm sure it's great, Laurie. I just don't know much about fashion, that's all." She looked at the racks. "Is this stuff in stores yet?"

"No, like I said, it's Spring. You're seeing this before almost anyone else has."

"Isn't that risky?" She raised an eyebrow. "I could rip off all your ideas. I could be a spy sent by a rival designer, you know."

Laurie giggled. "Yeah, but you're not."

True enough. "So what's this all about? I'm guessing you didn't ask me to come here just to look at your designs."

"No, you're right." Laurie cleared his throat and assumed what Nicola guessed was his most businesslike expression. He looked like an especially stern kitten. "I was thinking how you mentioned yesterday that you were unemployed, and I thought I might have a job for you."

"I'm not going to be your assistant, Laurie."

He barked out a laugh at that. "What? No. God, no. That'd be *awful*."

"Well, then . . . ?"

"Research. That's what you said you did at Paramount, right? For like twenty years or something?"

"Sony, actually. And it was twelve years, but yeah." Nicola's interest perked up. Could be something here . . .

"Great. See, I'm jammed right now with this Spring collection—Fashion Week is coming up, you know—"

Nicola didn't know. Or care. "It's almost September. Isn't it early to be worrying about spring clothes?"

Laurie rolled his lined eyes. "You show Spring in fall, and Fall in spring. You need a lot of time for buyers to place orders and for you to actually manufacture the stuff. Obviously."

Obviously. "Okay. Where does the research come in?"

"Fall. I've got this great idea for a fall line, and I want to be ready to jump on it the second Spring is off my plate. I have loads of research—I mean, so, so much research, like a whole room full of books and magazines and videos, not to mention all the stuff that's out there on the web, I've got maybe a couple hundred bookmarks on my computer right now—and I desperately need someone to sort through it for me." He paused for air. "So will you do it?"

Nicola blinked. "Ah . . . fashion research? That might not be my forte."

"It's not really fashion so much. See, here's my idea." Laurie looked around and lowered his voice. "I haven't told anyone about this, almost anyone at all, but this is the concept: Let's say there was a nuclear attack back in 1984. Earth laid to waste, cities destroyed, human existence almost eradicated. Right?"

"Sure."

"Okay. So time has passed, almost thirty years, and people have started to rebuild. But things are still crappy, obviously, it's still a struggle to survive. So America has become this totally chaotic post-apocalyptic society." Laurie smiled in triumph. "And I want to design the clothes for that society. But, you know, make them *pretty*."

Nicola burst out laughing. Laurie looked injured, so she hastened to reassure him. "I'm not making fun of your idea, really. I actually think it's sort of brilliant."

"Really?" Laurie brightened, a plucked and wilting dandelion springing to life in a glass of water.

"Really. God knows I have no idea what people in your post-nuclear society would be wearing, but I'm pretty sure you do. That's great."

"Cool. Good." Laurie smiled. "So it's not really fashion research. I mean, there's plenty of that, in all honesty, but it's all sort of eighties-inspired, because that would have been when fashion *stopped*. Because of the bombs and all."

"Of course. Pesky bombs, messing up the natural progress of fashion like that," Nicola said. "So what exactly would you need me to do?"

"Just sort through all the stuff I have and put it into some kind of format where it'd be easy for me to pull out what I need. A database or something. You'd know better than I would what'd work."

Nicola considered. "Would I be working here?"

Laurie shrugged. "Everything's back at my place, the books and stuff. It'd be easiest for you to work there. I'll mostly be here, so I won't be around to bug you. I'd give you a key."

"Hold up. Are you really offering to give your apartment key to someone you met yesterday? Isn't that a little bonkers?"

He dismissed her concerns with another shrug. "I trust you."

The self-assurance, the snap assessments, all that reckless confidence . . . One of these days, Laurie Sparks was going to run into entirely the wrong person, would make entirely the wrong judgment call, and when it happened, Nicola could only hope he survived it. "What would this pay?"

"I don't know." The green eyes opened very wide. He looked baffled. "I don't have any idea. I guess what you got paid at Sony? Would that be okay? Would you need more than that?"

"Don't you want to know how much that was?"

Still baffled. "It's not really important. I can afford it."

"How would I get paid?" Nicola asked. "Would I be on a payroll?"

"I'd probably write you a check each week. That'd work, right? My accountant can make sure it gets taken out of the right place later." Laurie smiled. "Just make sure you remind me about it. It's the type of thing that will totally slip my mind."

"Yeah, don't worry about that. I'll definitely remind you."

"So you'll do it?"

A split-second decision. This seemed like a disaster in the making. On the other hand, it was a paid job, provided she could track Laurie down and get him to stand still long enough to write her a check each week.

"Sure. Sounds good." And hopefully it wouldn't be a colossal mistake. "Thanks for thinking of me."

"Hooray! Great. I'm so happy. Can you start tomorrow? Maybe just meet me at my place? I'm returning here in the morning, super-early, so it'll have to be like ten or so."

"Ah . . . okay." Had she made some terrible error, agreeing to this? "What's your address?"

He had his phone out. "I'm texting you it right now. I'm just on West 75th, it's super-easy to find. So cool. I'll see you early tomorrow morning. Ten, right?"

There was an air of dismissal to it. Nicola couldn't help feeling like there was more, much more, that needed to be pounded out with this arrangement, but Laurie clearly didn't share her feelings. With a quick wave over his shoulder, he headed off toward one of the work tables.

Nicola hovered for a moment longer, wanting to call him back over to discuss this further, but there seemed no point to it. Eventually, she turned and went down the stairs.

CHAPTER FIVE

LAURIE LIVED ON the Upper West Side, a short block over from Central Park, in a crazy old prewar building. Dark gray stone with black iron grates over the first-floor windows, copper awnings turned to verdigris. Gargoyles. It had gargoyles.

It also had a doorman, middle-aged and sturdy in a smart long green coat with brass buttons and a matching cap. He smiled when Nicola gave him her name and told him she was there for Laurie.

"Mr. Sparks said to expect you. Said we might be seeing a lot of you." He stabbed in an extension number on the phone box by the door. "I'll let him know I'm sending you up."

Nicola listened to the tinny electronic tone on the other end, ringing over and over. No response.

Jesus, Laurie.

The doorman gave her an apologetic smile and disconnected the call. "I'll try again in just a moment, give him time to wake up a bit," he said. "Sometimes Mr. Sparks can be difficult to reach."

"You don't say," Nicola said.

He punched in the number again, thick fingers flying expertly over the narrow keypad. More ringing, and this time Laurie picked up. Nicola could hear his voice over the electronic crackle of the speaker, groggy and thick with sleep. "Hi, Maurice. Tell Nicola she can come up."

The doorman held the door open for her. Heavy glass overlaid with an intricate pattern of wrought iron ivy branches. "Eighteenth floor, second unit."

"Thanks." The ceiling of the lobby was polished copper, shining like a just-minted penny, embossed with an ornate pattern. Green and gray inlaid marble floors, an old-fashioned bronze gate in front of the elevator. The elevator was tiny and cramped, about half the size of a standard elevator car, and was constructed of old, dark wood.

The elevator door slid open. Nicola pushed aside the gate and stepped onto the eighteenth floor.

A small foyer, a door on either side. Only two units on the entire level. Before she could knock on the door marked with a brass number "2", it swung open.

"'Morning, Nicola. Come in. I'm running late, *quelle surprise.*" Laurie held the door open and ushered her inside.

Laurie slept in ivory satin pajamas. This came as no shock. His sleep-mussed hair stuck up all around his head, making him look like a newly-hatched chick who'd been struck by lightning. His face looked odd. It took Nicola a second to realize she was seeing him without his makeup. He even had faint stubble, a pale fuzz that indicated he was a natural blonde. She wouldn't have predicted that.

"Good morning," she said.

He shook his head. "Don't look at me. I'm a mess."

"Almost didn't recognize you without your warpaint," she said.

He shot her a bleary, sleep-dazed smile. "I considered answering the door with a bag over my head."

Even stubbly and disheveled and makeup-free, he was cute. Boyish. His nose looked different, thicker. He probably usually contoured it with makeup somehow, to make it a smidgen less prominent.

"Could you make coffee? Strong. Really strong. My brain doesn't work right without it. Kitchen's over here," he said.

Nicola's first glimpse of his apartment was sensory overload, an explosive rush of gold and bronze. "Whoa," she said.

In the act of leading her to the kitchen, Laurie paused and turned to look at her. His feet were bare and bluish-white and looked fragile. His toenails were painted robin-egg blue. "What?"

"This is your place? Did you move?" She looked around his living room. "I watched an episode of *NYC Elite* last night. You didn't live here."

"You watched my show? What'd you think of it?" Some of the early morning fog in Laurie's brain seemed to lift. "Did you like it?"

"It wasn't really my thing." She'd watched half of an episode online on Donya's laptop. It had featured Laurie prominently, and by the first commercial break she'd known she wouldn't gain many insights into the real-life Laurie by watching his bitchy, arrogant alter ego on the screen. "But this wasn't your apartment."

Screen-Laurie had lived in a wide open space with white walls and floor-to-ceiling glass-block windows and huge, aggressively modern paintings on the walls. Screen-Laurie had swept grandly down a staircase made of floating glass and lolled about on a stark white chaise lounge, all while fretting and grousing dramatically about the state of his collection. Nothing like that here. This place was . . .

Rococo. That was the term she was looking for. Cluttered and intricate and elaborate, too many things competing for her attention at once. Thick Persian carpets with curling patterns in gold and blue covered great swaths of the inlaid wood floors. Gold-upholstered armchairs, walls papered with gold and violet stripes. Heavy bronze drapes blocked the outside light, forcing Nicola to squint to see anything other than a soft glimmer of gold, gold, gold from every direction. It was nuts. She wanted to flee, and she wanted to stay here forever.

"Oh, sure. I can't film here. My co-op board won't allow it." Laurie shrugged. "So the production company rents that place for the show and pretends it's my apartment."

"But the two places are so different. The kind of person who lives here wouldn't live there, if you see what I'm saying. Doesn't it bother you?"

"Why would it?" Laurie looked genuinely puzzled. "It's just a *show*. I'm playing a character."

"Not really. You're playing yourself. Don't you at least want to play an accurate version of yourself?"

She could tell Laurie found the conversation both confusing and boring. "Why on earth should it matter?" He shook his head. "Coffee. Need. Kitchen's that way."

He flailed a hand in one direction, then padded toward the stairs and headed up. A massive staircase, with a carved and curving banister of dark wood running up to another floor. A high balcony ran all around this second level; Laurie disappeared through a dark doorway into what Nicola guessed was his bedroom, leaving her to fiddle around his kitchen.

The kitchen was modern. Granite countertops, stainless-steel refrigerator, restaurant-grade pots dangling from ceiling hooks. Nothing more than props; Laurie wouldn't cook. Nicola knew that much about him.

The coffee maker looked like a robotic spider, with shiny black handles and chrome nozzles sticking out in all directions. A minor swell of triumph when she finally managed to cajole it into spitting strong black coffee into a dainty glass carafe.

It took Laurie a long, long time to emerge from the wilds of upstairs. Shaved and showered, makeup on, dressed in a pink silk poet shirt and black leather pants. He smelled like lemon cupcakes. He accepted a heavy white ceramic mug from her and wrapped both hands around it. "Bless you. Thanks." He moved to the fridge, added a good inch of cream to his mug, moved to a canister on the counter, added another inch of sugar.

He opened a drawer. Chaos emerged, a compressed mass of takeout menus and matchbooks and champagne corks and loose batteries. Nicola had a drawer in her kitchen with very similar contents. Maybe everyone did. Maybe junk drawers were the great equalizer of modern American society. Laurie pawed around and produced a key on a long silver tag.

"This is yours. If you lose it or something, just tell Maurice or whoever's at the door and he can get the super to let you in. I guess it's not a big deal if you lock up or not, since nobody goes in the building who's not supposed to be here."

"I'll lock up. You should, too. How well do you know your neighbors?"

Laurie made a scoffing noise. "You're too suspicious," he said.

Nicola fought an urge to sit Laurie down and give him a comprehensive lecture on personal safety. She said nothing, stewing in a cloud of disapproval.

"Come on. Let me show you all my stuff."

She trailed him up the stairs. He led her into what had probably been his home office before this current project had wholly taken it over. Cases with sagging shelves of books, more stacks of books on the floor and piled on the vast oak roll-top desk. Huge, glossy, coffee-table books mostly, dealing with fashion and film history. Magazines, tons of them. Lopsided stacks of newspapers, ratty old paperbacks. DVDs: Nicola glimpsed *Road Warrior, Escape From New York, Solarbabies, Night of the Comet,* old *Max Headroom* episodes. All of it meaningful to Laurie, all of it giving him some spark of an idea for his future collection.

"I don't really know what I want you to do with all this," Laurie said, before she could formulate a question along those very lines. "I just need you to find some way to help me make sense of it. You can use my computer." He motioned toward the desk. Computer, printer, scanner. Good.

"You'll probably want some kind of catalogue of all this, right? A searchable database?"

Laurie was nodding before she'd finished speaking, though Nicola had the sense he wasn't paying close attention to her words. "Sure, yes, whatever you think would work best. I'll leave it up to you."

Laurie *seemed* like the world's most laid-back employer, but Nicola knew from past experience that this could be problematic. If she and Laurie weren't on the same wavelength, if he didn't like the direction she took, if he refused to pay her . . . This could be disastrous for her, if it went sour.

"So I'm going to take off now, unless you've got questions," he said.

"Hey, Laurie, wait. I'm going to need to have an agreement on paper about what we're doing. I can draw something up today, something very straightforward." There'd be templates online, she knew, and instructions for drawing up a basic contract. "And I'm going to sign it, and then you're going to sign it. You can have your lawyers or anyone you want look over it first, but we need to have it in place, just to avoid any trouble later."

"If that makes you happy, fine, I'll sign anything. But I think you're being fussy. Like I said before, I trust you."

What was it like to go through life like that? Nicola could only stare after Laurie in frustration tinged with amusement as he flitted down the stairs, leaving her to figure out what, exactly, she was supposed to do with herself in her new position.

CHAPTER SIX

LEFT TO HER own devices in Laurie's bizarre, ridiculous, glorious place, Nicola gave in to the temptation to snoop.

She opened doors one by one. Laurie's bedroom contained a king-sized bed—four-poster, gold canopy, an ivory satin coverlet and an assortment of gold tasseled throw pillows propped up against the monstrous headboard, which was covered in gold leaf. One of the doors led to a sewing room. Sewing machine, dressmaker forms, bolts of fabric. It was hard to imagine him sitting here, tackling the nuts-and-bolts of clothes-making, stitching fabric together and cutting out patterns and tacking down hems. He seemed far too flighty, far too stuck on the impractical and infuriating side of the creative process. Nicola had met plenty of creative types in Los Angeles. She'd mostly loathed them.

One of the rooms had been retrofitted into a gigantic walk-in closet with long racks and shelves bearing loads of garments. His own clothes, mostly, all his tiny tailored suits and bright satin shirts. Rows of shoes; Nicola picked up a green snakeskin loafer and confirmed that, yes, her feet were much bigger than Laurie's. There was also a wide assortment of women's clothes, mostly evening gowns and cocktail dresses and long coats. Nicola initially figured these were Laurie's own designs, and then she noticed the labels, which were an encyclopedia of fashion names: Dior, Armani, Chanel, Yves Saint Laurent. While she couldn't rule out a side interest in cross-dressing, most of the clothes were far too large for

Laurie. He kept them as inspiration, probably, things to look at for ideas for his own line.

Bathroom. One of those walk-in stone showers Nicola thought were only found in luxury hotels. A built-in stone bench at the end, upon which rested an assortment of bath products. Two types of shampoo. Something fussy and expensive that could only be purchased in salons or from chic salesgirls at high-end department stores, and a half-full bottle of a generic drugstore brand.

Laurie wouldn't trust his fabulous hair to that. No way. The good stuff was his; the other was for . . .

He lived alone, right? There was a guest bedroom, done in shimmering greens and golds, but it looked unused and immaculate, and the air in there was stale. He had a boyfriend who stayed over sometimes, probably. Could even be a girlfriend. Seemed unlikely, but not impossible.

Not that Laurie was much of a sexual being at all. For all his beauty, there was something pristine about him, untouched and untouchable.

A rattle of keys from downstairs, a commotion at the door. Laurie had returned home for some reason, and here she was, snooping away. She slipped out of the bathroom and stood at the railing.

The door opened. Not Laurie. Definitely not Laurie. Startled, Nicola drew back and observed the mystery visitor.

A young man. Early twenties. Very tall, very slender, with an admirable shock of dark hair that fell into his eyes. Probably hadn't visited a barber anytime that summer. Skinny black jeans that made his long, long legs look like bicycle spokes, black plastic-framed glasses that somehow managed to draw even more attention to his high, sharp cheekbones. He was carrying a lidless banker's box; from her overhead perspective, Nicola caught a glimpse of the contents. Books, mostly.

Nicola knew exactly who this was, from the crappy half-episode of *NYC Elite* she'd watched. Jonathan. This was Jonathan, Laurie's former assistant.

It wasn't too surprising he'd have a key to Laurie's place, considering how Laurie gave out keys like candy on Halloween, but the timing of his arrival, so soon after Laurie had left, was a little strange. He wasn't expecting to find Laurie home—he hadn't knocked, hadn't announced his presence in any way. Had he been outside, watching the door, waiting for Laurie to leave before entering? If so, was he up to mischief?

Didn't seem to be, or at least not mischief Nicola could identify. He crept about the living room and, as she watched, removed items from his box and placed them on shelves and end tables. Books. An iPod. An umbrella, slipped into the brass stand by the door.

Huh. Nicola stepped up to the railing. "Hi there," she called down to him.

He froze and looked up, eyes wide behind his glasses. He took a moment to compose himself before he spoke. "Ah . . ." he said. "Ah. Who are you?"

"I'm Nicola. I'm doing some work for Laurie." She headed down the stairs. Jonathan was still frozen in place, the box still in his hands. He looked more than just surprised to see her. He looked guilty. "You're Jonathan?"

"Yeah. Hi." Realization dawned across his face. "His research, for his whole apocalyptic thing. You're doing that?"

"Yup." She stopped in front of him and examined him. A beautiful guy, really, all that astonishing bone structure beneath the outer trappings of someone who didn't give a damn about his appearance. No wonder he was, as Nash had claimed, such a popular character on Laurie's show. "Are you supposed to be here?"

"Sort of." Jonathan smiled. "Yes in the sense that Laurie refused to take back his key, which indicates to me that he doesn't mind if I stop by. No in the sense that I'd rather you not mention you saw me today."

Nicola gestured with her chin toward the box in his hands. "What's that?"

"His junk." He hoisted the box a little. "I moved out of here in a hurry. I was pulling crap off of shelves and throwing it into boxes, and some of his stuff got mixed in with mine. Now that I've cooled off a little, I thought I'd return it."

He'd moved out. He'd lived there. Aha. Nash had been wrong; Laurie and Jonathan were a couple. "Were" seemed to be the operative part of that equation, though.

He shifted the box in his hands. "You mind if I do this?" he asked.

"Knock yourself out," she said. It wasn't her apartment, and Laurie sure seemed nonchalant about people tromping around his place while he was away. It didn't seem right to leave Jonathan unsupervised, though, so she informally trailed him, followed him up the stairs, watched as he returned a stack of books to the library and a couple of kitschy knickknacks to the office.

Jonathan looked back over his shoulder, amused to find her shadowing him. "I'm not going to steal anything, you know."

"I'm sure you aren't," she said.

"How well do you know Laurie?" he asked.

"I interviewed him two days ago. That was the first time I met him. He hired me yesterday," she said.

Jonathan smiled. A flash of dimples, incongruous in that stream-lined, angular face. "If I were still working for him, that's the sort of thing I'd try to talk him out of doing."

"Yeah. He's very trusting."

"That's an understatement," Jonathan said. "I don't think it occurs to Laurie that there are people out there who maybe don't want the very best for him."

"Must be nice to go through life like that."

Jonathan shrugged. "He's had an easy time of it. His mom dotes on him. Anything he wants, it's his. He never went to design school, just scored a few hotly-coveted apprenticeships with big designers after high school. Learned a lot, and to be fair, he knows his stuff. So his mom gave him the cash to launch his own line, and wouldn't you know, his very first collection was a hit."

"I don't know much about the fashion world, but I gather that's unusual?"

"Almost impossible. A lot of it is because he's a fantastic designer, that's only fair to point out, but a lot of fantastic designers go nowhere. A lot of it is that he had the right connections and enough money behind him. And a lot of it is just force of will. Laurie wants something, he bulldozes his way through to it, and he's cute and charismatic enough to pull it off. Since that technique has worked pretty well for him, he's never learned there are other ways of doing things."

Jonathan sounded frustrated. "Is that why you broke up?" Nicola asked. His blue eyes went frosty, and she found herself backpedaling. "Why you broke your arrangement with him, I mean. Your arrangement to be his assistant."

A pause, and he defrosted. "You got it right the first time. We broke up. Though, point of sober fact, I'm also no longer his assistant." He exhaled heavily. "That's part of it. Mostly, it's that goddamned show. It's taking over his life, and he's entirely unaware of it. Or maybe he knows, but doesn't think it's something he needs to stop."

"I watched the show, very briefly," she said. "I like Laurie okay in real life. I don't like him on television."

Jonathan nodded emphatically. "Yes. Yes. Exactly. And that's the Laurie he's shifting into. The Laurie who needs the eyes of the world on him, the Laurie who pitches hissyfits at the slightest provocation—"

"The Laurie who isn't dating you?"

"Yeah." Jonathan's bony shoulders slumped, an origami crane folding in on itself. "Though that's mostly on me, if I'm being honest. Laurie wanted our relationship to be a part of the show, and I nixed it. Because on the show, it wouldn't be real. It'd be just like that fake-ass apartment they pretend is his."

"How long were you a couple?" Nicola asked.

"I've known Laurie since we were kids. We lived in the same neighborhood, our parents were friends. We went to the same boarding school in Wilkes-Barre," he said. "We've been soulmates from the start, we've been together since we were sixteen. Maybe it's dumb, but I absolutely believe, more than anything, we'll be together again."

Ah, yes, that conviction that could only come from being twenty-two and certain his love was stronger and more special than anyone else's. Nicola hadn't been Jonathan's age in a while, but she remembered that feeling. "You think that'll happen?"

"I know it will. Not any time soon, though. He needs to grow up a little first." He smiled at Nicola. "Sorry. I'm being sappy. Is he doing okay, you think?"

"He seems fine. I don't know what he was like when he was with you."

"Can you do me a favor? Keep an eye on him. Make sure he doesn't play in traffic, that kind of thing." It wasn't quite a joke.

"That's not what I was hired to do," she said.

Jonathan smiled. He looked both wise and wistful. "Actually, I sort of think it was."

LAURIE ARRIVED HOME around seven. Lost in work, Nicola was startled to hear the front door open. She came out to the railing and looked down at him. "How was your day?" she asked.

He looked up. He seemed confused at first, as though he had no idea who she was or what she was doing in his apartment. "Productive, I think," he said at last. "I'm not sure. Maybe. I didn't really get anything done, but it felt like I laid the groundwork for getting things done in the future. Does that make sense?"

"More or less," she said. "Come up here for a second. I want to show you what I'm doing."

"I'm sure it's fine," Laurie said. He obligingly climbed the stairs and trailed her into his office.

It looked faintly less chaotic than it had this morning. She'd spent most of the day sitting on the floor sorting through the stacks of books and miscellany and mulling over ideas for the best possible organizational system. "I've assigned a cataloging number to each book, each movie, each magazine, everything. I've set up the bare bones of what will eventually be the mother of all databases here on your computer. Does this look like what you had in mind?"

Laurie looked around the room, glanced once at his computer screen, nodded. "Yes, just like that. That's perfect. See, I knew I made the right choice in hiring you."

"Okay, cool. For the next few days, I'm just going to keep doing exactly this. After that, I'll start filling in details and writing up summaries of the information. A lot of these books have references to other sources that I'm not sure you have, so I can work on tracking those down as well, if you want."

"Fantastic. Phenomenal. I don't want to cut you off, but I haven't eaten anything today, and the eighty-seven cups of coffee are finally starting to wear off, so I need to order something up, because I think my stomach's starting to digest itself."

He did look a little wan, not that it was easy to tell under his makeup. Nicola's first impulse was to offer to fetch dinner for him, but that was ridiculous. Laurie got people to do stuff for him by seeming helpless and ineffectual, most likely because he *was* helpless and ineffectual, and she'd be doing him no favors by encouraging this. "I'll just see you tomorrow, then." She tapped a finger on a two-page document on the desk. "I'm going to leave this with you. It's a very basic agreement I put together about our working arrangement. Sign it after you've gone over it, or let me know if you want to make any changes."

Laurie glanced down at it, flipped to the second page, picked up a pen, and added his signature to the bottom with a big flourish.

"No, Laurie. Read the damn thing first."

"I trust you," he said stubbornly. "That's not the way I do things."

She wouldn't win this battle. "Your choice," she said with a shrug.

Laurie placed the pen back down, then paused. He picked up something from the corner of the desk.

A child's toy, a metal-suited and helmeted action figure, probably from some cartoon that hadn't existed when Nicola was a kid. Laurie turned it over in his hands. "Jonathan stopped by, huh?" he said.

"Yeah."

He nodded. "Did he say anything about me?" he asked.

"We didn't really talk," Nicola said.

Laurie didn't respond. He seemed smaller than ever, crumpled almost, and Nicola thought he might be close to tears. "Do you need anything else?" she asked.

He didn't say anything, just shook his head. She had a crazy impulse to pat his shoulder, or comfort him in some way.

No. Wouldn't be appropriate, and it wasn't her job. She couldn't think of anything else to do or say, so she just left, leaving Laurie alone in his crazy, amazing apartment, clutching that silly action figure and looking like someone had just punched him in the stomach.

CHAPTER SEVEN

THIS REALLY WASN'T a difficult job. In fact, it was fun.

Nicola was good at this, sorting through boundless crap and making sense of it, pursuing fragmented leads and wheedling out grains of information. She was becoming an expert on mid-eighties fashions, felt she could write a reasonably impressive doctoral thesis on cheeseball eighties apocalyptic films. She was giving Laurie good value for his money, not that he seemed at all concerned with that.

Some days she saw Laurie, some days she didn't. Usually their paths crossed in the morning, but as Fashion Week drew nearer, he worked later and later in his studio, refining his designs for his upcoming runway show. For such a flaky little thing, he did seem to have a good work ethic. Whenever she asked about his collection, he'd either whine about nonspecific flaws or assure her it was staggeringly brilliant, depending upon his mood.

She'd been working for him for just over two weeks now. She'd received two paychecks. Laurie dutifully wrote checks to her from his personal account whenever she asked, filling in the amount she specified without question.

A rustle at the door. She glanced at the time in surprise. Only a bit after four. She came out to the railing.

"You're early," she called down to him.

He tilted his head back and looked up at her, then flopped down on one of the gold-covered sofas in his living room. "I'm bereft," he said. He flung a hand over his eyes to accentuate his point. "I am a fraud and a colossal failure, and I will be exposed as such the second my clothes hit the runway."

"Sure you will." Nicola headed downstairs. "Rough day?"

He stared at her from between his spread fingers. "Have you ever devoted every waking fiber of your being to something only to realize you've produced naught but a pile of unmitigated horse pucky?"

"Can't say I have," Nicola said. "Buck up, little sailor. You've just been working on this too closely. Look at it fresh tomorrow. I'm sure your clothes are fine."

"Easy for you to say." Laurie tilted his neck back over the edge of the couch and stared up at the ceiling, his expression morose. "My brain is a mass of congealed jelly, and right now I want nothing more than to drink vast quantities of champagne while watching Duran Duran videos for renewal of purpose. Are you in with me?"

"Soundtrack of my formative years. You bet," Nicola said.

Which is how they found themselves sprawled in his living room, watching videos on Laurie's extravagantly large flat-screen television, warm and tipsy off of their second bottle of Veuve Clicquot. Laurie gestured with his glass toward the screen. In lieu of flutes, he favored the saucer-shaped glasses, the ones that were allegedly modeled after Marie Antoinette's tits, and somehow this all made Nicola feel very decadent and louche. "Say what you will, those bitches knew how to *dress*," he said, pertinent to their present entertainment.

"I'll drink to that." Nicola raised her glass up and back and waited for him to clink against hers. She sat on the floor, her back resting against the couch, with Laurie draped luxuriously behind her. They'd ordered up the champagne from the liquor store on the ground level of the building. It was a chic little storefront with gruesomely marked-up prices that the well-heeled Upper West Side clientele paid without flinching, and Nicola had argued that it was ridiculous for Laurie to pay an additional fee to have it sent up when he could scamper downstairs and fetch it himself in two minutes. Laurie counter-argued that he was, in fact, preposterously wealthy and could swallow the delivery fee no problem, and besides, he didn't want to move from the couch. Nicola had no worthy rebuttal to that.

Something cold drizzled down her neck. Laurie giggled. He'd tried to clink, missed, and dumped the contents of his glass on her head. "Sorry, sorry. Hand-eye coordination is always the first thing to go, right?" He patted her head with his hand in a half-assed attempt to mop up the mess.

"Don't worry about it. Certainly not the worst stuff I've had in my hair."

He kept on patting. "You have really pretty hair," he said. "I mean, that's a terrible cut, and the color's boring, and your styling is for shit, but it's really thick and healthy."

"Thanks." Under other circumstances she'd object to anyone, her employer most particularly, petting her like this, but Laurie was just . . . Laurie.

"You know what we should do?" he said. "Makeovers. We should do makeovers tonight. Totally."

"No. No, no, no, no, no. Terrible idea, Laurie."

"I didn't mean that I'd give you one," Laurie said, though she was pretty sure that was exactly what he'd meant. "I can call up Marcos, he's my hair guy, he comes here all the time to do my hair. He can do yours right now. Really, he'd know exactly how to get it looking less awful."

"No. I hate makeovers. Hate the idea, hate the whole makeover industry. No."

"Why? I love them. I love people fussing over me and making me look pretty. Prettier," he clarified.

"And that's where you and I are different." Nicola set down her glass on a side table and got to her feet. "I should be getting home, Laurie. Thanks for the bubbles."

Laurie struggled up to a seated position on the couch. "Don't go," he said. "Stay. Please? We can order dinner and watch movies or something. If it gets too late, you can just sleep over."

A slumber party at Laurie's. Great merciful Zeus. There'd be toenail painting involved, she just knew it. "Sorry. I'm cooking dinner for my roommate tonight. We already made plans."

Laurie looked crushed. The kid was lonely, and while his fervent need to cultivate her friendship was flattering, it wouldn't last. He'd been devastated when Jonathan left, and for whatever reason, probably because she'd dumped him into a taxi when he'd been drunk and helpless, he'd glommed onto her as someone who could take care of him.

Not really what she needed right now.

"Goodnight, Laurie," she said. She looked around for her coat. It had been a crisp September morning, the first almost-chilly day of the season, and she'd thrown on a lightweight jacket over her t-shirt and jeans before leaving her apartment. Ah, there it was, draped over the back of an armchair. She struggled into it.

Laurie opened his mouth like he was going to try to wheedle her into staying longer, then stopped. "Cool coat," he said. "Can I see that?"

He'd never commented on anything she'd worn, and she was thankful for that. It had probably taken him some effort to refrain from snarking on her old jeans, her loafers, her shapeless t-shirts, all of it functional and none of it stylish.

"Sure." She slipped the coat back off and handed it to him. It was one of Donya's that had been too roomy around her shoulders. Rather than getting it tailored to fit, she'd passed it along to Nicola. It was a satin-lined belted trench that stopped at mid-thigh, made from soft, stretchy, greeny-blue material, with an oversized hood and deep slash pockets. The back featured exaggerated darts at the waist and strange folded flaps of fabric arranged in an X pattern, which created a very flattering silhouette: wide shoulders, tiny waist, curvy hips.

Laurie examined it. Really examined it. Turned it inside out, tugged at the seams, held the hem up close to his eyes. "Where'd you get this? There's no tag," he said.

"It's my roommate's. I have no idea."

She glanced at the inside collar. Laurie was right, no tags. There was something on the lining, though, some marking in wide-tipped black felt pen, barely visible against the dark blue. HOH. Someone's initials, maybe, like a child's mother marking his clothes before sending him off to sleep-away camp.

"Can you ask her where she got it?" he asked. "Right now, can you call and ask her?"

"I suppose." Laurie seemed almost manic. A new light in those pale green eyes. "Why is this important?"

"Because of Caprini's 1984 collection," Laurie said. "Kip Caprini. His 1984 collection, he showed this coat."

"So it's a vintage piece?" Nicola asked. "Is it valuable?"

Laurie shook his head. "No, you don't get it, it's not vintage, this is brand new. This stretch satin in the lining, that's a blend, it's only been around for the past twenty years or so." He looked at her, focused and sharp. "Kip Caprini's 1984 fall collection was weird. It didn't look much like anything he'd shown before that, and nothing he's done since then has looked like it, either."

Kip Caprini. Nicola knew the name. He'd been popular years ago. She hadn't known the Caprini brand was still in existence until recently, when she'd spotted the company logo in blocky gold letters above one of the posh shops on Fifth Avenue. "So?"

Laurie pointed at the X in the back. "That use of darts. Notice how it almost looks like folded paper, like origami. It wasn't the kind of thing he did. Wasn't the kind of thing anyone was doing at the time."

"Okay, I get that. But what's the big deal? You seem upset or something."

"Because Caprini didn't design that line." Laurie looked at her, earnest and passionate. "He couldn't have. I'm surprised more people haven't pointed it out, but he sent stuff down the runway that season that wasn't his."

"Wait a minute, Laurie. Do you know this, or do you just think it?" There was no danger in Laurie airing his private theories to her—who would she repeat them to?—but it wasn't a good idea for him to be casually categorizing other designers as frauds.

"I know it. I mean, I can't prove it, but I know it. Wait, I'll show you what I mean." He scampered upstairs. Nicola wondered how soon she'd be able to slink away. When Laurie had an idea in his head . . .

He returned, a nylon garment bag draped over his arms. He flopped it across the back of the sofa, yanked down the zipper, and pulled out its contents.

A long trench coat, done in dark maroon with a gray silk lining. It was longer than Nicola's coat, but the style was nearly identical. Same X in the back, same deep pockets set into the seams.

"I bought this at an auction last year. This walked down the runway in 1984, this exact coat," he said. "It's gorgeous. It *speaks* to me. And none of Caprini's clothes speak to me, ever, so I know he didn't make it."

"That's evidence for you," Nicola said. "So, what's the theory? You think someone's producing knockoffs of that 1984 line?" She tapped on her coat.

"It's not a knockoff," Laurie said. "It's too well-made. Look at the care that went into those seams, the quality of the fabrics. That's the original. That was made by the same designer." He gestured to her. "Call your roommate and ask her where she got it."

That was bossy. Bossy people always brought out the worst in Nicola. "Ask her yourself."

"Fine. Give me her number, I'll call her now."

Nicola shook her head. "Nope, no good. She's still at work. You can ask her in person tonight."

"In person?"

"In person. Come have dinner with us. At our apartment."

"In *Queens*?" Said with a mixture of petulance and panic that made Nicola laugh out loud.

"Yep. Just an easy train ride away, a hop across the river. Cake."

"But you can just call her now. It's only a quick question." He sounded whiny, which strengthened Nicola's resolve to mess with him a little.

"I can, but I won't."

"I'm your boss. I could fire you," Laurie said. It lacked conviction, and it only made Nicola laugh harder.

"Go ahead. But you'll never find out anything about the coat." She picked it up and dangled it in front of him, teasing a kitten with a dangling ribbon.

Laurie jumped at the bait, as she knew he would. "Fine. We should take a cab, though. It's faster."

"Nope. Subway or nothing."

Laurie wanted to argue some more, she could see that in his face, but more than that, he wanted to find out more about the coat.

Which is how they ended up on a crowded Queens-bound train, in a car jam-packed with commuters, a sweaty mass of humanity, everyone crammed right up in everyone else's business.

Laurie looked stricken and panicky at the crush of bodies. Nicola felt a pang of guilt. He was a celebrity, sort of, and getting trapped in a crowd might be dangerous for him. Not that anyone on the train appeared to know or care who he was.

They got separated at a stop, forced apart by the crowd when a swarm of fresh bodies flooded on. Nicola looked around in alarm until she spotted the white-gold top of his hair. She jostled and elbowed her way through the car, which earned her more than a few glares, until she reached his side. He had nothing to hold onto, nothing to brace himself against except other passengers. He seemed fragile and vulnerable, like he could easily fall and get trampled, so she wrapped one arm around his shoulders and pulled him up against her.

He looked startled at first. Then he grabbed hold of her coat with both hands and clung to her, creating their own stable island in the sea of bodies.

CHAPTER EIGHT

"THIS IS MUCH less horrible than I thought it'd be," Laurie said as he looked around the apartment.

"Gosh, thanks," Nicola said. "The décor's all Donya's. I've had no hand in any of this."

"I can tell," Laurie said cheerfully. "It's *nice*."

They drank red wine and cooked dinner. Or rather, Nicola cooked while Laurie gouged and mangled the pile of vegetables she'd given him to chop for the salad. He had no finesse in the kitchen, none at all, though at least he seemed enthusiastic.

This was an easy meal, nests of angel hair smothered in a quick white sauce of clams and herbs. A garlic ciabatta loaf was in the oven, and Donya was due to arrive any minute.

"Donya's your roommate? The one who bought the coat, right?" Laurie's eyes were bright and his cheeks were flushed. The red wine on top of all the earlier champagne was making him especially sparkly and bright. "When you say roommate, do you mean roommate, or . . . ?"

"Just a roommate. We both worked at Sony in L.A. She moved out here a year ago, and when I got the job here, she offered to share the place."

Laurie cocked his head to the side and observed her over the rim of his wine glass. "Girls or boys?" he asked.

Nicola smiled. "Men," she said. "I'm forty. Boys are both off-limits and unwanted."

"But you don't have a boyfriend, do you?" Laurie asked. "That's probably why you're cranky all the time."

"Naah, I've had boyfriends. I was cranky all the time then, too."

Donya came home just then. Nicola probably should've taken a minute to text her about their surprise dinner guest, because she looked flabbergasted at the sight of the sparkly pixie in their kitchen, who was trying his hand at tossing the salad. More lettuce ended up on the counter than in the bowl, which sent him into fits of giggles.

Donya set down her purse by the door. "Ah . . . hi?"

"Hey, Donya. Meet my boss. Laurie Sparks. He's joining us for dinner. Laurie, this is Donya."

Donya looked at Nicola, looked at their wine glasses, then smiled at Laurie. She stepped forward and extended a hand.

"Hi, Laurie. Nice to meet you. Nicola's been mentioning you a lot lately."

Laurie shook her hand. "Are you the one who called me a mouthy little fameball?" he asked.

Donya raised her eyebrows at Nicola, then smiled at Laurie again. "I am. And it's just terrific she told you about that."

Laurie brushed that aside. "It's okay. I've heard worse."

"Laurie has something he wants to ask you," Nicola said.

"The coat. The one you gave Nicola." Laurie trotted into their attached living room, where Nicola had draped the coat over the back of an armchair. He picked it up and brandished it in front of Donya. "Where'd you get this?"

Donya looked surprised at Laurie's sudden intensity. Behind Laurie's back, Nicola rolled her eyes at her. "It's sort of an involved story, but it's important to Laurie," Nicola said.

Donya stroked the coat. "It's pretty, isn't it? I wish it fit me better. I got it when I was in Los Angeles last spring, when I was freelancing at E!," she said. "It's from that thrift shop on Washington, near Sepulveda. Nicola, did I ever take you there? The studio wardrobe resale place?"

Nicola shook her head. "Despite my deep and devout love of clothes shopping, no, I've never heard of it."

"They buy up wardrobe from films and television shows and resell it. You can get a lot of cool designer stuff that way for pretty cheap prices."

Laurie looked confused. "So this was worn in a movie?"

"Or on a TV show. Yeah, probably. That's what their whole inventory is."

Laurie nodded. "Okay, so what's this from?"

"I have no idea." Donya took the coat from him and looked at the lining. She pointed to the "HOH" penned inside the collar. "The shop has its own code for which items come from which production. This 'HOH' probably means something, but I don't know what."

"Could you find out?" Laurie asked.

Before Donya could answer, Nicola jumped in. "She could, but she won't, because she doesn't work for you, kiddo. It should be easy enough for you to find out. You can just call the place tomorrow and ask them."

Laurie still looked determined, almost maniacal. He was a little frightening when he got an idea stuck in his fluffy head, a tiny satin-clad tyrant. "Can you go?" he asked Nicola. "To Los Angeles? You could show them the coat, and then you could buy up anything else they have from the same show for me."

Donya looked surprised. Nicola wasn't. She was growing familiar enough with Laurie that she was starting to understand how his mind worked, which was sort of a frightening thought.

Still, it was a ridiculous suggestion. "Yeah, I could go," she said. "But I'm not sure you'd get your money's worth. And it would be your money, by the way, in advance; I couldn't front the cost of a plane ticket or a hotel or whatever it would take to buy the clothes."

"No big deal, I'll talk to my money people tomorrow morning. They'll know the best way to get you to L.A. Do you think you could leave tomorrow?

Donya looked at them like they were plumb crazy, and maybe they were, but the way Laurie did business was starting to grow on Nicola. And she did want to see Los Angeles again, sort of.

"Tomorrow would be fine," she said.

DINNER TURNED OUT to be a blast. Laurie was on his best behavior, bubbly and charming, and he and Donya hit it off immediately. By the time the second bottle of wine was opened, they were giggling together like best girlfriends, and Nicola was starting to feel a little charmless and superfluous. She had no claim to Laurie, she reminded herself, no ties to him apart from their temporary work arrangement.

Still, watching them with their heads together at the other end of the table, two shiny mops of great hair snickering over something ridiculous, made her chest hurt a little.

She might be going to Los Angeles again, soon. Then again, maybe in the morning, when the buzz from the wine had worn off, maybe Laurie would reconsider. It was equally possible he'd forget all about it.

At the end of the evening, Nicola called a car service to pick up Laurie. It was tough hailing a cab on her street, and there was no chance she'd trust him to navigate the subway alone. She poured him into the back seat, made sure he had his wallet on him, made sure he had a credit card inside his wallet to pay the driver, and saw him safely off.

Back in the apartment, Donya washed dishes. Nicola gathered up their empty wine glasses from where they'd left them on the coffee table after dinner and placed them by the sink. "So that was Laurie Sparks," Donya said.

"That was Laurie Sparks." A pause. "What do you think?"

"He's adorable." Donya smiled. "He's got the survival skills of a bunny rabbit, though. I worry that the world is going to crush him at some point."

She was silent for a moment. She added a long squirt of dishwashing soap to the hot water in the sink. Nicola knew Donya wanted a place with a dishwasher, wanted a place with central heat and new pipes, wanted a place in Manhattan. When the lease was up in January, she'd probably look to upgrade her living situation. Nicola was fine with their current place. One apartment was as good as another. "Is he really sending you to Los Angeles, do you think?"

"I don't know. I put it at fifty-fifty," Nicola said.

Donya glanced at her. Her expression was sharp. "If you go, you're not going to see him, are you?"

Nicola didn't pretend to misunderstand. "I'm not planning on it."

"You're not going to drive past your old place, you're not going to drop by the office to say hi to everyone, you're not going to hang out at any of your old haunts on the off-chance you'll run into him, right?"

"Give me some credit," Nicola said. "If I go—which, I remind you, is kind of a big if—it'll just be to pop into that shop, find out what I can about the coat, then fly back here. I'm not keen on opening old wounds."

"Good." Donya looked like she didn't believe her. Nicola couldn't say she blamed her.

CHAPTER NINE

A LITTLE TO Nicola's surprise, she really did find herself flying to Los Angeles the next day. Even more surprising was that Laurie went with her.

Laurie explained he'd need to see the inventory at the resale shop in person, because Nicola wouldn't be able to tell if any other garments bore a resemblance to Kip Caprini's 1984 fall collection. Made sense, though Nicola suspected he was looking for an excuse to take a break before Fashion Week, which kicked off on Monday.

He'd be multi-tasking in Los Angeles. The Emmys were tomorrow, Sunday, and he had an invitation to a big post-awards bash hosted by *NYC Elite*'s production company.

They flew first class. Nicola squawked about the exorbitant and unnecessary expense of this; Laurie calmly replied that she was welcome to switch her ticket to economy, if it made her feel more at home, but he wanted champagne, leg room, and hot lemon-scented towels. Nicola fought down pangs of guilt and sat beside him in a comfortable leather seat with a fold-down footstool and a portable entertainment system in the mesh pocket in front of her. They boarded early; when the rest of the passengers trudged past them en route to the back of the plane, she felt like a fraud. Laurie just swaddled himself in a gigantic cashmere blanket, donned a blue satin sleep mask, and napped, an untouched flute of champagne resting on the tray table built into his armrest.

Upon arrival at LAX, Nicola helped Laurie retrieve his three oversized pink suede suitcases at baggage claim. At the rental car counter, she shot down his insistent demands that she rent them something flashy. She would be doing all the driving, as Laurie didn't have a license, and flashy was not high on her list of priorities.

Their hotel was in Beverly Hills on Burton Way, a yellow brick structure with cheerful red awnings and a courtyard filled with jasmine bushes. Their rooms were on opposite ends; Nicola had a single room on a low floor, while Laurie had a suite on the highest level. The wealthier the guest, the closer to godliness.

After checking in, she drove their unflashy rental vehicle to the studio resale shop in Culver City. A Saturday afternoon, warm and sunny without being oppressively hot, and the traffic on the 10 Freeway moved swiftly. Something about the open space of the road and the gradual sprawl of the city surrounding it made the sick knot she'd felt in her guts all summer begin to lessen.

The shop was on Washington, tucked away in a strip mall between a Cuban restaurant and a Coffee Bean. Nicola retrieved the coat from the backseat and, with Laurie at her heels, entered the store.

A single spacious room with high ceilings, almost like a warehouse. Nothing but circular racks of clothes placed too close together, leaving little room for aisles or walkways. Nicola headed straight for the sole cashier, a willowy young man in a blue suede shirt, and draped the coat across the counter.

"Hi," she said. "My friend bought this here. We were just wondering what production it was from?"

The young man glanced at the "HOH" marked inside the collar and nodded. "*Holmby Hills*," he said.

"What's that?" she asked. In the three yards between the front door and the register, she'd somehow managed to lose track of Laurie. Ah, there he was, riveted by a display of glittery costume jewelry.

"Show on The CW last year. Lasted maybe half a season. You didn't miss much," he said. "Terrible stuff. Like *Dynasty* for teens, only they were trying too hard to make it campy, and that sucked all the fun out of it."

He was much too young to be using *Dynasty* as a pop-culture touchstone. "Thanks. Do you have other clothes from that show here?" she asked.

He shrugged. "We got a huge shipment from them, but that was maybe four months ago, so most of it's probably already gone. Go ahead and look around—everything will be marked with that same code." He bent down over the counter and nodded at Laurie by the jewelry case, his voice low and conspiratorial. "Over there. Is that Laurie Sparks?"

Nicola didn't bother to turn around. "Uh-huh. He's my boss."

"Really?" The young clerk gazed at Laurie, his expression dazzled and dazed, and Nicola mentally rolled her eyes. "He's so *stylish*," he said, the last word coming out as a faint dreamy sigh.

Nicola collected Laurie. "Come on. We're looking for anything with "HOH" written inside the collar. *Holmby Hills*."

Laurie looked around the store. His nose wrinkled. "It smells funny in here."

It didn't. It smelled like a bunch of used clothes crammed into one space, which maybe wasn't the freshest odor in the world, but it wasn't bad. She pointed at a rack. "Start looking. You start on that side of the room, I'll start at the other, and we'll meet in the middle."

She searched and searched, systematically working her way through the racks, reading the three-letter code inked on each collar of every garment. She glanced over at Laurie, who'd opted for a different approach. He'd circle each rack once, then pull out items of clothing at random for a closer look.

It took them just under two hours to go through the entire store. Nicola found a total of eight items with the appropriate mark. Some bore labels from other designers, which would presumably rule them out, but she grabbed them anyway in the interest of completion. Three dresses, a pair of slacks, three women's dress shirts, one men's suit jacket. Laurie found one dress, something in a dusty violet satin.

"What'd you get?" Laurie asked. She passed her bundle over to him. He spread them out across the top of a rack and went through them one by one. "Not it. Not it, not it, not it. No way." The dress shirts, the jacket, and the slacks all got tossed in his discard pile after a quick glance. After a longer look, he rejected one of the dresses as well.

The remaining two dresses, a navy coatdress and a pale green sheath with a mandarin collar, received more appraisal. Laurie examined the seams, turned them inside out, searched for tags or labels, found none. Laurie nodded. "These three dresses. Same designer who made your coat."

He bundled up the dresses in his arms and headed for the register, where the willowy young man was thrilled to wait on him. His demeanor was composed, even aloof, but Nicola noted the spots of color in his cheeks, the shy glances he slid in Laurie's direction whenever Laurie wasn't looking. He remained silent for the entire transaction until the very end, when he scrawled something on the bottom of the receipt before handing it over. "That's my number," he said to Laurie. He shrugged. "I'm Stuart. Just, you know . . . just in case. Whatever."

His entire face was bright red by the time he finished, and he was too embarrassed to look directly at Laurie. Laurie beamed at him. "Thank you, Stuart," he said.

Back in the car, Nicola nodded at the receipt still in Laurie's hand. "You planning on doing anything with that?" she asked.

"The plan is never to date again, ever, until death renders the whole question moot, so . . ." He crumpled up the receipt. "Sorry, Stuart."

She glanced at him. "You want to talk about it?"

He shook his head. "Nope."

She backed out of the parking lot. He pulled the plastic sack containing his newly-purchased dresses out of the backseat and spread them across his lap. He fingered the fabric of the violet dress, his brow furrowed in thought.

"How can you tell these are by the same designer?" she asked.

He considered. "I don't know how to answer that. It's obvious to me. From my perspective, I guess the question is why can't you tell?"

"It's really that clear, huh?"

"If you were presented with a bunch of different paintings by a bunch of different artists, you could pick out a Mondrian, right? You do know what a Mondrian looks like, right?"

"Yes, dear. No need to be condescending."

"Sorry. Didn't mean to be. But that reinforces my point. Mondrian's paintings are distinct. So are these dresses."

They still just looked like clothes to her, but Laurie seemed adamant. "What do we do now?"

"I don't know. Talk to whoever was in charge of the wardrobe for that show, I guess." He tapped the dresses. "These weren't bought off the rack. They were custom-made. So we need to find out who ordered them from who."

Nicola headed east on Washington. "Shouldn't be too hard to find who that is, right? You've got your phone on you?"

"Sure." Laurie slipped it out of his pocket. Web-enabled, naturally. Mighty convenient. She needed to get herself one of those.

"Try Googling it," she said. "See what comes up."

Laurie looked over at her, baffled and helpless. "What would I type?" he asked.

"You'll have to experiment around. Maybe '*Holmby Hills* wardrobe' will do it. Or try 'costumer,' if 'wardrobe' doesn't get you what you want." She waited as Laurie typed something on his tiny keypad. "What'd you get?"

A long, long pause while Laurie scrolled through his results, so long that Nicola was tempted to tell him not to bother, that she'd do it herself when they got back to the hotel.

"Molly Gable," he said at last, triumph in his voice. "How do we contact her, though? The show's been canceled."

"Don't know. Google her and let's see."

Laurie obeyed. Another long pause while he sorted through the results. "I think she's got a Twitter account," he said. He sounded uncertain.

"Good, that's a start. Is it the right Molly Gable?"

"I don't know. It just says 'Molly Gable.' How can I tell?"

"Check her profile. What does it say?"

Another long pause. "Ha! *Wardrobe superstar and all-around amazing chick,*" he said. "Hey, she follows me! Weird."

Not too weird, really. Laurie was a fashion designer, and Molly Gable's career centered around clothes. "Great. Tweet at her, will you? Tell her you want to talk to her about the *Holmby Hills* clothes."

Laurie bent his head over his tiny keypad and typed away with both thumbs. "Done. Now what?"

"Now we wait for her to tweet you back. When she does, ask for her phone number. If we do this entirely through Twitter, it's going to take forever."

"We should meet her in person, shouldn't we?" Laurie asked. "She'd probably be more likely to give us information."

"If you'd rather do that, sure."

"It'd be better. I tend to go over really well in person, because I'm pretty and famous. The effect gets diluted over the phone."

"Sure, but I think your best quality is your modesty," she said.

Laurie shrugged. "I'm not being conceited. I really *am* both pretty and famous. It's not like it's even an opinion."

Nicola glanced over at him, so beautiful and self-satisfied and oblivious, and said nothing.

MOLLY GABLE RESPONDED to Laurie's tweet later that afternoon. Laurie showed Nicola the message, which started out with "OMG! I LOVE YOU!" before Molly got control of herself and turned off the caps lock long enough to suggest meeting at seven at a bar in Hollywood. The details were hashed out through an exchange of tweets. Nicola winced at that, because anyone reading Laurie's Twitter would know exactly when and where he'd be that evening. She wanted to suggest he take more care with his personal information, but he'd probably just roll his eyes and shrug off her warning, which would make her feel old and stodgy.

Molly was adorable. Short red hair which she tried to wear in a sleek, sophisticated bob. Her natural curls had other ideas, and even as Nicola and Laurie talked with her, squeezed into a corner booth in a hot and crowded nightspot, they struggled to revert to a corkscrew shape.

Molly was in her early thirties, probably, which made her too old to be sending anyone all-caps messages beginning with "OMG!", but she was so clearly smitten with Laurie that Nicola was willing to assume hormones had overridden common sense. Nicola sipped a glass of red wine, Molly nursed a mojito, and Laurie, bless his fluffy little soul, was making his way through a fluorescent blue bubble-gum martini. Couldn't drink champagne all the time, she supposed.

Molly wasn't much help. She seemed crushed about this. When Laurie showed her the dresses and the coat, she nodded. "Okay, yeah, I was hoping you weren't going to ask about those," she said. "Those were all from Gina's wardrobe. Gina Davenport."

"Gina Davenport was in *Holmby Hills*?" Nicola asked.

"Yeah, she played the main character's mom," Molly said. "Anyway, some of her wardrobe was custom-made by a personal friend, which usually isn't the sort of thing we'd do, but she convinced the producers because, well, she's Gina Davenport. Also because the stuff was pretty good. I mean, that purple dress is gorgeous, right?"

"Do you know the name of this friend?" Laurie asked.

Molly shook her head. "I don't remember. It was a weird arrangement. I didn't have anything to do with it. I saw her name and address on invoices a couple of times, but I never met her or anything. I know she lived in Nevada, for whatever that's worth."

"It was a woman?" Laurie asked. "You're sure of that?"

"Yeah. I think her name was . . . Joelle?" Molly looked uncertain. "Joelle. I think that was it. Complete blank on her last name, though. And it was definitely Nevada, I know that. I'm not sure about the town, but it was someplace I'd never heard of. Not like Vegas or Reno or anything."

"Was it sent to a home address, or in care of a company?" Nicola asked. Laurie's eyes met hers over the rim of his martini glass. He looked approving, like he was glad she was asking smart questions. Strange how having Laurie's approval seemed to matter.

"Just a street address, no company name. I noticed that specifically, because that's not usually the way it works. I mean, it's not like I deal with the designers directly, obviously. We always go through a representative at their business office, or I purchase stuff outright from a boutique or department store."

"Are you on good terms with Gina?" Laurie asked. "Would you feel okay asking her for the name of her friend?"

Uncertainty crossed Molly's face as the impulse to make Laurie happy warred with a reluctance to promise more than she might be able to deliver. "I don't know. Gina's totally cool, but I don't know her all that well."

"You could try calling her though, right?" Laurie asked. "I mean, worst that could happen is she'd say no."

Molly still looked torn. "Now that the show's canceled, I don't know how to get in touch with her."

"Would someone at the production company have that information?" Laurie asked. "You could call one of the producers. They'd know how to reach Gina."

"I could probably do that, I guess." Molly started to look unhappy, which meant it was time for Nicola to step in.

"If it's any trouble, don't worry about it," she said. "Laurie and I can try getting in touch with Gina Davenport on our own."

Laurie glared at her. She ignored him. Molly looked relieved.

"Okay, great," Molly said. "I mean, I'll definitely ask around. I just don't know how much help I'll be. Everyone's kind of moved on, you know?"

"Lot of that going on these days," Nicola said. Beside her, Laurie gave her a curious look, but said nothing.

IN THE CAR back to the hotel, Laurie looked glum and prickly. "Well, *that's* probably a dead end," he said.

"Maybe, maybe not. I wouldn't worry about it," Nicola said. "If Molly can't help us, we'll take a different approach. Maybe we can try to track down Gina Davenport's agent or something." She threw a side glance at Laurie. "Gina might want to meet with you, what with you being so pretty and famous."

Laurie didn't rise to the bait. "It's possible," he said.

"If not . . ." Damn it. Here it came, the same urge to please Laurie that Molly had experienced earlier. "If all else fails, I might know a way to meet Gina. Might."

Laurie perked up. He glanced at her. "Oh? Do tell."

She shook her head. "I said might. I also said if all else fails. Let's see if Molly gets anywhere first."

"You've been holding out on me, Strozyk," Laurie said cheerfully. "I didn't know you had *connections*."

Something about that made her feel a little sad and pitiful, like she'd been overselling herself just for Laurie's approval. "I don't," she said. It came out curt, which drew a startled look from him. "So what's this thing you're going to tomorrow night?"

"Our production company is throwing a big swanky shindig at the Peninsula. Fancy people in fancy dress. It's the type of thing that'd make you break out into hives." He grinned. "I considered asking you to go with me, just to get back at you for dragging me to Queens."

"I'm glad you restrained yourself. Does your production company think *NYC Elite* is going to sweep the Emmys?"

"Sadly, zero nominations. Until they create a category for Most Glamorous Reality-Show Participant, we're doomed to get overlooked," Laurie said. "No, they produce other shows, too. That one about boring old married people doing boring old married things, the one that's a remake of that boring old show from the eighties? They produce that one. It won a bunch of crap last year. It'll probably win a bunch of crap this year, too."

Nicola puzzled it out. "Are you talking about the *thirtysomething* reboot?" she asked.

"Yeah. That's the one. Have you watched it? It's awful. Why do people get so dull as soon as they hit their thirties?"

Nicola would take offense at this, but her brain was occupied with other matters. "Clarion Studios, right? I didn't realize your show was produced by Clarion."

"Yeah, that's it." He glanced at her. "What's up? You look weird."

She shook her head. "Nothing. Clarion's production offices are located on the Sony lot, that's all. I used to work in the same building with them." Deep breath. She shouldn't ask. She shouldn't ask. She shouldn't ask.

"Could I go with you?" she asked. She focused on the road, couldn't look at Laurie. "Do you have a plus-one?"

She couldn't see Laurie, but she could almost hear the gears in his brain start to whir as he tried to figure this one out. "I do," he said at last. "Why do you want to go?"

"I like parties every now and then. It could be fun."

"Liar." Amusement in the single word. "You want to see someone, don't you? As soon as you found out it was a Clarion party, that's when you decided you wanted to go." He thought for a moment. "Is it *thirtysomething?* One of the actors? Do you have a crush on an actor?"

"I just want to go to the party, Laurie." She sounded nonchalant. Good. "If you don't want me to go with you, that's totally okay. It just sounded like fun."

"Uh-huh." Long silence from the passenger seat, and then Laurie spoke again. "One condition."

"Shoot."

"I get to give you a makeover," he said. "Dress, hair, nails, the works."

"Laurie . . ."

"That's my deal," he said. "Makeover. Dictated entirely by me. Take it or leave it."

Hell. Crap. Hell. Surrendering herself to Laurie's concept of what she should look like would be an exercise in ritual humiliation.

Then again, she sure hadn't packed an appropriate dress or shoes for such an event, so she'd have to go shopping anyway. Her self-respect fought a battle with some primal, mortifying, long-buried urge. An urge to look *pretty.*

Self-respect did not win. "Okay," she said.

"Really?" he asked. The surprise in his voice suggested he'd been bluffing. "Really, really?"

"Sure. Might be fun."

"Awesome. So cool. Get me up super-early tomorrow, will you? This is going to take all day." He sounded thrilled, almost giddy at the prospect of getting his dainty hands all over ugly-ducking Nicola.

Lord help them all.

CHAPTER TEN

LAURIE DIDN'T RISE until after noon. Nicola had already breakfasted by herself in the chic little coffee shop in the lobby, had already gone for a long jog in the narrow park that lined Santa Monica Boulevard along the glossy heart of Beverly Hills, had already called up to Laurie's room twice and received no reply, was already giving some consideration to finding a place for lunch, when he finally texted her to meet him up in his suite.

At her knock, he flung open the door and ushered her inside. He was swaddled in a huge white bathrobe that enveloped his tiny body like a hungry fleece amoeba. "Come in. Do you need breakfast? I ordered a lot from room service."

Nicola looked down at the linen-covered cart, which bore great porcelain platters of crisp waffles and sliced fruit, a huge pitcher of orange juice, a graceful silver carafe of coffee. She'd had coffee, but she could use more. And there was no reason waffles couldn't make a perfectly decent lunch.

"I overslept. I was up most of the night," Laurie said. "I watched that entire *Holmby Hills* series online, start to finish, every episode." He looked both bleary and manic.

"Was it any good?" Nicola asked.

"I don't know. After the first ten minutes, I turned the sound off," he said. "I was just watching for the clothes."

He produced a sheaf of handwritten notes, scrawled on a notepad embossed with the hotel's logo at the top. "I examined all of

Gina Davenport's outfits. These are the ones I think were by the same designer who did Caprini's 1984 collection."

Nicola flipped through the notes. They were incoherent to her, and Laurie's handwriting was awful.

"I thought of something last night, too." Laurie looked triumphant. "Gina Davenport was the face of Caprini in the mid-eighties. Remember? Those jeans ads?"

She did remember, now that Laurie mentioned it. Caprini designer jeans, featuring a very young Gina Davenport, sitcom star and everybody's teen sweetheart, long legs and big white teeth and waves of dark feathered hair. "You think Caprini designed Gina's *Holmby Hills* dresses? Maybe just as a favor to her?" she asked. "That would make sense, wouldn't it?"

"Except it's not Caprini. It's whoever designed his '84 collection, and that wasn't him. And Molly specifically mentioned that Joelle person."

There were undercurrents here that made Nicola uncomfortable, like Laurie was pursuing some vendetta against Kip Caprini by trying to mark him as a fraud. Maybe that wasn't it at all, maybe his intentions were good, but still, was there anything that could be gained here? If she thought too much about it, it seemed like an unworthy endeavor.

"If you say so," she said. "But I'm not sure what more we can do right now, other than wait for Molly to get back to us."

"Oh, no. We're not working on this today." Laurie seemed surprised. "Are you kidding? We've got a party tonight. Today is all in the service of that."

He looked around his pretty suite. His drapes were pulled back, offering a view of the Hollywood Hills, iconic sign and all, rising up to meet that endless blue sky. "I had an idea last night . . ."

He rummaged around the closet, disappeared into the bedroom, wandered back into the living room, looked around in helpless confusion. Nicola was just about to ask him what he was looking for when he gave a triumphant yelp and picked up the violet dress, which was folded in a soft, shimmering heap on the coffee table right in front of him.

"See if this fits you," he said.

Nicola took it from him. Her initial reaction was to tell him she couldn't wear it, but why not? It'd save them the trouble of shopping for a new dress.

"Hang on," she said. She disappeared into Laurie's bathroom and shed her clothes. Slipped the soft, featherweight folds of violet over her head and pulled it down as carefully as she could to avoid tearing or snagging the fabric. She tugged the seams straight on the sides and looked at herself in the mirror.

The fit was better than she'd expected. Not perfect—tight around the waist, loose across the hips and bust—but not bad. She had worse-fitting garments in her closet. The dress fell to her knees in a full, flowing skirt. If she twirled in a circle, it'd probably fly up to her waist.

She did not twirl in a circle. She went out to see Laurie. "What do you think?"

The brow creased. "Stand up straight. Can you hold your arms out to the sides?" he asked. He examined her from all angles. He pinched a loose fold of fabric across her hips, he tugged the straps into place, he gave her stomach a quick pat. He nodded.

"We can work with this," he said. "I can make some alterations super-fast. It's going to be a little tight across the belly, though. There's not enough of a seam for me to release it. Gina's got a smaller waist than you."

"Yup. Kind of gathered that," Nicola said. "So should I just not breathe all evening, or . . . ?"

"You can breathe as long as you keep your gut sucked in." It didn't sound like he was kidding. "Okay, take it off and put it back on inside-out. I want to pin you." He picked up a plastic carrier and popped open the top. It contained a pincushion, scissors, spools of colorful thread.

"You brought your sewing kit with you? Very forward-thinking."

"I called the concierge last night and told them what I needed. They sent it up," he said. Of course. In Laurie's world, anything he needed was promptly brought to him by other people.

The day was a flurry of personal grooming and Nicola-improving, much of it done in the privacy of Laurie's suite, thanks to the aid of the unseen, ever-helpful concierge. Laurie's hairstylist of choice in Los Angeles, a briskly competent middle-aged woman named Kimberly, sat Nicola down in the middle of the living room, spread towels around to protect the carpet, consulted briefly with Laurie, whipped out a pair of scissors, and started hacking away at her dry hair.

When Kimberly and Laurie finally let Nicola look in a mirror, she was pleasantly surprised by the result. Her indifferent mop had been transformed into shaggy layers that looked full and healthy. Kimberly spritzed it with a conditioning spray that made it shine like a mink stole and smell like the perfume counter at a high-end department store.

"Ideally, you should go darker," Kimberly said. She scrutinized a hunk of Nicola's hair. "Or lighter, even. You're such an indeterminate shade of brown."

"I think she'd look amazing as a blonde," Laurie said. "But we don't really have time for it today.

Small blessing. She'd look silly as a blonde.

A manicurist came up to the suite next, a young Asian man laden with a metal cart of supplies and clean towels. He soaked her feet in a warm, soapy solution, sanded her heels, filed and buffed and painted her toes. Same ritual for her hands. Her short nails were painted a soft pink. While this took place, Laurie curled up on the embroidered cushions on the window seat, catlike, and hand-stitched alterations to her dress, before surrendering his own dainty mitts to their manicurist's expert ministrations. "Isn't this fun, Nicola?" Laurie asked. He didn't seem to mean it ironically.

Laurie did her makeup himself, Nicola sitting on the sofa while he perched on the edge of the coffee table in front of her. He plucked her brows and painted her eyes and layered goopy beige crud on her skin, then used a thick, stubby brush to dust a pale shimmering powder all over every inch of her face and throat and clavicle.

His touch on her face was light and expert. He sat back to look at his work and smiled.

"You're so pretty," he said. Nicola felt an odd tightening in her chest, the way she sometimes felt when looking through old yearbooks or hearing the music that was popular during her teen years, transported back to a time when *pretty* seemed important or even necessary.

CHAPTER ELEVEN

IT WAS TIME-CONSUMING, this business of looking present-able. The production company sent a limousine to pick them up at eight, and Laurie fussed around right until that moment. A quick detour to a shoe store on El Camino to grab a pair of open-toed high-heeled silver sandals, which made Nicola grateful for her fresh pedicure, and then they were headed to the Peninsula.

Nicola's first trip in a limo was a short one; even counting the vital shoe detour, the distance from their small, swanky hotel to the bigger, swankier Peninsula was less than a mile. Not enough time to pop the cork of one of the half-bottles of Schramsberg stashed in the mini-bar.

Clarion's post-Emmy bash was held up by the rooftop pool, a gorgeous rectangle of shimmering blue surrounded by crisp white canvas cabanas which sheltered the tables of catered food from the elements. Laurie stood and posed dutifully in front of a backdrop splashed with the Clarion name and the logos of various sponsors by the entrance to the roof garden while cameras clicked and journalists shouted questions at him. Nicola stood to the side and observed Laurie. He ignored all the questions, just struck poses in his snow-white suit with the red fur collar and matching cuffs and his shiny red boots while looking haughty and untouchable.

Champagne was proffered on hammered bronze trays by white-suited waiters. Laurie went through glasses like a marathoner swilling water at an aid station. Nicola resisted the temptation to match pace with him. She focused her attention on the fabulous buffet: huge cold prawns served with lemon aioli, rice balls filled with an oozing center of warm herbed cheese, tiny fried chickpea cakes topped with chopped pear tomatoes and purple kalamata olives.

She watched the crowd. The awards show itself would be over by now—it took place in the late afternoon, so East Coast television viewers could watch it during prime time—but no one who'd attended the ceremony had made it to the after-party yet. If there were celebrities here besides Laurie, she hadn't spotted any.

"Laurie Sparks!" A barrel-chested man in his thirties with a broad stubbly face and a head full of rough brown curls came over to them. His hand was locked around the slim wrist of his date, a dead-eyed blonde in a strapless fuchsia patent-leather dress; he half-dragged her over to them. "How the hell are you?"

"Bennett. Good to see you." Laurie and the man hugged, Laurie almost disappearing into the other man's huge chest. When Bennett released him, Laurie placed his hand on Nicola's upper arm. "Bennett, this is Vanya, my bodyguard. She's from Chechnya. She's got an AK-47 strapped to her thigh. Vanya, this is Bennett Wheeler. He produces my show."

Jesus. She should've cut Laurie off from the bubbly stuff a couple glasses ago. "It's Nicola, actually. I'm doing some work for Laurie. Nice to meet you, Bennett." They shook hands. Bennett laughed.

"I like the Russian bodyguard story better. You got a Slavic look to you, you know. Like one of those Russkie models from some dirt-poor village in Siberia or wherever." He winked at her. "You from New York? Lot of those girls end up there."

"My father's family was from Warsaw," she said.

"Yeah, yeah, I can see that, you got that whole Pole thing about you. I was seeing this Polish girl once and she had a jawbone like yours. Knew how to work that jaw, too."

Bennett's date had disentangled her wrist from his grasp and wandered off during this exchange. Nicola spotted her a few paces away, trying to flag down one of the champagne-bearing waiters. Seemed like she had her priorities in the right place.

"So what kind of work you been up to for Laurie?" Bennett asked her. He winked. "I'd say it was something very professional in nature, if you know what I mean, but unless you're packing more than an AK-47 under that dress, Princess Laurie isn't going to be interested, am I right?"

While Nicola was still considering and shooting down a million possible responses to that, Bennett turned his attention to Laurie. "So, hey. Looks like we're definitely on for a second season. There won't be an official word for a while yet, but I didn't want to leave you hanging."

"Well, it's not like it was really in question, was it?" Laurie sounded bored and bitchy. He'd shifted personalities slightly, in some way Nicola couldn't really pinpoint, but she had a sense of him putting on an act, like Bennett's behavior had triggered something dormant and unpleasant in him.

"Naw, but MTV brass had some issues. We're looking at some cast changes, maybe. Not you, bro, you're golden, but they've made a few good suggestions."

"Tell me those suggestions involve getting rid of Valerie. *Please* tell me I won't have to put up with her stupid fat face any more," Laurie said.

Valerie. Nicola cast her mind back to the episode she'd watched. Valerie was a performance artist, a dour, heavyset young woman who'd made a lot of serious proclamations about Art and who made Nicola glad she was no longer in her early twenties, back when she knew everything and made sure everyone around her knew it. It was the inalienable right of twentysomethings everywhere to be insufferable twits. As far as Nicola was concerned, those who went through that phase on television were more to be pitied than reviled.

Laurie and Bennett thought otherwise. "You got it, bro," Bennett said. The mind boggled at Laurie being called "bro" in an unironic sense. "Don't tell anyone, obvs, but she's pretty much dunzo."

"MTV decided viewers didn't really want to spend their time watching fat, ugly heifers? There's a shock." Laurie sipped his champagne, glossy pink lips somehow managing not to leave any trace of lipstick behind on the rim. Nicola wasn't holding a glass, which was probably good, because she'd be tempted to throw the contents in his pretty, pretty face.

Bennett barked out a laugh. "I know, right? Ol' Valerie made good television, I guess, but that face . . ." He made a retching noise. Laurie giggled, the song of angels. Nicola gripped the edge of her dainty porcelain hors d'oeuvre plate so tightly she thought she might reduce it to sand.

Bennett clapped Laurie on the shoulder. "I gotta schmooze, bro. Good seeing you here. Nice meeting you, Polish girl, whatever your name was," he said to Nicola. He disappeared into the crowd.

The party filled up, the noise from the cluster of journalists near the entrance grew louder. Laurie looked around. "I think the people who were at the ceremony are arriving now."

"What the hell was that, Laurie?" Nicola asked.

Laurie looked guilty but unrepentant. "What, the Vanya-from-Chechnya bit? Sorry. I just thought you looked like a sexy Russian spy in that dress. Bennett agreed."

"Bennett also thought I looked like a hooker, possibly one with a penis, but that's not what I'm talking about. I mean the fat jokes," she said. "Really?"

Laurie stared at her for a minute, color rising in his face. "Valerie is a very unpleasant person," he said. "Really. She's been a huge bitch to everyone, me included." His voice was loud, too loud. "And she's fat. That's a fact, that's not me being bitchy."

"Are you kidding me? That's one hundred percent you being bitchy. And it's really not a smooth move to talk that way with one of the show's producers."

"Bennett obviously agreed with me. Obviously." Laurie was very red now. He looked defiant and embarrassed.

"Sure. And Bennett struck me as an astute judge of character," she said.

"I don't know why you think it's such a big deal. You can be so judgmental sometimes," he said. He sounded like a petulant child. He looked around for a waiter. "I need more champagne."

Drop it and move on. Laurie was her boss, and he was also a dumb kid, and that combination meant she would never, ever win any arguments with him.

"Ooo, look!" Laurie said, his sudden funk forgotten. He pointed near the door. "Shiny things."

A couple had just passed the media gauntlet and had entered the sanctity of the pool area. The woman wore a floor-length gown in emerald satin; her date wore a classic tux and carried a shiny gold Emmy statuette. It was this that had attracted Laurie's magpie-like attention.

"She's on some TV show, right? I've seen her picture on bill-boards," Laurie said.

"She's on *thirtysomething*," Nicola said. "Marissa Kestleman." Her throat was dry, ashes and sand in her larynx, and damn it, she really could use some champagne to get things lubricated.

"Is it hers or his?" Laurie asked. "Is he someone?"

Nicola just shook her head. Laurie wasn't looking at her, his attention fixed on the new arrivals. Probably for the best. Her expression could freeze him to stone just now.

"I'm going to ask if I can hold it," Laurie said. He bounded off.

"Laurie, wait—" Too late. He zipped his way through the crowd. Nicola hesitated—*last chance to get the hell out of here*—then charged after him.

"Hi! I'm Laurie Sparks. Oh my God, that's gorgeous, congratulations, can I hold it?" One blur of words. The couple looked delighted and irritated, like someone's adorable Pomeranian was getting his muddy paws all over their brand-new sofa.

"I suppose. Be careful. It's surprisingly heavy." The man passed it over to Laurie with a trace of visible reluctance.

"So totally cool. I want one of these," Laurie said. "Is it yours?"

"It's his," Nicola said. "Hi, Alex."

The man stopped staring wistfully at his Emmy and looked at Nicola. His smile froze. "Oh, hell," he finally said.

"Marissa. How are you?" Nicola said to the woman.

Marissa was faster to recover than Alex. Well, she was an actress, and though it pained Nicola to admit it, a damn good one. "Nicola! Wow. You look so different. I love what you've done with your hair. I had no idea you'd be here."

"It was a last-minute thing. I've been doing some work for Laurie here," she said. "This is Laurie Sparks. He's on *NYC Elite*."

"They probably already know that," Laurie said.

Alex finally spoke. His voice sounded strained. Good. "You were in New York," he said.

Seeing Alex unsettled like this made her feel hard and flinty. "I still am. This is just a business trip." She nodded at the statuette in Laurie's hands. "I see you won. Congratulations."

"Thank you." Alex swallowed, his Adam's apple bobbing. "Ah, this is weird, isn't it?"

Laurie was looking from Alex to Nicola, the Emmy forgotten in his grasp. "So what's the story here? How do you all know each other?"

"Laurie, this is Alex Weinberg. He's the EP and showrunner for *thirtysomething*. And that's Marissa Kestleman, of course. His leading lady."

A confused fumbling of hands as Laurie tried to pass back the statuette and shake hands and balance his empty champagne flute all at the same time. "Nice to meet you. Nicola never told me she knew anyone famous."

"Alex has an office at Clarion. That's where we met. We also lived together for ten years," Nicola said. "He moved out five months ago and bought a house with Marissa."

Laurie's eyes opened wide. "Oh," he said. "Oh!"

"Nicola . . ." A warning note in Alex's voice. Marissa looked friendlier than Alex, but her smile had the tension of a buzzing power line. This could easily devolve into a huge, awful scene.

It wouldn't. Nicola wouldn't do that. Marissa was a nice person, that was maybe the worst thing about this whole mess. Alex was nice, too; she couldn't have loved him so much for so long if he wasn't. Their actions had been indefensible, but no doubt they both felt awful about poor old Nicola, who ended up on the sidelines when they discovered their beautiful love for each other. She smiled, a rictus grin that was supposed to reassure them, but which probably inspired cold terror.

"I'm glad I saw you, Alex," she said, "because I wanted to ask you a favor. Are you still in touch with Gina Davenport?"

It took Alex a moment to recover enough savoir-faire to switch trains of thought and answer her question. "Sure. We don't hang out or anything, but I have her number."

To Laurie, Nicola said, "Before *thirtysomething*, Alex produced that *L.A. Law* revival that was on a couple years ago. That was a Clarion show, too." Gina Davenport had played the sexy senior partner at the firm. Seven episodes were produced; the network yanked it from the schedule after only three had aired. Alex took it hard. He and Nicola went on a road trip to Napa while he nursed his wounds. They'd stayed at a bed-and-breakfast and ate pheasant stuffed with chestnuts and dried cherries and drank excellent local wines until Alex had decided he was ready to face the world again.

Laurie had looked baffled by the whole encounter. Now that Gina's name had entered into it, his focus returned. "I need to ask

Gina some questions about her outfits," he said. "It's super-important for my new line."

"If you can get us a meeting with Gina, that would be great," Nicola said. *You owe me.* "It'd have to be soon, though. We're not going to be in town long. Laurie is showing a collection at Fashion Week."

"Okay. Okay, sure. I can text her right now," Alex said. "I'll give you a call when I hear from her."

"You've still got my number? It hasn't changed," Nicola said.

"I've got it, Nicola." Alex looked defeated. Did she feel good about that, or not?

"Nice seeing you again, Nicola. Nice meeting you, Laurie. I love your clothes, really. I have one of your coats, and I wear it all the time," Marissa said. She smiled and shook hands with them again. So nice. So goddamned nice.

And then Marissa and Alex had moved on, no doubt to collect their wits and compare notes on the weirdness of being ambushed by a wronged and pathetic ex-girlfriend on Emmy night. Nicola exhaled, then remembered she couldn't breathe out all the way without the dress pinching her waist.

"Well," Laurie said. "Well, well, well. That was interesting." He grinned. "You should have given me some warning in advance. I would have come up with some fabulous lies about how we'd met. We could have convinced them we were having a scorching affair."

"I'm going to go," Nicola said. "I'm just going to catch a cab out front. I'll see you back at the hotel."

"I'll go with you," Laurie said. "There's no one famous here anyway."

He took her arm, which was nice of him, and walked with her out through the back exit. A conversation with a suited valet, and their limo appeared in a few minutes.

Tricky to climb into the limo in those absurd heels, and the satiny folds of the skirt kept tangling around her knees. She ended up flopping into her seat. She was stupid and graceless, covered in clown paint in an attempt to look like someone she wasn't.

As soon as they were ensconced in the backseat, a dark glass partition separating them from the driver, Nicola felt a little of the panicky pressure in her chest recede at last. Laurie looked at her. "You okay?" he asked.

She nodded, not trusting herself to speak. Laurie observed her in silence for a moment, then leaned back in his seat. "You settled, you know," he said.

Nicola looked at him in confusion. Laurie continued. "Alex. The shows he produces are total crap, Emmy or no Emmy. I mean, seriously, *L.A. Law? thirtysomething?* What's next on his slate—a triumphant revival of *China Beach? Hill Street Blues: The Next Generation?* Real innovative there, Alex."

Nicola didn't say anything. Laurie continued, warming to his subject. "He's not even that good-looking. You're so much prettier than he is, it's not even funny. He's going to be bald within the next five years, guaranteed. That hairline is a danger zone."

"He's a good guy, mostly," she said. Her voice sounded very distant. "We had a nice time together."

Laurie smiled at her, drunk and sloppy and somehow very endearing. He'd smudged his makeup, dark smears of liner under his right eye, and it made it look like he'd been punched. "You can do better than him," he said. "So, so much better."

The weight inside her threatened to dissolve and unleash a torrent of tears. Nicola felt an urge to lean against Laurie and sob, but she'd get his white suit messy with smeared makeup and snot, and her self-respect had already suffered enough blows for one day. She settled for patting him on the arm once, then leaning back into the leather seat and staring out at the posh streets of Beverly Hills.

CHAPTER TWELVE

ALEX CALLED THE next morning. Nicola was a little surprised to hear from him.

"Gina's invited us over for lunch," he said. "You, me, and Laurie. Does two o'clock work for you?"

"That'd be great."

"She's in Topanga Canyon. Should we just meet there?" Alex read off the address; Nicola scribbled it down on a pad on the bedside table.

"We'll be there," she said. "Thanks, Alex."

"I think Gina's looking forward to it. When I mentioned Laurie's name, she sounded a bit giddy."

"That tends to happen with Laurie."

"I have to say, I have a hard time wrapping my mind around you working for him. You've never been big on fashion, you know."

"I do know, in fact. It's just a job." A near-palpable strain, this simple conversation, for both of them. "We'll see you at two."

"Sure. See you then." The relief in his voice at the prospect of ending the call came through the phone. Nicola hung up. She felt exhausted and unwell.

She glanced at the violet dress, which hung neatly in the closet, the silver sandals placed beneath it. A dress made by an unknown designer, one Laurie was intent on tracking down, regardless of the cost. Nicola had a flickering thought, a weird hunch trickling around the back of her brain, that the cost might end up being higher than he guessed.

GINA DAVENPORT LIVED in a sprawling house—not a mansion, not by Los Angeles standards, but roomy nonetheless—atop a bluff along a winding road in Topanga Canyon. Alex was already parked outside when they arrived. He got out of his car, the same old silver Saab he'd bought five or six years ago, back before he'd become the industry's latest It Boy, and walked over to meet them.

"Hi, Nicola. Laurie, nice to see you again." Alex gave Laurie a bewildered glance, as though startled to realize his makeup and fancy clothes were part of his everyday image and not something he just whipped out on special occasions. Today, Laurie had paired a black velvet t-shirt with lavender satin Capri pants. Almost conservative by his standards.

Alex looked good, whatever Laurie might have said about his hairline. An inch taller than Nicola, with long, lanky limbs. In jeans and a button-down shirt and his usual wire-rimmed glasses, he looked brainy and sensible, like the Yale English major he'd once been.

It hurt to look at him.

Gina Davenport met them at the door. Barefoot, in skintight jeans and a flowery chiffon tunic. She had a wineglass in one hand, filled with something pale and bubbly. She smiled at them, veneers and dimples flashing. "Alex! Sweetheart, so nice to see you again! Come in, all of you." She ushered them inside.

Nicola glanced around. Gina's home was open and airy. High ceilings with exposed beams and rustic wood floors made from misshapen boards, pieced together jigsaw-style.

Gina and Alex hugged and bussed cheeks, smiling all the while. Gina had to be approaching fifty now, though she looked at least a decade younger, even without makeup. Smooth skin pulled tight across her cheeks and brow, breasts high and full.

"Gina, this is Laurie Sparks. And Nicola, my . . . friend."

The dimples flashed on them, and Nicola found herself dazzled by the force of her personality and charm. Gina shook her hand. "Nicola, so nice to meet you. And this gorgeous little one, of course, I already know." Her attention shifted to Laurie. "It's so amazing to have you here, in my very own home. I have gobs of your clothes in my closet, I'll have to show you later. You're such a talented little thing!"

"Oh, wow. That's so cool, coming from you. You're a total fashion icon." Laurie sounded like a star-struck kid, which was a big improvement over his world-weary sophisticate act the previous night. "That's really an honor, thank you."

"I have lunch set out on the patio, just through here." Gina padded across the boards and led them out the sliding doors. The wooden patio was built out over the edge of the bluff; if Nicola glanced through the gaps in the boards, she could see the rocky ground far below. A panoramic view of the city, the horizon brown with smog under that blue, blue sky. "I'm having a wine spritzer, but there's water, too, if anyone would rather."

Lunch consisted of apple slices arranged in a neat spiral on a plate, an accompanying spiral of sliced cheddar, and an unopened box of rye crackers. Gina giggled in apology as she gestured toward the spread.

"I know this looks pretty rinky-dink, but I wasn't planning on entertaining today. Being way out here in the middle of nowhere, it's an ordeal getting anyone to deliver in a timely manner."

"Looks great, Gina. We're just glad you could meet at the last minute like this," Alex said.

At Gina's insistence, they sat around the table. Gina poured out white wine for everyone, then added a healthy dollop of seltzer to each glass. Hard to see the point of wine spritzers, really; adding the seltzer damaged the taste and diluted the delightful capacity for intoxication. Reduced the calories, though, and that was probably what Gina, as a working actress, was concerned about.

Gina sipped at her watery wine-beverage and fluttered long lashes at Laurie. She leaned forward and rested her chin on her palm, elbow on the table, languid and slinky. "You are just so pretty I can't stand it. You almost make me wish I had a cock, just so I'd have a shot with you."

Laurie looked startled. Maybe a little annoyed, though he hid it well. "That's . . . nice of you to say."

"I'm addicted to your little show," she said, her manner confiding. Girl-talk. "You're just so cute. I have a huge weakness for bitchy little queens. If you're ever looking for a fag hag, I totally volunteer. I just want to cuddle with you and keep you as a pet."

Well, this was getting creepy fast. Across the table, Alex cleared his throat.

"We don't mean to take up much of your afternoon, Gina," he said.

Gina ignored him, her attention focused on Laurie. "So, darling boy, Alex has been a little cagey about the purpose of this meeting, but I gather you wanted to talk to me about clothes?" Flirtatious banter, flirtatious body language. It was playful, sure, but it seemed like there was a genuine, and aggressive, attempt at seduction in it, too.

Laurie sipped at his wine spritzer. He looked unruffled, but his color was high beneath his makeup. "I did. I'm obsessed with the gorgeous clothes you wore on *Holmby Hills*. I was just wondering if you could tell me anything about who designed them."

An immediate reaction, sharp and unexpected. Gina's body language changed. In the middle of making goo-goo eyes at Laurie, she froze, a mouse spotted by a swooping eagle. It looked like she stopped breathing. The change in her demeanor was striking enough that Alex frowned and set his glass down on the table.

"Why?" Gina straightened up. She stared at Laurie. "Why on earth would you be asking about that?"

Laurie opened his eyes wide. "Because they're fabulous, that's why. You must've gotten loads of comments on them."

"The show wasn't on the air long enough for anyone to comment," Gina said with a hint of acid. She sighed dramatically. "Darling boy, I wore a lot of different clothes by many, many different designers, and I couldn't possibly keep track of all of them."

"We talked to Molly Gable in the costume department," Nicola said. "We got the impression from her that some of your wardrobe for the show was provided by you personally."

Gina looked at Nicola, and for the first time Nicola detected animosity, sweeping and poisonous, paired with something she couldn't peg. Alarm, maybe.

"I don't know why she'd tell you that," Gina said. "That's silly. That's not how these things work. Alex, you of all people should know that. Stars don't provide their own wardrobe."

Alex shifted on the wooden bench. He looked from Gina to Nicola, brow creased. "Gina . . ."

"If it helps, I made a list of the clothes I'm specifically interested in finding more about," Laurie said. He extracted his sheaf of handwritten notes from the back pocket of his satin pants and passed them to her.

Gina didn't take them. She stared at his notes like they might bite her. "I told you, I don't know anything." She looked at Alex. "You didn't tell me this was what they wanted to see me about."

"I didn't know." Alex looked dazed. "Why does it matter? If you don't know where your clothes came from, no problem. No harm done, right?"

Gina got herself under control. The smile returned, flirtatious and warm. "Of course. It's fine, really." She took a sip of her wine. Her hand shook. "I guess I'm still feeling a little sensitive about

Holmby Hills getting canceled. I didn't mean to sound like such a diva there, but there's really nothing worth talking about now."

"Okay, then." Alex sounded bright and cheerful. "I guess that's that. Gina, can I pour you more wine?"

"You know what, I think I'm coming down with a headache," Gina said. She smiled again. Her famous dimples weren't flashed quite as deeply as before, but her smile was still lovely. "Sorry if I seemed bitchy. I'm really not feeling well at all today, but I was trying to put on a brave front for my visitors. I guess it didn't work. Silly of me."

Laurie nodded. He seemed wholly sympathetic and concerned, like the dimples had worked their spell on him. "Of course. I'm so sorry for bothering you about this. I just thought your clothes on the show were really pretty, that's all." He flashed his own dazzling smile.

"You're such a sweetie." Gina reached across the table and laid her hand on his. "You'll have to come over some time when I'm feeling more like myself. Though I warn you," she said, lashes fluttering for all they were worth, "I might get you drunk and try to take advantage of you."

Laurie laughed and disentangled his hand from hers. He got to his feet. "We'll get out of your hair so you can take care of your headache. I hope you feel better soon. Thank you so much for taking the time to meet with us."

"Sure, honey, no problem. I'm sorry I wasn't more help." Gina proffered her hand; Laurie and Nicola shook it in turn.

Alex rose as well. "I'll walk them out, Gina, then I'll help you find something for your head," he said. "If you need anything, I can run into town and pick it up for you."

"Thanks, Alex. You're a doll." A few more exchanged niceties and apologies, and then Alex was escorting Nicola and Laurie back through the house.

No one said anything until they reached the front door. With a quick glance toward the patio to make sure Gina was out of earshot, Alex asked in a low voice, "Anything going on I should know?"

"No more than what Laurie said. We're just interested in whoever made her clothes, that's it."

"Want me to see if I can find out what that was about?" Alex said. "I can talk to her after she's calmed down."

She still *liked* Alex, damn it. She knew she still loved him, loved him almost as much as she detested him, but she hadn't realized how much she'd missed his shrewd intelligence and his kindness . . .

Scratch that. Starting an affair with Marissa hadn't been kind, not at all.

She nodded. "If you can."

"I'll call you." He shook hands with Laurie, seemed to consider giving Nicola a hug, then compromised by patting her on the shoulder.

Alone in the car once more, Laurie turned to her. "You look weird," he said. "Is it Alex, or Gina?"

She considered. "Both. Gina, mostly." Checked for oncoming traffic, pulled off of the shoulder, flipped a careful U-turn on the precarious canyon road, headed downhill. "I think I might owe you an apology."

"Why?"

"I've been assuming you've been making more of this than it warranted. This whole business with the coat and the dresses, I don't know that I believed there was anything worth investigating. But Gina's reaction . . ."

"I know. Bizarre, right?" Laurie seemed unruffled by her lack of faith in him.

"So what do we think that was about? What's going on with the clothes?"

Laurie thought, chewing on his lower lip, brow creased. "Either Molly was lying and/or didn't know what she was talking about when she said Gina's clothes were designed by a mysterious friend in Nevada, or Gina was lying and/or didn't know what she was talking about. Of the two, I trust Molly. Gina's creepy."

"No argument here." She glanced over at him. "She got a little weird with you."

He shrugged. "It happens. She's not the first."

"You mind?"

He seemed to choose his words carefully. "There's no point in minding. If I want to dress the way I dress, look the way I look, then I can't really have a problem with getting noticed, can I? People sometimes don't respond to me the way I want them to, that's all."

He shrugged, like the subject was boring him. "Do you think Alex will be able to find out anything more?"

"He might. He can be pretty sneaky when he wants to be."

"He's okay," Laurie said suddenly. "I can see why you were with him. I mean, I hate his guts because he cheated on you and dumped you, but he's okay."

"Yeah, he is. Except when he's not." Turning onto Mulholland now, heading toward the freeway, leaving the scenic vistas and multimillion-dollar homes behind. "What's the plan now?"

"I'll call Molly again. Maybe she'll know something. I guess we wait to hear from Alex, too."

Nicola glanced over at him. "Fashion Week kicks off today."

"Well aware, thanks. I'm not showing my collection until Thursday."

"I know, but maybe we should think about wrapping it up here?"

Laurie stared out the passenger side window. "We'll fly back tomorrow, probably. Wednesday would be fine, too."

"Is everything going okay with your collection?" she asked.

"Of course it is," Laurie said. "Why would you ask that? It's very, very good." He sounded offended.

Nicola lifted her fingers up off the steering wheel, keeping her palms in place, as a show of surrender. "I'm sure it is. You don't seem to be thinking about it much lately, that's all. I just wondered if that was normal."

"It's great. It's fantastic. I'm not thinking about it much because I don't have to. It's too *late* to think about it, for that matter. Trust me, I know a whole lot more about this sort of thing than you do."

"Unquestionably. No need to be a snot about it."

He didn't say anything, just shot a covert glance over at her. Despite his denials, Nicola wondered.

CHAPTER THIRTEEN

"KIP CAPRINI," ALEX said. Even over the phone, he sounded triumphant.

Nicola raised her eyebrows. She wished Laurie could listen to this, but he was up in his own room, napping. "You sure?"

"No, but I've got some pretty good circumstantial evidence. After you left, I took a run to the market to pick up some groceries for her. I was in her kitchen fixing her something more substantial to eat than apple slices, and her landline rang. I glanced at the kitchen extension, and Caller ID read Kip Caprini, no joke. I figure she called him while I was out, and he called her back."

"You hear any of her conversation?"

"No, she was in the living room, and I thought it would be ungentlemanly to pick up the extension and eavesdrop, not to mention difficult to explain if I got caught. But still, that seems significant, doesn't it? Laurie asks her if she can name the person who designed her wardrobe, she freaks out, then immediately calls a big-name designer. A certain cause-and-effect is suggested, don't you think?"

"I'll fill Laurie in." She exhaled. "Thanks, Alex. I appreciate it."

"No problem." A long pause. "Hey, are we cool now?"

"Are you kidding me?"

"Sorry, that was wrong. I withdraw the question. It was good seeing you. I'm glad you're doing well. I've been worried about you."

"Don't be," she said. "I'm no longer your concern."

It was true, but it didn't mean it didn't sting.

THEY SQUANDERED THE rest of the day. Laurie tweeted at Molly again, asking if she'd had any luck on her end, but received no response. It seemed likely she hadn't been able to find out more about the mysterious Joelle in Nevada and was too embarrassed to tell Laurie.

Nothing more to do in Los Angeles, and it was time they returned home anyway. Nicola called the airline and booked seats on a flight leaving the following afternoon.

Which is why she was presently sitting in the hotel lobby, her carry-on bag on the floor beside her, waiting for Laurie to meet her downstairs so they could drive to LAX and return their rental car and catch their flight. Laurie had assured her he was all ready to go, that he just needed to throw a few things in his suitcase and he'd be right down. That was forty minutes ago.

If they left within the next ten minutes, if there was no traffic on La Cienega, if the security lines at LAX weren't awful, they could still make their flight, maybe. She was giving some consideration to marching up to his suite and carrying him downstairs kicking and screaming when the strange man approached her.

He was young, late teens or early twenties, with a close-cropped hairstyle, like a buzz cut that had started to grow out. Thin and wiry, clad in jeans and work boots. He looked out of place in this hotel, though Nicola wasn't sure why. Los Angeles wasn't a fussy city, and even here, in the heart of Beverly Hills, jeans were common. Appropriate, even. Something about him, though, didn't fit. Maybe it was his air of tension, the way he looked at Nicola, then looked around, eyes darting left to right, as though he expected to be attacked from behind at any second.

The man—kid, really—plopped down onto the loveseat beside her. He nodded. "Hey," he said.

"Hey," Nicola replied, the default Los Angeles salutation. She gave an impersonal smile and glanced at the clock on her phone's display screen. *Come on, Laurie.*

"Just visiting?" the kid asked. He gestured at her carry-on.

"Business trip," she said.

He nodded. "Me, too," he said. He had a canvas duffle with him, which should lend credence to his words, but he wasn't a guest of the hotel. Nicola would swear to it. The tension he gave off alarmed her. He kept looking around the lobby, even while talking to her, and when he did meet her eyes, his focus would snap into place, like she'd become the most important thing in the world to him, until his eyes started roaming again. It was unsettling.

"Hey, can I ask you something?" he asked.

"Sure." Short replies, trying to discourage conversation without being outright rude.

"I saw you in the lobby yesterday. You're here with Laurie Sparks, right? The designer?"

Aha. She glanced at his canvas bag. It could contain a camera. Was he a paparazzo, maybe, waiting to ambush Laurie? Not that Laurie was a huge enough star to warrant photographers staking out his hotel, but it seemed like the most likely possibility.

"Nope," she said. "I'm here on my own."

He stared at her, as if he knew that was a lie. She saw something in his face, something that scared her a little. "Huh," he said at last.

She smiled at him. "Excuse me," she said. She rose to her feet, shouldered her bag, and headed off to the ladies room in the corner of the lobby.

Once inside, she dialed Laurie. He picked up on the first ring. "I'm out the door, I swear," he said without preamble.

"Change in plans. Stay where you are for just a second, will you?"

"What's up?"

"I don't know. There's someone in the lobby asking about you. Might be a photographer. I figure it's best if we wait until he leaves."

"I don't exactly try to avoid publicity, you know." Laurie sounded amused. "If he wants to ambush me, why not? I'm looking especially pretty today."

"Do me a favor and stay put, okay? I'll call you right back."

She slipped out of the ladies room and lingered in the recessed alcove beside the courtesy telephones and the rack of sightseeing brochures, then peered into the lobby. The kid was still there. He stared at the elevators, like an English Pointer fixed on a target. Waiting for Laurie.

She picked up the courtesy phone and dialed zero for the front desk. It was all of five yards away from her, which was a little ridiculous.

When someone answered, she spoke in a rush. "Hi. This is Nicola Strozyk, I just checked out of room 208 about an hour ago. Do you see the young man in the jeans and brown t-shirt in the lobby? He's sitting facing the elevators."

A pause. "Yes, I do, Ms. Strozyk." A brisk male voice. She couldn't see the front desk from her position in the alcove, but when she'd checked out, it had been staffed by a well-groomed and highly efficient young man.

"He was asking me questions about one of the guests, Laurie Sparks. Laurie and I don't know who he is or what he wants. Laurie's going to come down from his room and check out in a few minutes, and if that man isn't a guest of the hotel, we don't want him to still be here."

"We'll take care of it right now. Thank you for calling, Ms. Strozyk." Coolly practical, like there was nothing at all odd in her request.

Had that been high-handed of her? Even sort of a dick move? The kid could just be a fan, hoping for a glimpse of Laurie, and

Nicola had asked to have him booted out in what was probably a wild excess of caution.

She peeked out again. A man in dark suit with a powerful upper body and a wireless earpiece approached the young man and talked to him. The young man responded. Low voices, everything seemed civil. Smiles and nods on both sides, and the young man got to his feet, picked up his canvas duffel, and left through the sliding glass doors in front.

Nicola waited a minute, then called Laurie. "Coast is clear. Come on down. And don't dawdle; I'm already going to have to speed if we want to make our flight."

"If we miss it, we miss it. There's like forty-eight flights a day to New York," Laurie said. "What was that all about?"

"I'll explain on the way to the airport. Get your tiny ass down here."

She approached the front desk. "Hi. Nicola Strozyk. Did I just talk to you?"

She received a brisk smile from the uniformed young man. "You did. Our head of security talked to the gentleman and determined he was not a guest of the hotel. He said he had just stopped in our lobby to get out of the sun. He's gone now. I'm sorry he disturbed you."

"Thanks for that. I'm sorry for causing a fuss," Nicola said. The elevator doors opened just then, and a uniformed bellboy wheeled out a bronze trolley stacked high with Laurie's ridiculous pink suitcases, which meant Laurie would be following soon enough.

Good. It was time to get out of Los Angeles.

CHAPTER FOURTEEN

NICOLA SURPRISED HERSELF by enjoying Fashion Week. It consisted mostly of crowds and lines and long waits followed by short bursts of activity, of sharp-tempered women in high, high heels barking orders into cell phones, of confusing signs pointing around a maze of white canvas tents set up in Damrosch Park, but for all of that, it was almost fun.

Laurie had placed her name on the list to see his show, a coveted front-row seat right next to his mother. His only condition was that she'd have to wear whatever he picked out for her. He hadn't made her look too ridiculous at the Emmy party, so she agreed.

She stopped by his apartment on the morning of the show. He was already at Lincoln Center, so she let herself inside and changed into the outfit he'd left for her. Heavy black stovepipe pants that made her legs look freakishly long, a cream-colored tunic, a black wool jacket. All from the LSD label, all of it a good fit, all of it flattering. He'd even provided footwear, teetering black boots that pinched her toes and made her feel like an Amazon warrior. It was only a short distance from Laurie's place to Lincoln Center, but after one block she realized she wouldn't be able to walk there without amputating her feet afterward, so she hailed a cab.

Maggie Sparks greeted her effusively at Laurie's tent, clasping both of Nicola's hands in hers and kissing her on both cheeks. "Nicola, sweetheart, lovely to see you. I'm excited to see what Laurie's been up to."

"Me, too." She hadn't seen his collection since her first visit to his studio. Maybe she'd think more of his clothes when she saw them on the runway.

She didn't. The show started forty minutes late, which could only be Laurie's fault, but it was fun. Pounding electronic music blasted in the background, something that sounded like it had played in all of Europe's most fabulous discothèques in 1982. The show itself was quick, a rapid procession of forty or so outfits that came down the runway, modeled by a series of languid, ethereal creatures.

His whole punk-graffiti thing, the neon squiggles and splashes on the black streetwear, the appeal was still lost on her. The crowd applauded for every outfit, and the fashion journalists in the seats surrounding her scribbled notes and typed furiously away on tablets, but it left her cold. Still, she stood up alongside Maggie and applauded when Laurie took his victory lap down the runway, a fairy prince in blue velvet pants and a gold blouse with puffy sleeves.

She had to fight to get close to him afterward, so thick was the throng of well-wishers surrounding him. His cheeks were kissed; microphones were thrust in his face. Nicola could do little more than give him a pat on the arm and reassure him she enjoyed the show. Laurie looked disappointed when he realized she wasn't going to stick around, but then a journalist from *WWD* caught his attention, and Nicola was forgotten in the crowd.

REVIEWS FOR LAURIE'S show were fine. Nicola went through all the fashion blogs the next morning, one by one, surprised by how emotionally invested she felt. "Women will want to wear these clothes," read one. "A crowd-pleaser from fashion's reigning *enfant terrible*," another proclaimed. The worst she could find was a blogger who claimed it lacked the visual impact of his debut collection two years ago. Nothing there to upset Laurie.

She was already entrenched in her work for the day when a still-groggy Laurie appeared in the doorway to her makeshift office. He was makeup-free and in his pajamas, his coffee mug cradled between both hands. "Guess what we're doing today," he said.

"I couldn't possibly."

"We're crashing a runway show. Or trying to, anyway. Kip Caprini is showing at two o'clock, and his crabby old assistant refused to put me on the list, which is actually sort of totally my fault, because I didn't even think about it until last night, at which point it was way too late. It took me forever to even find the right person to call. I think I woke her up. She was *mean*."

"It's possible you need to hire a new assistant, kiddo."

"Entirely possible. I've been making my own arrangements this week, and between you and me, I kind of suck at it." Laurie grinned. He seemed buoyant, even while only half-awake, as though being done with his runway show had lifted a burden from him. "So my new plan is to show up at Caprini's tent and charm our way inside."

"As long as you do all the necessary charming, I'm in," she said. "Any particular reason we're crashing?"

"Maybe we'll get a chance to talk to him. You need to wear that coat of yours, by the way," he said. "See if he has any reaction to it."

In all the Fashion Week chaos since their return from Los Angeles, the whole Caprini business had been abandoned. Still no reply from Molly Gable, which definitely meant she was avoiding them.

Back to Lincoln Center, back to the canvas tents. A tall, snotty woman with a clipboard and headset denied them entry to Caprini's show. "No. Uh-uh," she said. "You're not on my list, you don't have seats, and we're one hundred percent at capacity."

"What about standing room?" Laurie said. He gave her his most charming smile. "We'd stand right at the back, out of the way."

"No way. There are *fire laws*, you know," she said. She was very young, and model-pretty, and Nicola couldn't blame her for trying to do her job, though it probably wouldn't hurt her to ratchet back the attitude a few notches.

There was a long line of people waiting behind them, people with legitimate seats. Nicola tugged on Laurie's arm. "Come on. We're getting nowhere," she said.

Laurie didn't budge. "Do you know who I am?" he asked. In response, the young woman rolled her eyes. Nicola was pretty firmly on her side now. There might, just might, be someone out there who could utter that particular phrase without sounding like a jackass, but Laurie was not that person.

"Laurie . . ." Nicola added a hint of warning to her tone. Laurie scowled. He looked on the verge of throwing a tantrum.

"Excuse me." An elegant young man jostled his way to their side and addressed the woman with the clipboard. "Sorry. I couldn't help overhearing. Are you Sasha?"

The young woman looked startled. She nodded. "You are . . . ?"

"Galen Ming." He smiled at her. "We've spoken on the phone several times, I believe. I worked in Mr. Caprini's business office earlier this year?"

"Of course. Hi," she said. Her gaze dropped down to the list of names on her clipboard. "You're right here. You can go straight inside and one of the other girls will show you to your seat."

"Thank you." Another smile. Galen Ming had impossibly smooth skin and thick black hair, kept longish in the front and very short in back. He wore a simple black sweater and pants, and he was one of the most beautiful people Nicola had ever seen. "But I think I might have a solution here. May I?"

Before Sasha could object, Galen gently eased the clipboard out of her grasp. He flipped the page, glanced at the seating chart, then flipped back to the list of names in front.

"Marie Adzwell and Mark Romanus won't make it. They're already seated at the Petroski show, which hasn't started yet. You can safely release those seats now and give them to Laurie Sparks and his friend. On the incredibly distant chance they do show up, you can certainly release the seats you have reserved for Carly Obel and her plus-one; she's still in Los Angeles, and she hasn't made it to a single show this week." Another smile. "Will that work? I'm quite sure Mr. Caprini would want Mr. Sparks to view his collection."

Sasha glanced at her list again, her bottom lip caught between her teeth. "I'll get in trouble," she said.

"You won't," Galen said. "Of course you won't. I give you my personal assurance of that."

He radiated trust and good intentions. Sasha relented. "You can go in," she told Laurie and Nicola. She sounded grumpy. "Tell Janice—she's the one in the houndstooth tights—I said to give you the Obel seats."

"Thanks so much." Laurie smiled at her, every trace of petulance gone.

They slipped through the entryway into the tent before she could change her mind. Laurie turned to their mysterious benefactor. "Thank you. That was totally cool of you." He held out a hand. "I'm Laurie. This is Nicola, my associate."

Galen clasped Laurie's hand and held it just a little longer than necessary. He was as petite as Laurie, and almost as lovely. "Galen Ming. It was my sincere pleasure, Laurie," he said. Meaningful eye contact. "I'm a fan of your designs."

"Maybe we could talk after the show?" Laurie asked, but Galen had already released his hand and slipped off into the crowd.

They found their purloined seats. Nicola secretly fretted that someone would boot them out, but no one challenged them. Laurie kept looking around the massive tent, scanning the rows and rows of folding chairs. He could be looking for fellow designers or celebrities. More likely, he was looking for the beautiful and efficient Galen Ming.

Thumping techno music and strutting models. Caprini's fashions differed greatly from Laurie's, long gowns with plunging necklines and pantsuits in tight, shiny leather. All of it was bold and aggressively sexual, heavy on crisscrossed straps and leather collars and exposed cleavage.

Laurie kept still during the show, for once not fidgeting, his attention focused on the clothes. When it was over, when Caprini had taken his bow, Laurie grabbed Nicola by the wrist.

"Let's see if we can talk to him," he said.

He pulled her through the crowd. Nicola, stuck in heels for the second day in a row, wanted nothing more than to go back to Laurie's place and take her shoes off, but Laurie seemed determined.

A tap on her shoulder. She turned and saw Galen Ming smiling at her. "It's Nicola, right?" he asked. "Did you enjoy the show?"

"It was fantastic. Thank you again for the seats."

"Are you and Laurie going to the after-party?" he asked.

At the sound of Galen's voice, Laurie ceased his attempts to burrow through the crowd surrounding Caprini. He perked up. "We'd definitely go if we knew anything about it," he said.

"It's at his store on Fifth. Nine o'clock tonight," Galen said. "I'm on friendly terms with his assistant. It'd be no problem at all to put you both on his guest list."

"Will you be there?" Laurie asked.

"Of course," Galen replied. He smiled. Laurie smiled back. Nicola would swear that, at the present moment, he wasn't thinking of Kip Caprini at all.

THE CAPRINI SHOP on Fifth Avenue was aggressively sleek, an open space with shiny black walls and a minimalist steel staircase that led up to a second level. The party was up there, past a bouncer; he glanced down at the screen of the tablet he carried, found Laurie's name, and gestured for them to go up the stairs.

Gowns and blouses hung on dark wood hangers spaced at even intervals on chrome bars set into alcoves in the walls. Soft recessed lighting showed off the clothes to full effect. There were low square chrome platforms set up around the room. During the day, they were probably used to display shoes and accessories; for the party, they'd been pressed into service as impromptu seating areas.

Nicola was in the violet dress again, at Laurie's request. If Caprini really had designed it, he theorized, seeing it might provoke a response.

Flutes of champagne were arranged in neat rows on a linen-covered table by the door. Another table was laden with platters of fruit and cheese. The food was surprisingly basic, but maybe people in the fashion world didn't eat much. Too bad. Nicola was hungry. She and Laurie collected flutes and did a quick reconnoiter of the room.

There he was, the party's host, Kip Caprini himself. Caprini was in his mid-fifties and holding up well. Very tall, a smooth shaved head, broad shoulders. He wore tight pants and a tighter black shirt that showed off his muscular upper arms. He was smooth and unlined, rugged yet polished. He draped his arm around the waist of a leggy blonde woman in a silver column dress. She had the starved, unearthly beauty of a model, and she looked familiar.

"Is the woman he's with anyone in particular?" she asked Laurie.

Laurie nodded. "That's Sofia Lee. Former Victoria's Secret Angel, current face of Caprini, also currently his wife."

"Wife?"

"It happens." Laurie's tone was dry. "Even in the fashion industry. Let's introduce ourselves, shall we?"

He led the charge through the room. It was a small gathering, only forty or so guests, and presumably most were not complete strangers to the host. Maybe they'd get kicked out. Maybe the big man with the tablet would be called upstairs to escort them out of the party.

Caprini conversed with a middle-aged woman in a gray fur coat, her silver hair chopped into a blunt, immaculate bob. He looked up and spotted Laurie. He patted the woman on the shoulder once, then leaned down and said something Nicola couldn't hear. The woman laughed and moved on.

"Laurie Sparks." Caprini stuck his hand out. He smiled. Capped teeth, tanned face, the skin a little tight over his nose and cheeks. Up close, it was obvious he'd been recently lifted, and his new face hadn't yet had time to settle. "I noticed your name had magically appeared on my guest list."

Laurie shook his hand. "I begged and pleaded and wheedled my way onto it," he said. "I wheedled my way into your show this afternoon, too. I thought your collection was amazing. The bronze gown with the mandarin collar? Gorgeous."

Ah, good. Laurie was on his best behavior.

"That's very flattering." Another tight smile from Caprini. "I have to say, compliments from the up-and-coming crowd always make me wary. I can't help feeling like an aging wildebeest surrounded by slavering young jackals."

He didn't introduce Sofia, who gave the new arrivals one bored glance out of spider-lashed eyes, then snuggled in closer to her husband and bit him on the earlobe, hard enough to make him wince. She disentangled herself from him and sauntered off without a word. Kip gave her a firm slap on her twitching silver backside, then turned his attention back to Laurie.

"This is Svetlana," Laurie said. He took Nicola by the elbow and pulled her forward. "She's my personal life coach and spiritual guru."

So much for good behavior. "Nice to meet you. I enjoyed your show," Nicola said.

Caprini barely glanced in her direction. Zero interest in her, zero interest, she'd swear, in the violet dress.

He *was* interested in Laurie, though, that was clear. He shifted a step closer, until they were almost chest to chest. Laurie didn't back away. He was nearly a foot shorter than Caprini, so he had to tilt his head up to meet him in the eye. "You showed yesterday, right?" Caprini asked. "Fashion reporter friend of mine saw it. He said it was a little shaky. Not bad, but shaky. I think 'spotty' was the word he used." He took a drink from his glass. Scotch, no ice.

"Opinions are going to vary, of course. I was pleased with it. So were others. There was a very flattering write-up in the *Wall Street Journal* this morning." Laurie seemed unruffled. "I think your friend had the minority opinion."

"Mmm." Caprini regarded Laurie. Dark eyes glittered. "Piece of advice?"

"Always welcomed."

"Drop the reality show shit," Caprini said. "It damages your credibility as a designer. Damages all our credibility, actually. It cheapens us."

"Have I done that?" Laurie cocked his head to the side, coquettish yet shrewd. "I'm not sure I can take credit for bringing anyone down besides myself. And the show's been fantastic from a branding standpoint. I'm not just a designer, I'm a star."

"It's more a question of staying power, though," Caprini said. "Frankly, I think you're fighting an uphill battle. I say this as something of a supporter—I thought your debut collection had some promise. But you're working in a limited range with a limited skills set, and even with all the money your rich mommy can throw at you, I'd be surprised if we heard much further from little Laurie Sparks."

"We'll see, won't we?" Laurie tone was mild.

"We will indeed," Caprini said. "Me, I'm betting the industry will soon grow weary of pretty little clothes designed by pretty little boys who want to look like pretty little girls." He raised a hand and brushed his thumb across Laurie's painted cheek.

Nicola felt her thigh muscles twitch at the physical contact, her body reflexively bracing for action. Laurie remained still, implacable and intractable.

"As I said, opinions will vary," he said. "Plenty of people do seem to like my pretty little clothes."

Caprini smiled down at him. Lots of teeth. "Kid, right now I think 'pretty' is mostly what you have going for you. Even me, I might let you suck me off, but I sure as hell wouldn't wear anything you designed."

"Of course not, unless you're into drag. I don't do menswear." Laurie sipped his champagne. "I'm not interested in sucking you off, either, but thanks for the offer, I guess. And thanks for all the advice."

"Oh, of course. My pleasure. Nice meeting you, kid. Feel free to crash my parties any time." Caprini clapped his hand down on Laurie's shoulder and shook him once before releasing him.

That physical contact again. It wasn't friendly, and it pissed her off. Nicola took Laurie by the arm and half-pulled him away from Caprini, anxious to put some distance between them.

"He didn't notice your dress," Laurie said when they were safely out of earshot. "Did you see that? He didn't even look at it at all."

Nicola stared at him. "Is that your takeaway from that whole encounter?"

Laurie looked confused. "What do you mean?"

"I mean he was a total dick to you. I wanted to punch him. Almost did, in fact."

"Good thing you didn't. I was fine." He took another sip of his champagne. "You're not really my bodyguard, you know."

"No kidding. I just didn't like him getting in your face like that. And he really shouldn't have touched you."

"Don't freak out about it. It's not a big deal. It's not like he was going to take a swing at me or anything," Laurie said. He grinned. "I've never gotten into a fistfight before. It might've been fun."

"You would have lost," Nicola said. "Badly. Now that we've talked to Caprini, you want to get out of here? I don't think we're welcome, I'm starving, and the hors d'oeuvres suck."

Laurie glanced around the crowd. "In just a little bit, okay? I want to mingle first."

Nicola smiled. "I haven't seen him." At Laurie's look, she clarified. "Galen Ming."

"I wasn't looking for him." His cheeks were pink. "It's just, you know, fashion people. There are a lot of fashion people here. My peers. I should talk to them."

"Uh-huh. A likely story, kiddo."

"I'm sure I don't know what you're talking about," Laurie said with great dignity.

"Laurie!" A voice behind them, a pale hand on Laurie's shoulder. Laurie and Nicola turned. Galen Ming, as lovely and elegant as before, flashed his pretty teeth at them. At Laurie, really, but Nicola was included by default. "I'm glad you could make it. Both of you, of course."

"Hi, Galen." Laurie went a deeper pink. "It's good to see you. Can I get you a glass of champagne?"

Galen shook his head. "I'm not sure how long I'm planning on staying," he said.

"Nicola and I were thinking of taking off soon. We were going to find dinner somewhere," Laurie said. "Would you like to join us? Unless you have other plans, of course."

Galen beamed at him. Nicola thought she heard Laurie's heartbeat quicken, heard the celestial choir singing in his head. "I don't want to interfere with your evening," he said.

"No interference at all. We'd love to have you along," Laurie said. "It'd give us a chance to thank you for all you've done today. Right, Nicola?"

"Absolutely." Nicola looked from Laurie to Galen, from Galen to Laurie, and sighed to herself. It was young love, or young lust, or at least young mutual attraction. It was adorable and heartwarming and maybe just a little nauseating. "You know what, maybe you two should just go someplace together. I've been running a bit of a headache this evening, and I think an early bedtime might be a good idea.”

She expected Laurie to put up at least a token objection to this. She was wrong. “Okay. Good thinking. Feel better. See you Monday?”

“Monday,” she said. “Good night, both of you. Galen, nice seeing you again.”

Galen and Laurie murmured goodbyes. Nicola slipped down the stairs and past the bouncer, then headed out the front door.

Fifth Avenue was heartbreakingly pretty at night, the skyscrapers forming a glittery canyon on either side of the street. Nicola walked up to the subway stop on 59th, the damned silver sandals cutting into her feet with every step. So Laurie had a crush, and how nice for him. Given the maniacal enthusiasm Laurie directed toward new projects, his romance with Galen would probably move fast. That was good. Healthy, even. Maybe he’d finally start getting over Jonathan.

Odd how lonely that made her feel.

CHAPTER FIFTEEN

MONDAY MORNING. BACK to Laurie's place to continue working on her project. It couldn't go on forever—she'd be finished in a few weeks, and then where would she be?

She entered his apartment quietly. Now that Fashion Week was over, he didn't need to get to his studio early. He'd probably still be asleep.

She made coffee as noiselessly as she could, then crept upstairs to her makeshift office. Laurie's bedroom door was closed. There was a possibility Galen was behind it. Wouldn't that make for an interesting morning?

Searching, labeling, fleshing out the information in her database. This was pleasant work. The last pieces were falling into place. It'd be in great shape for Laurie, whenever he started his new collection.

A soft knock on the door frame. "Good morning."

She looked up and saw a pajama-clad Laurie, hair rumpled from sleep. "Good morning. Get coffee, then come back here. You can tell me all about Friday night."

"I have no idea what you mean." Laurie smiled and withdrew. He returned shortly, mug in hand, and sat down on the floor in the lotus position, spine straight, tiny bare feet propped up on his thighs. Flexible little show-off.

"Did it go well?" Nicola asked.

"It did, actually. We went for tapas at a cute place in Hell's Kitchen. He's super-nice. Really interesting, too." A long sip of his coffee. It seemed like he was mulling over how much to tell her. "He's worked for a whole bunch of designers, Kip Caprini included. He travels all the time. He just got back from Milan last month."

"Did you talk about Caprini at all?"

Laurie shook his head. "His name came up a couple times, but no. I didn't want to seem like I was pumping him for information." He cleared his throat. "He'd been doing a freelance gig in the IMG offices lately, helping them with Fashion Week, but now that it's over, he's out of work."

Ah. That was where this was heading. "You offered him a job as your assistant, didn't you?"

"He's very well qualified," Laurie said. It was a touch defensive. "And he'll be good at it. You saw how he charmed us onto the list for Caprini's show. That's exactly the sort of thing I need someone to handle for me. Plus, he's super-cool and smart. He even said he wouldn't mind having television cameras follow him around all day for my show."

"I bet he wouldn't." That was something she hadn't considered: Laurie's assistant would become something of a television star, too. Jonathan hadn't cared for that part, but others would consider it a perk. "Not that it's my business, but are you seeing him, too? Romantically, I mean?"

"Oh. No. Nothing like that." Color rose in his cheeks. "I mean, he's cute, but I don't even know that I'm interested. Or that he's interested. It'll strictly be a working relationship." The pretty eyes met hers, pale green and earnest.

"That's probably best. It's just that it might get a little tricky, mixing your work life and your personal life like that." Again.

"Yeah, that was my thought, too. It's better if we keep it professional," he said.

"So I was doing some thinking about Kip Caprini over the weekend," she said. "You still haven't heard anything from Molly?"

"Nothing. I pestered her too much, and it must've ticked her off," Laurie said. "It's a dead end."

"She's not the only possibility. We've only been looking at the *Holmby Hills* side of things," Nicola said. "Maybe we should start looking at Caprini's 1984 collection instead. You still believe he didn't really design it, right?"

"I know he didn't. It flabbergasts me that no one else knows it." He seemed so intense, a tiny high-powered laser beam of certainty.

"Someone knows it. Someone must. Other people worked with him on that collection, assistants and sewers at the very least. If he wasn't working from his own designs, someone would know."

Laurie straightened up. Still in the lotus position, he held his mug cupped between both hands. In his ivory pajamas, he looked like a very small and glamorous Buddha. "Right. But it's been almost thirty years. How are we supposed to find out who worked for him? Call him up and ask him?"

"Sergio Sarmento," she said. "I was busy this weekend. I looked for anyone with ties to Caprini in his early years. There was a profile of this guy Sarmento in *Vogue* four years ago. You know him?"

"I know his line, though I haven't heard much about him lately. He used to do all this military-inspired ready-to-wear. Camouflage pants and French Foreign Legion hats. He's South African or something."

"Angolan. Emigrated to England with his family as a kid, moved to New York in the eighties. He mentioned in the profile that he got his start apprenticing for, you guessed it, Kip Caprini." Nicola shrugged. "I can't guarantee he helped with the 1984 collection, but as near as I can tell, the dates seem right. Might be worth talking to him."

"It might indeed. Is he still local?"

Nicola shook her head. "Can't tell. Some department stores carry his line, but he doesn't have his own boutique. I thought I could try to get in touch with buyers. Maybe they can give me a line on him."

"Cool. Do it. Good thinking, Nicola." Laurie got to his feet. "If you need help, ask Galen. He's stopping by this morning, then he's going to the studio with me."

"Are you going to give him a key?" Nicola asked.

A half-smile. "Already did," he said. "Friday night."

"Ah. I don't suppose you asked for references?"

"Give me a break. You saw him at Caprini's show. The girl at the door knew him. He's obviously legitimate."

That blind trust, that terrifying faith in human nature . . . Then again, Laurie didn't investigate her bona fides before hiring her, and that turned out fine. The way Laurie did business clearly worked for him, so she should just focus on her own job and stop fretting over him.

THE ASSOCIATE BUYER in the women's casuals department at Macy's was named Irene, and she was very friendly. After Nicola explained that she was working on behalf of Laurie Sparks, Irene was more than happy to chat about Sergio Sarmento.

"We've carried his line for more than a decade now," Irene said. "Not every season, not every collection, but quite often. Our customer base responds well to his designs."

"Do you have any way to contact him? Laurie is very interested in meeting him."

"I can't give out that information, of course. But if you want, I can email Mr. Sarmento and ask him on Mr. Sparks's behalf."

"You're a peach, Irene."

"No problemo. I'll do it right now." A pause, then: "Do you mind me asking? What's Laurie Sparks like in real life? He's *hilarious* on television."

Not hard to guess what Irene wanted to hear. "Pretty much the same. Larger than life. Fabulous, gorgeous, all of that."

"It must be fun working for him." Irene giggled. "I'll email you if I hear from Mr. Sarmento, would that work?"

"Perfect. Thanks so much."

The reply came later in the day: Sergio Sarmento currently lived in Paris, and he would be delighted to hear from Laurie Sparks. His personal telephone number was included in the email.

Nicola stared at the message, then called Laurie at his studio. "How's your French?" she asked.

"Actually, it's not bad," he said. "I had the mandatory four years at my boarding school, of course, and after my parents got divorced I spent a few summers at my dad's chalet in Rhône-Alpes."

She was sorry she'd asked. "Good. I'm forwarding you an email with Sergio Sarmento's phone number in Paris. You can call him and ask about Caprini."

"Why don't we go there and ask him?" Laurie asked. "Like I told you before, I work better in person."

"Yes, your whole 'pretty and famous' shtick, I remember," Nicola said. "Are you sure it's necessary? This is something a quick phone call could resolve."

"Strictly speaking, it's seldom *necessary* to go to Paris, but it sure is fun." Laurie giggled. "Come on, it'll be awesome. Have you ever been?"

"I haven't. Are you seriously offering to take me to Paris?"

"Why not? I'm between collections, and I need to celebrate. Besides, this way I'll look really good to Galen. I'll be the cool boss who takes him to Paris on his first week at his new job."

Of course Galen would be going with them. Personal assistants did, in fact, travel with their high-powered bosses all the time, to smooth the road and make all necessary arrangements. His presence would ensure that Nicola didn't get roped into doing personal tasks for Laurie, and that was a huge plus.

"Hey, you haven't told Galen about your Kip Caprini conspiracy theory, have you?"

"Nope. But if he's going to Paris with us, we should fill him in."

"Don't," Nicola said. "He's got strong ties to Caprini, he's still good friends with Caprini's assistant. That's how he got us into the party, remember? If you tell him things, he might feel obligated to pass them along."

"Galen would be totally cool with keeping it secret, I'm sure," Laurie said. "Whatever. He doesn't need to know, so I won't tell him." His tone indicated that he thought Nicola was being a ninny. Maybe she was, but word didn't need to get back to Caprini that Laurie suspected him of being a cheat. Having met Caprini, she felt safe in assuming he wouldn't take it well.

CHAPTER SIXTEEN

GALEN WAS EVERY bit as frighteningly competent as his dealings with Sasha at the Caprini show had indicated. Within minutes of Laurie briefing him on the situation, he'd booked them on an Air France flight to Paris, had reserved rooms in a hotel in Montmartre, had called Nicola to make sure her passport a) existed, b) was current, and c) was presently in her possession. He also grilled her extensively as to her preference re: window versus aisle seats, the existence of any food allergies, and whether she'd be comfortable renting a car in a foreign city. Galen, like Laurie, couldn't drive. This made Nicola feel vital and a little smug.

Another first-class flight. Galen and Laurie sat next to each other, with Nicola across the aisle. The boys kept their heads together for much of the voyage, giggling at private jokes.

Chauffeuring the boys from de Gaulle to the hotel in their rental Audi took all her concentration. She couldn't relax enough in Paris traffic to enjoy her first view of the city. The other cars—boxy yet sleek, vastly different from the gas-swilling behemoths that owned American roads—whizzed past her, gliding and merging. Laurie sat in the passenger seat, a road map spread across his lap. In lieu of navigating, he spent the trip leaning into the backseat to practice his French on Galen.

Galen was fluent. Of course he was. He and Laurie chattered away, bursting into peals of laughter at Laurie's occasional mispronunciations. Nicola, who'd had three years of high-school Spanish in migrant worker-heavy Modesto, felt unsophisticated compared to the worldly and glamorous boys.

Their hotel was on Rue Gabrielle, with a gorgeous view of the Sacré-Coeur Basilica. Cobblestone streets and steep hills, even trickier to navigate than the Autoroute from the airport. Their hotel was a flat-roofed white building with a cherry red door and a green striped awning. In the lobby, Galen looked at Laurie anxiously, as though concerned it wouldn't be up to his standards.

"I hope this is acceptable," he said. "I thought you might be sick of the big luxury hotels on the Champs-Élysées. I find them so impersonal. This might appeal more to your artistic side, I thought. I've stayed here several times, and I've always found it to be very romantic and charming."

"I despise big luxury hotels," Laurie said, the rotten little liar. "This is perfect." He smiled at Galen. Galen smiled back. Nicola's stomach churned, just a little.

Three rooms, all on the same floor. Laurie's room was at the far end; it was the biggest of the three, and it had the best view of the Basilica, all curves and arches and turrets. His room, while not a suite, had its own enclosed bathroom; Galen and Nicola would be sharing the communal facilities down the hall. Comfortable beds with white down comforters and crisp white coverlets, blue-and-gold patterned carpets. It was cute and clean without being at all luxurious. Were Laurie not so enchanted with Galen, he'd probably grouse up a storm about it.

Galen set up an appointment for Laurie and Nicola to meet with Sergio Sarmento later that afternoon. After being assured by Laurie that Nicola could drive them there and back, Galen agreed to stay at the hotel. "My phone will be on at all times, should you run into problems," he said. If he felt slighted at being left out, he showed no trace of it.

Sarmento had a flat in a gray stone building on Rue Valette in the Latin Quarter. More precarious cobblestone streets. Were she by herself, or here with anyone but Laurie, Nicola would have ditched the Audi long ago in favor of taking the Metro.

The exterior of Sarmento's building was cracked and crumbling. No intercom system, but the front door had warped in its frame and stood permanently ajar. The building didn't have an elevator, so they walked up three flights of stairs covered in threadbare gray carpet. Nicola rapped her knuckles against Sarmento's door.

A broad, brown man in a white sleeveless shirt and wide-legged cotton pants answered the door. He had bumpy skin and a warm, crooked smile. Before Nicola or Laurie could speak, he was already ushering them into his flat. "Hello, hello. I think you must be the beautiful Laurie Sparks?"

"That's me. This is my associate, Nicola. Are you Sergio Sarmento?"

"Yes, yes. Please, it is Sergio. It is a great pleasure to meet you, beautiful Laurie." Sergio placed his large hands on Laurie's slim shoulders and kissed him on both cheeks. "And his friend Nicola, it is always an honor to meet beautiful women." More kisses. Sergio smelled like bay leaves and cloves.

"Please, both of you, please come in. We will drink *cafes*, and then perhaps Laurie Sparks will tell me what it is that makes him come all the way from New York City to speak to me."

Sergio's flat was small and tidy. Unfinished wood floors were covered with faded Persian rugs, the once-vivid colors transformed into dusty pastels through time and wear. A coffee table stripped and sanded down to the bare wood, a pair of armchairs covered in worn rose corduroy. A dressmaker form in the corner, a vintage treadle sewing machine beside it.

"Please, sit." Sergio gestured to the armchairs, then moved to the attached kitchenette. He poured coffee from a battered steel percolator into dainty china cups.

"I have done an investigation of you, Laurie Sparks," Sergio said over his shoulder. He grinned. He had beautiful eyes, dark brown and rimmed with long lashes. He wore thick eyeliner, maybe even false lashes. Nothing about him apart from those eyes could be considered beautiful, but there was great warmth and appeal to him. "When the very charming Irene from the Macy's department store said you were anxious to speak to me, I investigated to see who is this young American designer. And I found much, much information about you. You are a television star! A designer and a television star, all at once."

"I was a designer first," Laurie said.

Sergio nodded. "Yes, yes, of course. Your clothing, your collection, I view it online, it is all very good. You are very talented." He grinned. "I flatter myself that I am very talented, too. If I had a beautiful face like yours, maybe someone would make me a television star."

He placed the little cups on saucers on the low table between Nicola and Laurie. He drew a backless stool closer to them and sat down, his own cup held gracefully in one large hand.

The coffee was very strong and black and good. Nicola sipped hers in silence, waiting for Laurie to take the lead.

"Your clothing is beautiful," Laurie said. "Your military jackets this season, the ones with the knotted belts and the band collars, I wish I'd designed them."

Sergio smiled again. "Ah. You came all the way to Paris to pay me compliments?" His eyes twinkled. "It seems unlikely, this."

"No, you're right," Laurie said. He sipped his coffee; Nicola could almost see his mind working, choosing his words with care. "I'm interested in Kip Caprini, particularly his early collections. I understand you apprenticed for him in New York."

"Ah, yes. A lifetime ago, yes. I worked for Monsieur Caprini." He smiled. "But Caprini, he is in New York, not Paris. It would be far, far easier to ask your questions directly of him."

"Did you work for him in 1984?"

"Yes, in 1984." Sergio seemed curious and cautious.

"His fall collection. Belted coats mostly, with folded darts at the back forming kind of an X. Do you remember those?"

"But of course. They were most unusual, those coats."

Laurie set his cup on the table and leaned forward. "Are you absolutely certain Kip Caprini designed those coats?"

Sergio looked amused. "Now, what are you up to, beautiful boy?" he asked. He waggled a finger at Laurie. "There is mischief in what you say, and I do not want to be swept up in it. Even for you, lovely Laurie."

Laurie shook his head. "No mischief, I promise." His eyes looked very wide and earnest. Nicola had seen that expression recently, when he was denying any romantic interest in Galen. "I know Kip Caprini's work. I've studied all his collections, and I respect him tremendously. But it's because I've studied his work so closely that I'm convinced, absolutely convinced, that he could not and did not design those coats. They just aren't *him*."

It still sounded unconvincing to Nicola, no matter how many times he brought it up, no matter how emphatic and passionate he sounded on the subject.

Sergio considered. "They were . . . different, yes. I grant you that." Another long silence. He stared ahead, lost in thought. Finally, he shook his head.

"Monsieur Caprini, he did not have an easy time with that collection. He was young then, you will remember, no older than you are now. It was only his third collection, and he had been so very successful, so very quickly with his first two. Much like you. I think you have shown only three collections, yes?"

Laurie nodded. Sergio continued. "He started, he stopped, he changed it all many times, he yelled and cried and threw things around his workroom, he did all that. And in the end, he made those beautiful coats and those beautiful dresses, and we were all very happy." He shook his head. "I tell you now, I have given the matter no more thought than that. They were different from what

128

he had done before, they were different from what he has done since, yes, this is all true. But I do not know it means he did not create them."

Laurie nodded. "Thank you," he said. "I respect your opinion. That's all I wanted to know."

"What about Joelle?" Nicola said. It was the first time she'd spoken, and they both turned to stare at her in surprise. "Did anyone named Joelle work for Kip Caprini at that same time?"

Sergio's brows furrowed. "Joelle Sutton, do you mean?" he asked. He pronounced the last name very precisely, with the emphasis on the final syllable. It took Nicola a minute to understand what he had said.

"Who was Joelle Sutton?" Laurie asked. The laser intensity in his eyes was back.

"A very pretty and very unhappy girl," Sergio said. "Joelle was a seamstress who worked for Monsieur Caprini. A small girl, too much eye makeup and no flesh on her, none. Me, I like fat women and I like thin women, both are very nice, but Joelle, she was much too thin."

"She was a seamstress?" Laurie chewed on his lower lip. "Sergio, anywhere from six to eight sewers work for me. I hire them as needed when I'm working on a collection. They change all the time, season to season. I know some of them by name, sure, but some I never meet. I don't know for certain, but I think that's probably typical."

"Yes?" Sergio said.

"How come you remember Joelle Sutton so well thirty years later?" Laurie asked.

Sergio set down his cup on the dainty matching saucer. He exhaled. He looked weary and heavy. "I was going to say 'because she was sad,' or 'because she was pretty,' but no, there are many sad and many pretty young girls, and I do not remember them all. It was in fact because of Sabina that Joelle is in my memory still."

"Sabina?" Nicola asked.

Sergio nodded. "Sabina Petrescu. She was a model in New York. She may be forgotten, but there is a chance you know this story. Pretty girls who meet bad ends, they are often remembered. Sabina Petrescu, she was Joelle Sutton's special girlfriend. And she was murdered, many years ago."

"When you say girlfriend, do you mean they were lovers?" Laurie asked.

Another nod. "Yes, yes. It was not much public, but it was not much secret, either. Sabina would visit Joelle at Kip Caprini's design studio. They were very much in love, and Joelle, she was almost happy. And then Sabina, she was found. Someone hurt her, violated her, very bad, you see, and choked her, and left her in the water to wash up on the shore." His face was grave. "Joelle, she left after that happened. It was not pleasant, that."

"Who killed Sabina? Did they ever find out?" Nicola asked.

Sergio shrugged his broad shoulders. "I do not know. I think they might have found the monster, yes, but I am not certain. There was another pretty girl, another model, who was found in the water maybe a year, maybe two, before Sabina."

"Where did Joelle go when she left?" Nicola asked.

Sergio shook his head. "That, too, I do not know. Me, I did not see her again, ever."

They had a full name now, Joelle Sutton, and maybe this was the same Joelle whom Molly Gable had thought made Gina Davenport's *Holmby Hills* wardrobe. Locating a Joelle Sutton in Nevada might not be difficult.

"Danielle, she could tell you much about Joelle," Sergio said. "Danielle Marcin. She was a model then, and she was great friends with Sabina Petrescu. They shared a flat." Sergio made a face. "You know of what I speak, yes, the flats young girls who wish to model live in, the flats their representatives provide for them? We have them here, too, in Paris, and they are not much good. Six, maybe eight, maybe ten girls to one very small place. Danielle and Sabina, they lived in one of those."

"Do you know where we could find Danielle . . . is it Marcin?" Laurie asked.

Sergio nodded. "Marcin, yes, Danielle Marcin. She modeled my clothes in the past, on the runway, many, many times. She no longer models, she is a woman now, and it is a world for girls, but she is in Paris. She is a businesswoman, she owns a boutique. Rive Gauche, very chic. Danielle, she has done well for herself." He smiled.

"Danielle and I, we stay close. If I tell her Laurie Sparks and his friend Nicola wish to speak to her about Sabina Petrescu, she will say yes."

"Will you ask her for us?" Laurie asked.

"I will," Sergio said. "Because you are beautiful, Laurie Sparks, and because you look so very, very lovely when you say you will not cause mischief for Kip Caprini." A wink. "Even though I think you may not be telling the truth."

He rose to his feet. "I will stop by Danielle's boutique today, if you wish, and I will ask her. Mind you, there is some need for care. Sabina Petrescu may be gone many years now, but there is still pain when one so young dies in so terrible a way." A nod. "I will stop by, and I will call you, Laurie Sparks, and tell you what she will say."

"Thank you." Laurie rose to his feet; Nicola followed suit. "Thank you very much."

"It is my pleasure." The broad smile again, crooked teeth, too many for that wide mouth. A chaos of kisses at the door, and then Nicola and Laurie were going down the stairs, heading back toward the cobblestone street.

"He didn't say he was sure Kip Caprini designed that collection, did you notice that?"

Laurie's words jolted Nicola out of her thoughts, which were fixed on strangled models and sad, pretty girls. "He didn't say he wasn't sure, either. He said the idea that Caprini might've faked it had never occurred to him."

"It's occurred to him now, after I raised the possibility. He seemed uncertain." They headed down the hill to the Audi, which was parked, very poorly, at the curb. Blasted narrow streets. "He knows Caprini was so desperate to send something down the runway that would live up to the promise of his early collections that he'd use someone else's designs if he needed to."

"That doesn't mean he did, in fact, do that."

"Except I know he did. You keep overlooking that. Some faith in me would be nice for once, Nicola." Laurie was sounding peckish, which probably meant he was hungry. Too much of Sergio's strong coffee on an empty stomach would do that.

"Let's get lunch," she said. "We'll pick up Galen and go some-place nice. How does that sound?"

Laurie brightened at that. "Aubergine," he said. "Let's go to Aubergine. It's on Faubourg-Saint-Honoré, and it's so awesome it makes me cry. I'll call Galen now and see if he can get us reserva-tions." The prospect of outstanding French cuisine blasted all thoughts of Caprini out of his beautiful fluffy head. "It's right by the Louvre, have you been? If not we should totally go there after-wards."

"I've never been there. This is my first visit to Paris, remember?"

"That's really sad," Laurie said. "Everyone should go to Paris, all the time." He took out his phone and carried on a quick conversa-tion with Galen.

When Laurie was done with his call, Nicola glanced over at him. "I thought you handled yourself well with Sergio, by the way. I like you when you're being polite."

Laurie smiled. It bore a resemblance to a smirk. "You like me all the time."

True, though he didn't need to look so smug. "Hey, Laurie? How do you feel about the collection you showed last week?"

He looked at her. "You didn't like it. I knew you didn't like it."

"My opinion on matters of fashion is meaningless. You've made that clear often enough. I want to know what you thought of it."

Laurie was quiet for a moment. "I don't know," he said at last. "I think I pulled it off. The reviews were good."

"But . . . ?"

"But I don't know. I spent weeks leading up to Fashion Week feeling like I was going to barf all the time, because I hated that collection, and when I'd try to start over, I'd hate it more. I kept yelling at Jonathan about it. I was foul and awful, and he left me, but I just felt so bad about it, all the time. The first two collections came so easily to me and everybody loved me, and then this time, everything I touched was garbage. I felt so . . . ordinary." The last word came out like a curse. "And I'm not ordinary, I never have been. But maybe all the things that make me special are going away."

The words tumbled out in a rush. Nicola smiled.

"It's the curse of growing older, Laurie," she said. "You start realizing you're maybe not as goddamned special as you used to think you were. It's awful, but it's natural. You just have a steeper learning curve than most."

Laurie looked at her. "I don't get it," he said.

"I know," she said. "Don't worry about it. Your collection was fine. You pulled it off, and people liked it. Not as much as your earlier stuff maybe, but don't make more of that than you need to. This next collection, the one I'm helping you with, you can make that one as fantastic as you need it to be." She smiled. "And you really are pretty goddamned special, Laurie Sparks."

"Damn right I am," he said. He smiled, just a little, and settled back in his seat. He raised his chin and stared regally out at the passing Parisian scenery.

CHAPTER SEVENTEEN

A MESSAGE FROM Sergio Sarmento was waiting at the front desk for Laurie when they finally returned to the hotel, stomachs sated with duck sausage and *langoustines,* minds sated with world-class art. Laurie squinted at the scrawled French, stared at the implacable clerk behind the counter, then passed the message over to Galen, who translated effortlessly.

"It says Danielle Marcin would be most charmed to meet the beautiful Laurie Sparks tomorrow morning at nine at Bel Oiseau, Rue Saint-Guillaume, to discuss Sabina Petrescu." Galen looked curious, but neither Laurie nor Nicola enlightened him.

"Nine in the morning. Madness," Laurie said.

"Have you given any thought to this evening? I can make dinner reservations, if you've anyplace in mind," Galen said.

"Can you pick something? You know all the good spots," Laurie said.

"Make them just for the two of you," Nicola said. "I'm going to spend a quiet evening by myself. I don't think I'm up for a second gastronomically-exhilarating meal in the same day."

Laurie looked stricken. "Aren't you going to come along?" He seemed genuinely distraught, and Nicola was touched, until he continued: "We need you to drive us."

"Take a taxi. Better yet, try the Metro," she said. "You'll stand a better chance of arriving at your destination in one piece than you would with me at the wheel. Honestly, guys, I think jet lag is catching up to me."

"I'll hire us a car and driver, Laurie. It's no trouble at all," Galen said. Galen was far too polite to show it, but he might be happy at the prospect of time alone with Laurie.

"If you're sure," Laurie said. "I guess I'll just meet you here in the lobby tomorrow morning, and we can go to Danielle's shop together. Eight forty-five?"

"Eight thirty. And I'm going to pound on your door at eight to make sure you're awake. I'm wise to your ways, Sparks."

Laurie grinned, and all seemed well.

DEAD OF NIGHT, silent hotel, a couple of rowdy boys in the hallway. Nicola could hear Laurie and Galen erupting into giggle fits and talking much too loudly. "I told you not to keep your key in your pants!" For some reason, this produced a torrent of fresh giggles.

Nicola groped around the bedside table for her travel alarm clock and checked the time. Three fifteen. Christ.

She slid out of bed and yanked her door open. Outside the adjacent door to Laurie's room, the boys stared up at her, their faces bright with varying degrees of amusement and guilt. Laurie looked odd at first, his pale eyes appearing very dark, and then she realized his pupils were dilated.

She glanced up and down the hall, grateful none of the other guests on the floor had been roused by the ruckus. "Glad you made it safely back, Laurie. You might want to keep it down before they kick us all out of here."

"Did we wake you? Sorry." Another splutter of giggles. "I can't get my key to work."

"You could sleep in my room," Galen said. His face was red and sweaty, his eyes were glittery, and this was the first time Nicola had ever seen him with unkempt hair. He shot a quick, guilty glance at her. "I'd sleep on the floor, of course," he said.

Nicola took the key out of Laurie's hand. It was an old-fashioned metal one, attached to a bulky wooden tag with the room number painted on it. The locks in this place were old and stuck easily; Nicola had to apply her shoulder to her own door and wiggle the knob back and forth to get it to open. No surprise Laurie was having trouble with his.

Especially since he was clearly bombed out of his head on something.

She unlocked his door with no hassle and held it open. "There you go," she said. She looked at Galen. "Are you coming in?"

Galen shook his head. He straightened up, swept an errant lock out of his eyes, smoothed his hair into place. "I'll just go to bed now," he said. "Good night, Laurie. Sorry we woke you, Nicola."

"Good night, Galen," Laurie called after him, too loud for the empty hallway. Nicola pushed him into his room and pulled the door closed behind them.

She pointed to the bed. "Take a seat."

"What's up?" Laurie asked, even as he obeyed. He was a mess, as much as immaculate Laurie could ever be a mess. His mascara was smudged, his lipstick had worn off, and he was missing the top button of his black silk shirt. Beneath his pancake makeup, his stubble had started to grow, which added to his overall dissolute appearance.

She filled a glass of water from the tap and handed it to him. "You're just a little bit too sparkly right now, and I don't think it's just champagne. What did you take?"

Laurie looked indignant. "I get high on life," he said. A giggle broke through his affronted demeanor. "And the occasional whiff of magical pixie dust."

"That's terrific. You didn't travel with it, did you? Tell me you didn't bring cocaine across international borders."

"Of course not," he said, with great wounded dignity. "I'm not stupid. Galen and I went to this sparkly, awesome nightclub. You should have gone with us, except there were only boys there. Someone had party favors in the coatroom. It seemed like the thing to do, so Galen scored some for us."

The ever-efficient Galen. Laurie seemed fine, albeit a bit spazzy and giggly, so she patted him on the shoulder. "Okay, kiddo. Sleep it off. We're leaving to see Danielle in about five hours. And if you've got any more of that shit on you, get rid of it. I don't want to find myself receiving a crash-course in the French penal system because you and Galen decided to be a couple of idiots."

"You're upset with me. You disapprove, don't you?" Laurie asked. He looked hurt. "We've gotten drunk together, you know. It's not like this is any worse."

Nicola sighed. "Do whatever you want, Laurie. I'm not upset, but yeah, I disapprove. Call it a holdover from growing up in the Nancy Reagan era."

"I don't know what that means. Did Nancy Reagan do a lot of drugs?"

"God. Sometimes I forget you're an infant. No, Nancy Reagan did not, to the best of my knowledge, do a lot of drugs. Skip it. Just a thought, though: You are, as you never cease to remind me, famous. Ergo, there are things you might want to be careful about doing in public. This would be one of them."

"Ooo, doing lines in a Paris nightclub. Almost as scandalous as being an openly gay fashion designer." Laurie sounded scornful. Nicola felt tired.

"You asked if I disapproved. Just giving you an honest answer."

Laurie flopped back on his bed and stared up at the ceiling. His shirt slid up, revealing far too much of his pale, scrawny abdomen above the waistband of his red leather pants. "I got it. I guess I just forgot that you're *old*." The scorn again.

She left him to sleep it off. Or maybe he wouldn't sleep at all, maybe Galen would sneak back to Laurie's room as soon as they were certain she was gone.

It occurred to her, once she was back in her own room, crawling under the down comforter, that she needed to hang out with more people her own age.

CHAPTER EIGHTEEN

LAURIE WAS GRUMPY and prickly during the drive to Danielle's boutique. Could be the lack of sleep, could be residual peevishness at Nicola for not wholeheartedly endorsing his recreational pharmaceutical usage. Whatever the cause of his snit, Nicola couldn't work up much sympathy. She concentrated on navigating the Audi through the Rive Gauche neighborhood, through more cobblestone roads lined with decorously shabby shops.

Bel Oiseau—pretty bird, Laurie translated for her—was a tiny storefront boutique with flowing print skirts on display in the front windows. A wood sign with a painting of a sparrow dangled from the front awning. It didn't open until ten, but when Laurie rapped on the door, a tall, slender woman opened it. "Good morning," she said, in very clear English. "You are Sergio's friends, I think?"

"Bonjour. I'm Laurie Sparks. That's Nicola. Are you Danielle?"

"I am. This is my little shop. I arrive early today, for you." She smiled. "There is a café by the river where I like to take my breakfast. We will be able to speak there. I think it is not too far for you to walk, no?"

"Perfect," Laurie said. Laurie and Nicola followed her down the sidewalk.

Danielle was taller than Nicola, which was a bit of a feat, and her cork-soled platform sandals made her even taller. She wore a simple blue shirt paired with one of the long skirts she'd had on display in her windows. She looked unfussy yet elegant. Chic.

The café where she took them was chic, too. Tiny black tables and black leather chairs, yellow wood floors, large colorful paintings of beautiful women displayed high on the red walls. Danielle exchanged a cheery greeting with the proprietor, then led Laurie and Nicola to the back patio, which looked out over the Seine. A sunny fall day, the mildest of chills to the air. Nicola wore the *Holmby Hills* coat, because Paris was a stylish city and it was the nicest piece of clothing she owned, but it was already too warm for it.

They drank excellent coffee and nibbled on raisin-studded buns and hard white rolls served with butter and jam. Nicola observed Danielle and tried to mimic her posture and behavior as best she could, the way she sat up straight, legs crossed at the knee, and tore dainty bits off her roll before eating them.

Danielle was a knockout. Thick wavy hair caught back in a loose silk wrap and high, high cheekbones. She wasn't wearing makeup, or at least not any that Nicola could see, and she had lines under her eyes, but her skin was smooth and clear and her bone structure was stellar. She set down her cup, dabbed her lips with her napkin, and smiled.

"So," she said. "Tell me what it is you wish to know about poor Sabina Petrescu."

"Actually," Laurie said, "Nicola and I are trying to locate a woman named Joelle Sutton. Sabina's name came up when we were talking to Monsieur Sarmento. I understand Joelle and Sabina were close?"

"Joelle." Danielle made an odd tutting sound with her tongue against her front teeth. It sounded disapproving, though she looked only pensive. "Joelle Sutton, yes. Sabina and Joelle were lovers." She smiled. "This was all very long ago, you understand. Sergio, he told you of course, Sabina was murdered many years ago?"

"He did. I understand you lived with her?"

Danielle nodded. "With many, many girls. *Jolies filles*—pretty girls, we all were, so very pretty and so . . . *interchangeables*. New young girls would arrive all the time, each new girl younger and prettier than the last. I arrived in New York when I was fifteen. I did not know how to cook, I did not know how to shop, I did not know how to put my money in a bank account, I did not know how to be an adult. We all learned together, all the *jolies filles*." She smiled.

"Sabina, she was Romani, but she had been in New York for many years. She was older than us, and not as foolish as us, and she took care of us, very well. She told us how to eat, how to go to the Laundromat, how to take the train. We did not always listen to her, because we were young and we were foolish and of course we knew everything."

Did Laurie glance in her direction at that? Hard to tell. Nicola was watching Danielle, but she thought Laurie shifted in his chair beside her.

"Were you living with Sabina when she was killed?" Nicola asked.

Danielle nodded. "Yes. She went missing, four days she was missing, but the agency, they did not tell the police, they did not look for her. 'She is fine, she is with a boyfriend no doubt, she will show up soon,' they tell us when we say we are worried. She did show up, washed up on the shore in Long Island Sound. Her killer, he took her away from the city, and he kept her two days, and he raped her, and after he was done with her, he strangled her and dropped her in the water."

"Did they ever find her killer?" Nicola asked.

"No. At first, I do not know how hard they looked. There was another model, Alina, who had been killed the same way, one year before. Alina, they thought it was her husband. They lived in Greenwich, you see, very near where the bodies washed up, and they had a bad marriage. He was not arrested, there was no proof. But when Sabina was killed, the police, they look at him once more, they think he is their man." Danielle sipped her coffee. "But he did not know Sabina, and he did not kill her. He had a . . . I do not know this word in English. *Alibi?*"

"Alibi. Same word. Did the police have any other leads?" Nicola asked.

"If so, they do not tell me." Danielle smiled, knowing and resigned. "I bother them, still. I call Greenwich Police Department, I ask them, every year, because someone should still care about poor Sabina. I speak to the detective who is now handling this case. Every year, she tells me she is still looking, but she has found nothing more, there is no new evidence, there is no more she can do. And every year I write to Joelle and tell her this."

Laurie, who had looked sleepy and inattentive during Danielle's ghastly tale of murdered young women, sprang to life, the laser intensity returning for the first time that morning. "You're still in contact with Joelle?" he asked.

"But yes. It is, mostly, a one-sided contact, you understand. It is rare I hear back from Joelle, but that is expected. It was long ago, and Joelle and I are not friends."

"Do you mean you don't get along with her, or do you just not know her all that well?" Laurie asked.

"Joelle was . . . not pleasant." Danielle wrinkled her nose. "A *jolie fille* as well, this is true, but she was so sad, and, as I say, not pleasant. A rich, spoiled girl from a rich, spoiled family. Her problems were the problems of rich girls, and when I was so young and so poor, I did not care much for Joelle." A self-deprecating smile. "As I am spoiled and rich now myself, I am perhaps more sympathetic to her."

"What was wrong with Joelle? Sergio also described her as sad."

An expressive shrug. "Who knows? She was young and she was miserable, and she screamed and cried at poor Sabina too much. She took *héroïne*," and here Danielle did a quick pantomime of inserting a needle in her arm, so there could be no mistaking what she meant.

"Many did, many do, of course. She and Sabina, they fight about this, too much." A shake of the head. "Sabina, she would have been better off without Joelle. But it was love, and that was that."

She glanced from Laurie to Nicola and smiled. "So. You do not say why you are looking for Joelle?"

"We think she designed some clothes for a television show. This coat that Nicola's wearing, she might've made it. I want to meet her," Laurie said.

Danielle leaned closer and examined the jacket. "May I?" At Nicola's nod, Danielle fingered the collar and lapel and nodded. "It is good work, that. Joelle, she sewed, of course, for many famous designers, and she made her own designs, but I do not think she sold any."

She sipped her coffee, her mood thoughtful. "Fifteen years ago, Joelle wrote to me. Understand, I had not heard from her since Sabina, so it was a surprise. An American fashion magazine wrote about my little store, and Joelle read it and felt, I think, nostalgic. She lived in Las Vegas then and worked as a tailor. Not designing her own clothes, no, but sewing all the same."

Las Vegas. Joelle from Nevada, that was what Molly Gable had remembered. "Is she still in Vegas?" Nicola asked.

A shake of her head. "No, not anymore. Here, I will give you her phone number." A quick look, almost guilty. "I cannot give you her address without her permission, it is not right, and I am a little afraid to call her myself, to ask if it is okay. As I say before, we are not friends."

She took out her phone and scrolled through her list of contacts. Nicola glanced over at the entry. Joelle Sutton, a 775 area code. Danielle passed her phone to Laurie, who took out his own phone and copied the information into it.

"I hope what you say is true, that she designed your lovely coat, Nicola," Danielle said. She looked heavy and sad. "She was so unhappy, so aimless, for so long. I would be glad to know she has had some success in her life."

"If she designed it, she's a genius," Laurie said. "I only wish I could make something this good."

Nicola glanced down at her coat. If Joelle Sutton's designs could make Laurie feel pangs of humility, she must indeed be a genius.

CHAPTER NINETEEN

THERE WAS NOTHING more they could accomplish in Paris. They'd found out all they could, more than Nicola had expected, about Joelle Sutton. Laurie was enjoying himself, however, and seemed disinclined to return to New York, so they stayed on.

They moved out of the cute, shabby hotel in Montmartre. Because Laurie didn't believe in doing things halfway, they moved into the grandiose Plaza Athénée on Avenue Montaigne. Laurie ensconced himself in the most gorgeous suite Nicola had ever seen, a preposterous Regency-decorated cocoon in dusty rose and white-gold, aggressively sumptuous and posh. Nicola and Galen shared a smaller two-bedroom suite connected to Laurie's suite through a door, which Laurie insisted on keeping open.

Despite the cozy living arrangement, she didn't spend much time with Laurie and Galen during the second half of their visit. The boys wanted to shop; she did not. The boys would start their day in mid-afternoon, crawling out in their fanciest clothes and most expensive shoes to drop vast amounts of Laurie's cash at Galeries Lafayette and Le Bon Marché. They'd stagger back in the early evening to deposit their shopping bags in their rooms and engage in some vital primping before heading out to fine restaurants and discothèques.

Left to her own devices, Nicola decided to behave as a first-time visitor to Paris should. She visited the Picasso museum, Notre

Dame, the Eiffel Tower, the Arc de Triomphe, all the places the boys, seasoned travelers, shunned.

They'd been in Paris six days now, and Laurie showed no signs of wanting to leave. The lack of a firm plan was beginning to wear on Nicola. She couldn't do the job Laurie was paying her to do while she was away from New York, and in the meantime he was footing the very extravagant bill for her vacation.

Galen napped in his room of their suite, tuckered out from a long afternoon of schlepping Laurie's shopping bags around the city. Nicola curled up in an armchair in her own room and flipped through a guidebook while mulling over dinner possibilities.

A soft knock made her glance up. Laurie stood in the doorway, clad in a flowing white shirt with a flouncy ruffle down the front and ridiculously long cuffs that reached past his knuckles. He was barefoot on the plush carpet; his toenails were a pearly pink. A black rope-handled shopping bag with a gold logo emblazoned across the front dangled from his hand. "Hey, are you mad at me?"

Nicola straightened up and set the book aside. "Should I be?"

Laurie ventured into the room. He looked uncharacteristically unsure of himself. "You've been avoiding me for the past couple of days. I thought you were still upset about the other night. When I was high," he said.

"Long forgotten. You're an adult, Laurie. What you do when you go out at night is your own business."

"But you haven't been hanging out with me lately," he said. Almost a soft whine. "Aren't you having a good time?"

"I'm having a great time. Thank you so much for all this. I'm just feeling a little guilty for sponging off of you."

"But it doesn't matter," Laurie said. "I'm rich. I want to spend my money making you and Galen happy."

He seemed so crestfallen that Nicola had to fight down an urge to give him a big hug and assure him everything was fine.

Time to change the subject. "Have you thought about what to do with Joelle Sutton? Are you going to call her?"

"Tried that." Laurie flopped down on his stomach on Nicola's bed and plucked at the embroidered coverlet. "The number Danielle gave us has been disconnected."

"Might not be a big deal, now that we know her full name. We should be able to find her anyway, if she's still in Nevada." Nicola thought for a bit. "You know what, though, you should try Molly Gable again. See if she can confirm that 'Sutton' was Joelle's last name. We're just assuming it's the same person, but we might be on the wrong track."

"Seems like an incredible coincidence if there's two different Joelles. It's not that common a name," Laurie said. He took out his phone anyway. "Is it a reasonable hour to call someone in Los Angeles?"

Nicola did some quick time-zone math in her head. "She should be awake."

Laurie dialed. Phone to his ear, he kept talking to Nicola. "Molly never did call me back, you know. I doubt she'll pick up. She hasn't updated her Twitter, either."

"Huh. That's kind of odd."

Laurie pulled a face. "I'm getting voicemail. Again," he said. He spoke into his phone. "Hey, Molly, Laurie Sparks. Sorry to keep bugging you—this is the last time, I absolutely swear. I just wanted to see if you remember if Joelle's last name was Sutton? Does that sound right? If you could just call me back and let me know, that'd be totally awesome."

He hung up. "I think I pushed her too hard about trying to find out more about the designer," he said. He looked glum. "I always seem to make people mad at me."

He could be genuinely distressed about this, or he could be fishing for reassurance. Nicola didn't want to play that game. "We'll try her again when we get back to New York," she said.

"Almost forgot. Here," he said. He handed her the black shopping bag. "Peace offering. Just in case you really are mad at me."

"What's this?" she asked. She glanced inside and pulled out an enormous wad of gold tissue paper. A blue leather box rested at the bottom of the bag. Inside was a tank watch on a thick silver band, clunky and chic, masculine and feminine at once. "Laurie . . ."

"It reminded me of you, because it was sturdy and practical, but I thought it looked pretty, too." Laurie looked anxious. "Do you like it?"

"Thanks, kiddo. It's gorgeous." She would hug him now, really, but he was still sprawled on her bed, and she was still seated in the armchair, and there was too much potential for awkwardness if she got up and threw her arms around him. She'd never displayed any finesse with hugs. She settled for slipping the watch around her wrist and fiddling with the clasp.

CHAPTER TWENTY

BACK IN NEW York. About time.

Nicola returned to the status quo; Laurie returned to chaos. In his absence, buyers had whipped themselves into a frenzy trying to place orders for his recent collection; his studio had been overwhelmed with messages for him. Maybe Galen should have been dealing with this, but Laurie seemed determined to treat him more as a buddy than an assistant. Then again, he didn't treat Nicola like an employee either, so she had no grounds to disapprove.

Nicola resumed her research, back in her temporary office in Laurie's residence. After the full-tilt glamour of the Plaza Athénée, even Laurie's decadent New York abode suffered by comparison.

Joelle Sutton. A quick Google of the now-defunct phone number Danielle had given them showed that Joelle Sutton lived, or used to live, in a place called Decline, Nevada, which was about two hundred miles north of Las Vegas. Not much of an electronic trail on Joelle; if she was a working designer, she wasn't a successful one. Nicola's searches also brought up results for someone named Joel Sutton, who appeared to be a property lawyer in Manhattan. A brother? Father, maybe? Nicola made a quick mental note of this information, in case the trail for Joelle in Nevada was cold.

Still no word from Molly Gable. Nicola visited Molly's Twitter page and saw it was abandoned, hadn't been updated at all since they'd met with her nearly three weeks ago.

A tickling suspicion at the back of her neck that she tried to ignore. She Googled Molly.

A *Los Angeles Times* article from September eighteenth. She and Laurie had been in Los Angeles then. A quick news story, cold and factual: On the Santa Monica exit of the 405 Freeway just after one o'clock on Monday morning, an unknown assailant fired a single bullet through the front windshield of a BMW driven by a 33-year-old TV wardrobe supervisor from Westwood named Molly Gable. It struck Molly in the forehead, killing her instantly.

Jesus. Molly hadn't been dodging their calls. Molly, cute, helpful Molly, had been dead.

Even though it was after noon, Laurie hadn't yet left for his studio. He was still in bed, and under normal circumstances this was a line Nicola wouldn't cross. She knocked once on his bedroom door to give him a little warning, then went inside. "Hey, Laurie? Sorry to wake you, but you need to hear this."

Laurie lay on his stomach, slumbering beneath a mountain of silk sheets and velvet comforters, his face pressed into his pillow. He flopped over onto his back and made some unintelligible sound. One hand flailed around in the general direction of the lamp on his bedside table. Nicola leaned forward and switched it on.

He sat up. Hair sticking up in all directions, a red crease across his face from the ruffled seam on his pillowcase. "What's going on?" he said.

"Molly Gable was shot to death. Early in the morning after Emmy night, just a day after we met with her."

"Oh my God." Laurie was wide awake now. "You're kidding."

She shook her head. "I found a newspaper article about it. A shooting on the freeway. They haven't caught whoever did it. Theory seems to be that it was random. Someone shot down from the overpass and hit her while she was driving."

Laurie stared at her. "Coincidence," he said. "It has to be a coincidence, right?"

"Yeah, obviously, but the timing spooks me," she said. "It couldn't have anything to do with us, could it?"

"No way." Laurie shook his head, his hair waggling. "Uh-uh. We're not involved in anything that anyone would kill someone over."

"What about Kip Caprini, though? Gina Davenport seemed so freaked out when we talked to her, and we know she talked to Caprini afterward."

Another headshake. "That's stupid. If Molly was shot the night after the Emmys, that'd be before we even met with Gina. And seriously, no one would shoot someone over this. It's just *fashion*."

He was right, of course, but the news had been a jolt. "Yeah. Makes sense," she said. She exhaled. Still felt a little shaky. "Hey, I found Joelle's address in Nevada. I don't know if it's current, but the phone directory shows a Joelle Sutton in a place called Decline."

"Who on earth would name a city Decline? That's got to be a challenge for their tourism board."

"I looked it up. It's located on the side of a hill, and yes, before you say it, Incline would have been a much better name. Anyway, it's too small for a tourism board. Twelve thousand residents at last census."

"Oh, ugh," Laurie said. "I have a hard and fast rule about not visiting any city with a population under half a million. If it's not located in a coastal state, that figure goes up to a million."

Nicola stared at him. "That's the stupidest thing I've ever heard," she said.

"Nonsense. It's a very good policy, and it's served me well."

"In any case, Decline isn't a city. It isn't even a town. It's classified as an unincorporated area, whatever that means."

Laurie looked at her sternly. "That doesn't make it any better, you know."

Nicola smiled. "You know you're a snob, right?"

"I believe that fact is well established." Laurie raised his chin. "Can you go there and find Joelle? I'm really busy here. You can handle it on your own, can't you?"

"I can, but I don't want to. This is your deal, Laurie. You're the one who believes Caprini took credit for Joelle's clothes. You've already gone to two different cities to pursue your theory—why not go to a third to see it out?"

"Like you just said, Decline isn't a city," Laurie said. He sounded sulky. "Los Angeles and Paris are fun. Rural Nevada isn't." He brightened. "Hey, do you think Joelle would agree to meet us in Las Vegas? That's a good compromise, isn't it?"

"Joelle has no reason to compromise. She doesn't owe us anything. Besides, it's not like we could call her up and suggest it. Disconnected phone, remember?"

"Oh, fine." Laurie looked exasperated. "Since it's important to you, I'll go. But it seems irresponsible of me, leaving my company like this. I'm a businessman, you know."

"You're a businessman who's lounging in bed past noon on a Monday. Let's not get into a debate about irresponsibility, kiddo."

"Whatever." Laurie rolled his eyes. "Get me coffee, will you? I'll ask Galen to make travel arrangements when I'm more awake." At Nicola's warning look, he added, "Please?"

She headed off to Laurie's under-utilized kitchen, hating herself just a little for giving in to him so easily.

CHAPTER TWENTY-ONE

GALEN BOOKED THEM on a flight to Las Vegas, made arrangements for Nicola to pick up a rental car at the airport, and reserved rooms at the only hotel in Decline, Nevada that didn't have "Budget" in its name. A little to Nicola's surprise, he decided to stay behind in New York to deal with all the new chaos with Laurie's collection. He did insist on riding with them to the airport to help Laurie with his luggage.

"I can drop everything at a moment's notice and fly out if you need me," he said while they were waiting to check their bags at JFK. First-class line, only one person ahead of them. Life moved smoothly for Laurie. "I'm sure I can catch a Greyhound bus from Vegas to Decline."

"We'll be fine without you. I'm not planning on staying there any longer than necessary," Laurie said. Still grumpy at the prospect of leaving the city.

"Call me if you need anything. Anything at all," Galen said. He took Laurie's hand and squeezed once before releasing it. Laurie looked straight ahead, his expression blank, so Nicola pretended she hadn't seen that.

Their flight landed in early afternoon. That was disappointing. The Las Vegas airport was smack beside the glittery Strip, which looked a billion times better lit up at night than it did during the day. Vegas hadn't received the memo about the arrival of fall; it was ninety degrees when they landed. Laurie had dressed for New York temperatures in white leather pants and a matching jacket. While waiting on the curb at the rental car lot for their vehicle to arrive, he looked wilted and miserable.

The trek from Vegas to Decline took them through the heart of the desert. The rental car was beige and bland; Laurie was already too dispirited by the trip to grouse about the dullness. Before setting off, Nicola stopped at a convenience store to load up on chilled Pellegrino and deli sandwiches and cookies. Keeping Laurie fed and entertained would make their road trip pass smoother.

Honestly, it was like taking care of a five-year-old, this business of looking after Laurie. He was sulky and moody, hunched down in the passenger seat like a malevolent sprite, shoulders slumped, scowl fixed on his face.

The air conditioning was cranked. The car came equipped with GPS and satellite radio, which was a plus. "You want to listen to music?" Nicola asked.

A long-suffering sigh. "I don't care."

"Any preference as to the station?"

"Whatever," he said. He slumped against the door and stared morosely out the side window.

Nicola tuned it to an eighties station. It blasted A-ha's "Take On Me." Damn fine stuff. Music of her youth, it spoke to her soul. Laurie remained silent, but Nicola thought he perked up a little. By the time Berlin's "Metro" came on, he was singing along, poorly, at the top of his lungs.

They reached Decline at twilight. It was a dusty, sun-parched community located midway up a gradual hill, little more than a sprawl of fast-food restaurants and budget motels on either side of the highway. Nicola took the first exit and drove into town.

Nevada looked a lot like some parts of California, and Decline wasn't too different from Modesto, where she'd been born and raised. Not too pretty, all those indifferent strip malls and peeling stucco houses, but the landscape was wide open, nothing but low brown hills all around. Something comforting about that, the horizon sprawling in all directions.

The cool, impersonal female voice of the GPS informed Nicola that it didn't recognize the street address she'd input for their hotel. Laurie squinted at the display screen. "Are we lost? Did you get us lost?" he asked.

"Give me a break. This place is too small to get lost in." She glanced down at the printed information Galen had given her about their hotel reservation. "Keep an eye out, will you? We're looking for the Royal Yucca."

"Something tells me I shouldn't have my hopes too high about the 'Royal' part," Laurie said.

"Smart boy." She pulled into a Texaco station. "I need to top off the tank anyway. I'll ask for directions. Want to come in?"

"I'll stay here. Leave the radio on. And pick me up some cold seltzer, too; all the Pellegrino is warm," he said.

She glared at him, then unbuckled her seatbelt. She leaned across him and rolled his window down an inch.

"What are you doing?" he asked.

"Cracking the windows so you can get some air. I believe that's customary when leaving children in the car."

He rolled his eyes. "Hilarious," he said.

She was only gone a couple of minutes, but when she got back, there was trouble. Laurie had left the car. He'd taken off his white leather coat, and his aqua satin shirt glinted in the setting desert sun. He was leaning up against the passenger side door, and he was surrounded. Three men—kids, really, Laurie's age or younger—formed a half-circle around him.

Laurie said something she couldn't hear. He sounded calm. He moved forward, like he intended to walk straight past the kids.

"Go back to Vegas, fucking drag queen," one replied. He shoved Laurie, hard enough to make him stumble against the door.

No one should push Laurie around, ever. Nicola felt a sudden flare of fierce, fiery rage.

"Hey!" They swirled to look at her. She strode over to the car, keys clenched in her hand. "You. Don't touch him. Get away from him."

Laurie looked up at her. He seemed unruffled, she was glad to see. "Hey, Nicola. I was just having a chat with my new friends here."

She stared at the kid who'd pushed Laurie. White t-shirt, baggy canvas shorts, thick neck, the smug contempt of a lifelong bully emblazoned across his sunburned face.

"Laurie, get in the car," she told him. To the kid, she said, "Take a hike. Now."

"What are you going to do if we don't?" he asked, as she could have predicted he would.

Well, good question. There were three of them. "Grow up, all of you," she said.

"They come around here, lipstick-wearing sissy boys get the shit kicked out of them," one of the delightful little thugs said.

"Oh, you're brave, aren't you?" she said. Laurie hadn't moved, damn it. "Laurie. Get in the car. Do it," she said.

Without turning his back on his assailants, Laurie fumbled around behind him for the door handle. Despite his outward nonchalance, his hand shook. Nicola waited until he climbed inside and locked his door before moving around to her own side. One of the boys plastered his face right against Laurie's window and shouted something unintelligible at him. Laurie didn't flinch. Good for him.

Back behind the wheel, key in the ignition, starting the car. She was jittery from the adrenaline rush. She pulled forward out of the station; the kids moved to the side and gave her room. Good. If they'd tried to block her way, she didn't trust herself not to gun the motor.

"The guy behind the counter said we're close. We should have stayed on the state highway for another exit, but we can find the hotel if we just go straight from here. Keep an eye out for Yucca Road. Should be on the left."

Laurie didn't say anything. Nicola glanced at him. "You okay?"

He looked at her. "You want to know why I don't go to places with a population of under half a million?"

"I'm sorry that happened, Laurie," she said. "Maybe while we're here, you should consider toning down your sparkle."

"My gayness, you mean?" he said. His voice was thick with scorn.

"I said sparkle and I meant sparkle. Ditch the makeup and the satin and you'll attract a whole lot less attention."

"So I suppose that was my fault back there?"

She almost shot back an angry reply, but his challenging look stopped her. She thought about it a moment. "No. Sorry. You shouldn't get assholes jumping on your case no matter what you're wearing. That was a jerky thing for me to say."

A long silence. "You usually don't admit to being wrong." He almost sounded pleased.

"Don't get used to it. It doesn't happen very often." Yucca Road. About time. She swung left. "Here we are."

The Royal Yucca Hotel was, in sober fact, a motel. It consisted of two unconnected but identical two-story buildings placed at right angles to each other, with a separate one-story structure nestled at their juncture. This held the lobby and, more promisingly, a cocktail lounge. The hotel was painted burnt orange and dark brown, with a shingled clay roof and rusty iron security grates across the windows.

"Oh, ick," Laurie said. "Galen really thought this was the best of our options?"

"It's probably fine," Nicola said.

"It's still not too late to drive back to Vegas," Laurie said. "We could get a suite at one of the swanky casinos and order room service and loll around in our bathrobes all evening. Think about it."

"No dice, kiddo. This whole adventure is your show, remember?" She swung open her door. "Come on. Chin up."

Their rooms were right beside each other on the second level. Nicola had stayed in worse places, though she doubted Laurie had. A queen bed draped in a scratchy coverlet printed with daisies, gray stain-resistant nylon carpet, a television bolted to the heavy particle-board dresser. The remote control was tethered to the dresser with a plastic-coated steel cable, which Nicola thought was a nice touch.

Disheartened by the sight of his own room, Laurie trailed Nicola around while she did a rudimentary job of unpacking. There was a coffee pot and a complimentary packet of ground coffee on the bathroom counter. Already she felt kindlier toward the place.

"I need dinner. And a drink," Laurie said. "To fortify myself enough to spend an entire night in this misbegotten place."

"Someday people will write songs about your bravery," Nicola said. "Should we check out the options in the cocktail lounge?"

"God, yes," Laurie said.

The lounge was dark, the shades drawn low across the windows to block the glare of the setting sun. Formica tables and torn vinyl booths. They were the only customers in the place. The bartender looked up and nodded at them. "Sit wherever you want. I'll be right with you," she said.

They sat on the high stools at the bar. The bartender passed laminated menus to them. She had bronze skin, thick dark hair shot through with gray, and a strong nose. She wore a black leather vest, no shirt beneath it, and she looked tough and formidable. Her stare lingered on Laurie a little too long, but she didn't seem hostile, only curious. "Menu says we only serve breakfast until noon, but ignore that. Most people who come here get the huevos rancheros. Only thing the cook gets right. Everything else is pretty much shit."

Laurie looked alarmed. "We'll take two," Nicola said.

"Good choice. Drinks?"

"Do you have any champagne?" Laurie asked.

The bartender shook her head. "Sorry."

"Sparkling wine? Cava? Prosecco? Anything with bubbles?"

The bartender barely smiled. "I can drop an Alka-Seltzer in a glass of the house white, how's that?"

"Just the house white for us both. Hold the Alka-Seltzer," Nicola said.

The bartender plunked two small single-serving bottles of chardonnay on the bar. She gave a couple of glasses a quick polish and scooted them down to them. "Enjoy," she said.

She disappeared into the kitchen to deliver their dinner order to the chef. Nicola and Laurie dumped the contents of their miniature bottles into their glasses. "Cheers," Nicola said and hoisted her glass.

"To getting out of here in one piece." Laurie clinked his glass against hers. He drank. He scrunched up his face in distaste, but didn't comment otherwise. "Are we going to visit Joelle tonight? If we talk to her right away, we won't have to stay here very long."

"Easy, tiger. Let's start fresh in the morning. One night in scratchy sheets won't kill you."

"It might," Laurie said. He looked wilted and gloomy. "I have very sensitive skin."

Their food arrived. A stack of fried tortillas covered with eggs and melted cheese and chopped jalapenos and salsa. Looked greasy and disgusting, smelled like heaven. Laurie visibly recoiled at the sight. He broke off a small piece of tortilla with two dainty fingers and nibbled on an edge. Nicola dove in.

The bartender polished glasses down by their end of the bar, giving each one a firm swipe with her towel before replacing it under the counter. She kept looking surreptitiously at Laurie. "You folks coming from Las Vegas?" she asked.

"In a roundabout way," Nicola said. "We flew in from New York this morning, drove here from Vegas."

"Visiting friends?"

"Something like that," Nicola replied. Should she ask the bartender about Joelle Sutton? Decline was a tiny place; they might know each other.

"You want to hear something funny?" the bartender asked.

"Sure," Laurie said. He looked cautious.

"Maybe three weeks ago, this kid came in here. Ordered a beer, chatted a while. Said he was a bounty hunter from Vegas, on the trail of some guy who was wanted for passing a bunch of bad checks in the casinos. Didn't show me any credentials, not that I asked. He gave me the guy's name and a downright fascinating description and left me his number to call in case I spotted him. Said there'd be two hundred dollars in it for me."

She moved to the old-fashioned cash register and punched a key. The register drawer sprang open with a chime. She lifted up the drawer and withdrew a cocktail napkin with something scribbled on it in ballpoint pen.

"Problem is, this kid was operating on the assumption that we're a bunch of clueless hicks out here. And while we may not be on top of all the trends, we have, in fact, had MTV since 1984." She slapped the cocktail napkin on the bar in front of Laurie. "So how come somebody's trying to find you, Laurie Sparks?"

Nicola and Laurie leaned over the napkin. Laurie's name was scribbled on it, along with a phone number. A 323 area code. Los Angeles.

"Is this for real?" Laurie asked. His eyes were wide.

Nicola stared at the napkin, trying to piece this together. "You said this was about three weeks ago?"

"Yeah, probably about that. I don't remember the exact date. Long enough that I'd forgotten all about it until you two strolled in."

That was around when she and Laurie had been in L.A. "What did the guy look like?"

A shrug. "Youngish. Like I said, a kid. Early twenties. I don't remember too much about him, other than when he said he was a bounty hunter, I could sort of buy it, despite him being so young. He wasn't big or anything, but he looked ratty. What my mother would have called a marginal character, you know? He talked a good game, but as soon as he said your name I got suspicious."

"Thanks for telling me," Laurie said. "For the record, I'm not wanted for passing bad checks or anything. No bounty hunter should have any reason to come after me."

"Figured as much. Doesn't matter." The bartender grinned for the first time. It made her look much less intimidating. "My brother lost his job last year, so he and his kid moved in with me. She's fourteen. Loves that show of yours. She's always going on about how cute you are. She'd be pretty ticked at me if I handed you over to a bounty hunter."

Nicola picked up the napkin. "Can we keep this?" she asked.

"Sure, go ahead." The bartender placed their bill down on the bar. "That's for whenever you're ready. No hurry. Not exactly a rush for seats."

She moved down to the other end of the bar. Laurie turned to Nicola. His eyes still looked wide. "What—"

She shook her head. "Let's discuss it later."

Laurie picked up the bill. He glanced at Nicola. "Under the circumstances, I assume adding a two hundred-dollar tip would be appropriate, right?"

She finished her wine with a gulp and nodded at him. "Under the circumstances, that'd be an excellent idea."

CHAPTER TWENTY-TWO

WITH THIS NEW information, Laurie's suggestion of visiting Joelle Sutton right away instead of waiting until morning sounded like an excellent one. They hopped in the rental car and headed for Joelle's last known address.

"Who's looking for us?" Laurie asked. "Who left that note at the bar?"

Nicola exhaled. "I don't know. That phone number has an L.A. area code. Someone in Los Angeles knew or suspected we'd be going to Decline to look for Joelle Sutton."

"Gina Davenport," Laurie said. "Has to be."

"Okay, but why? Apparently she doesn't want us talking with whoever designed her wardrobe for *Holmby Hills*, but why on earth not? What harm could come of it?"

Laurie chewed his lower lip. "What if Molly really did manage to get in touch with Gina before our visit? We had that whole day where we were busy with Emmy stuff, so she would have had plenty of time. What if she told Gina we were looking for information about Joelle?"

"Huh." Nicola mulled it over. Molly had been shot that night . . . "I don't know, we're missing too many pieces here. Let's focus on finding Joelle right now."

"Are we in danger?" Laurie asked. He sounded scared. Nicola took a hand off the wheel and patted his leg in reassurance.

"We're fine, kiddo. But let's just talk to Joelle and get out of here, okay?"

The address for Joelle Sutton took them to a cul-de-sac on the outskirts of Decline. A smattering of small, nearly identical single-story houses were positioned in a rough circle around the end of a short paved drive. Not much in the way of landscaping, just sand and dirt and low, scraggly bushes.

"The houses look funny," Laurie said. "They're all the same."

"They're prefabricated. Trailer homes," Nicola said.

"This is a trailer park?" Laurie squinted out the passenger-side window. "They don't look like trailers."

"Not like what you're thinking, but yeah, they're modular. You buy them just like this and have them transported to a piece of property."

She parked. It was dark outside now, no street lights anywhere on the cul-de-sac. Not too inviting, this neighborhood.

At least the lights were on in Joelle's trailer, visible behind the Venetian blinds. Nicola and Laurie walked up the poured concrete walkway leading to the front door. The house was indistinguishable from the ones surrounding it, save for the well-maintained cactus garden underneath the front windows. Nicola glanced at Laurie and rang the doorbell.

After a pause, the porch light flickered on above their heads. The door opened a couple inches. A woman peered out at them. "Yes?"

"Joelle Sutton?" Nicola asked.

There was a pause. "Who's asking?"

Laurie came forward. "My name's Laurie Sparks. I'm a fashion designer from New York. I wanted to ask Joelle about some clothing she might have designed?"

The woman opened the door wider to get a better look at Laurie. A whiff of tomato sauce and garlic drifted out. In the background came the noise of a television, tuned to a cable news channel.

The woman was in her mid-forties, with dark hair cut short and indifferently. She examined Laurie and Nicola, then glanced at the dark street behind them. After a long moment, she stepped back and held the door open. "You can come in, if you want."

"Thank you," Nicola said. They followed her inside. The woman closed and locked the door behind them, then gestured toward the tiny living room.

"Go ahead and have a seat. I just finished my dinner. Can I get you a diet cola?"

The sofa was brown chenille with sagging cushions. Nicola and Laurie sat side by side in front of the television. Laurie looked unsure of himself. His spine was rigid, his hands folded in his lap.

"I think we're fine, thank you," Nicola said. "We're sorry for just barging in on you like this. I'm Nicola. I work with Laurie here."

The woman smiled. It didn't reach her eyes. No makeup, a plain face, bumpy sun damage across her nose and cheeks. She was barefoot, in cut-off jeans and a white tank top. There was a tattoo of a falcon in flight across her right bicep. She picked up the remote from the coffee table and clicked off the television. "I'm Cady. Joelle used to be my roommate."

"Then she doesn't live here any more?" Nicola asked.

"Joelle's dead." Cady looked tired. "I'm sorry you didn't know. It's been five months now."

Nicola heard Laurie's sharp intake of breath beside her. "I'm very sorry," she said. "Do you mind telling us what happened?"

Cady glanced from Nicola to Laurie. "You weren't friends of hers or anything, right?"

Nicola shook her head. "We'd never met her. We recently talked to an old acquaintance of hers, Danielle Marcin, who told us how we might get in touch with her."

Cady nodded her head. "I know that name, Danielle. She'd write to Joelle every Christmas. I remember her special because her letters came air mail from France." She smiled. "I used to collect the stamps."

She continued. "I only asked because if you were friends with Joelle, I'd probably be a bit nicer about how I told you this." She shrugged. "Joelle was a junkie. Had been since I met her, probably fifteen, sixteen years ago. We were both working at the same place in Las Vegas."

"Where'd you work?" Nicola asked.

"Cruddy little dry-cleaning place on Tropicana, over by UNLV. Joelle did some tailoring for them, alterations and stuff. I only worked there a couple of months. Went through a whole string of jobs, none of them much to write home about." She smiled. "I wasn't cute enough to strip. In Vegas. Just let that sink in for a bit. Anyway, Joelle had just come out from Los Angeles. We hit it off, and when I got a job at the bank here, she offered to move with me, split the rent. The cleaners had folded by then, and I think she'd pretty much had it with Vegas. Happens to us all sooner or later."

"Were you two close friends?" Nicola asked. She'd meant it to be devoid of innuendo, but Cady gave her a sharp look.

"We weren't lovers, if that's what you're asking." Cady slid her eyes over to Laurie, then looked back at Nicola. "I mean, I knew she was queer, but that didn't bother me much. She kept to herself. Didn't really have her shit together enough to get busy with anyone."

"How'd she die?" Laurie asked. It was the first time he'd spoken since she'd invited them inside. Cady looked startled, as though she'd assumed he was a beautiful porcelain doll instead of a flesh-and-blood human.

Cady didn't answer at first. She picked up a glass of soda from where it rested on the coffee table next to a plate containing the remnants of a spaghetti dinner. The table had a glass top over a white wicker frame. Her glass left a circle of moisture on the surface. She took a sip and set the glass down again, placing it so it lined up precisely on the circle.

"She messed up," Cady said. "She got herself in the wrong place at the wrong time. She was buying stuff she shouldn't have been buying from Ricky Sanchez—that's Lara Sanchez's kid, they live here on the circle—and someone came along and robbed him. Back-shot Ricky, shot Joelle for good measure." She shook her head.

"Dumb," she said at last. "The whole thing was dumb. Buying crystal from some jackass teenager. I mean, she was fifty years old, for Christ's sake."

Nicola's throat went dry. Should've taken Cady up on her offer of a beverage. She swallowed once. "They find who did it?"

Cady shook her head. "They did, they never told me. You'd have to ask Sandy—that's Sandy Cowell, over in the sheriff's office. He could tell you more about it. I just know what was in the paper mostly, and that's enough."

Laurie shifted on the sofa. "She was doing some work last year, wasn't she? Like a lot of sewing for someone?"

"Uh-huh. She was making some clothes for a client. Paid her some decent money, too, though it all seemed to go straight to Ricky." Cady shrugged. "She always did a little bit of that on the side, even in Vegas. Running up gowns for prom, *Quinceañera* dresses, costumes for strippers, that sort of thing. But in the past year or so, she'd upped her game. Started doing sewing on a larger scale. She played it pretty close to the vest, snapped at me the couple times I asked about it, so I didn't bug her too much. Just so long as she paid her share of the rent on time."

Cady waved a leathery hand in front of her face, as though brushing away the memory of Joelle. "She had a sad life. Could've done big things. Just a shame she was never able to make much of it."

"She was a really good designer," Laurie said. "She had an amazing talent."

Cady looked surprised at this. "Did she? I wouldn't know. I never was much for fashion. No, I guess what I meant was, she came from real money. Her father was some kind of big-shot politician or something. Fancy boarding schools and summers in Europe, the whole deal. Not that she ever talked about it. I found that out from her brother when he came to collect her things after her death."

She took another drink of her cola. "You want to know about Joelle, you could talk to him. Nice guy. They were twins, actually, Joel and Joelle. Seemed devastated by her death, though they sure hadn't been in touch lately. Joelle led me to believe she didn't have family left."

Joel Sutton. The property lawyer in New York. Probably the same guy.

"Do you still have any of her possessions? Stuff the brother didn't pick up?" Laurie asked. Cady looked confused and a little wary, so he clarified. "I'm just talking about clothes she might have designed. If so, I'd love to see them. Like I said, she was really talented."

"I boxed up everything that was hers. Her brother just took some personal mementos, photos and stuff like that. She did have a lot of clothes, which he didn't have any use for, so he left all that here." Cady shrugged. "It's still all stacked up in her old room. Been meaning to do a big Goodwill dump."

"Can I have it?" Laurie said. "Whatever you have of hers, Nicola and I will take it off your hands."

Cady frowned. The wary look shifted into outright suspicion. She shook her head. "No. I couldn't do that. I'd have to get permission from her brother. He says it's okay, then you can have it."

"He already said he didn't want it," Laurie said. Nicola winced at the petulance in his tone.

"If you push me, I won't let you have it at all," Cady said. "Her brother left me his card somewhere. When I find it, I'll give him a call, and then I'll let you know what he says."

Laurie glowered. He was going to squawk and complain and argue the point, and then Cady would refuse to help them. Time to make their exit. Nicola got to her feet and smiled. "That would be perfect. We appreciate it. Thank you," she said. She rummaged in her bag for a notebook and wrote down her number. She tore off the sheet and placed it on the coffee table, then handed the tablet and pen to Cady. "That's how you can contact me. If I could get your phone number too, that'd be great."

Cady looked grouchy at this, but she scrawled out a number and handed the pad back. Nicola smiled again. "Perfect. Thanks for talking to us, and we're sorry again for the intrusion. Laurie?"

Reluctantly, Laurie got to his feet. "Can you make sure you ask Joelle's brother, please? It's really super-important," he said.

"I said I'd call him, and I will," Cady said. It sounded snappish. Nicola couldn't blame her.

Cady stood in the doorway and watched until they were back in Nicola's car. Laurie buckled himself in. He glanced at the house, his expression peevish. "We should have stayed there and waited while she called the brother."

"Yeah, I don't think that would have gone over well. You do know we don't actually have a right to Joelle's possessions, right?"

"But she's not even using them. The brother didn't want them. She was just going to give them away."

"Doesn't matter. Still doesn't mean we're entitled to them. And you scared her off by getting so grabby about it."

Laurie stared at her. "Sorry," he said. It came out as a mutter. "It's just that it's important."

More than Joelle's death, more than Molly's death, this was what was important to Laurie: Joelle's designs. The kid needed to rearrange his priorities.

They drove in moody silence. Laurie heaved a sigh. "My stomach hurts," he said. "Dinner sucked."

"You barely ate any of it. I thought the huevos were pretty tasty."

"I barely ate anything because it sucked. Your palate is less refined than mine," Laurie said.

"Undeniably," Nicola said. "You want to stop for something to eat? I saw a Taco Bell on the way to our hotel."

This provoked the expected response. Laurie scrunched up his face in disgust. "Ew. No."

"It's not like our culinary options are unlimited here, kiddo," Nicola said. "We might still have some of the cookies in back. That should tide you over until we can scrounge up something else for you."

Laurie heaved a long-suffering sigh. He leaned over into the backseat, yanking at his shoulder strap to give himself enough slack to reach the cookies.

They were passing beneath the overpass of the highway entrance, and the front windshield exploded.

Chunks of safety glass flew at Nicola, bouncing harmlessly off her face and right shoulder. A chunk of the right side of the windshield was gone, wind rushing into the front seat through a fist-sized hole. From the passenger seat, still leaning into the back, Laurie squawked. It sounded like surprise, not pain.

She took a hard swerve to the right and hit the brakes, too hard. She skidded sideways on the loose gravel of the shoulder. The car slid down off the road and into the shallow ditch running alongside it.

A thunk of impact, a whoosh of inflating airbags, a fierce pain across her ribs where her shoulder strap kept her from flying forward. The airbag hit her in the face and chest. Fully inflated, it seemed to fill the entire front seat, vast and inflexible, blocking her vision.

They were tilting to the right, though the left wheels were still on the ground. The car hadn't toppled onto its side; it was just wedged in the ditch lining the road, pitched against the slope. Laurie's door was blocked.

Laurie . . . Nicola looked over. Behind his own airbag, Laurie made strange gasping noises, something between a whimper and a hiccup. "Laurie? You okay?"

"What happened?" he asked, his voice high-pitched and shaky.

"I think someone shot at us from the overpass." Shot at Laurie, technically; the bullet had gone through his side of the windshield and would probably have gone through Laurie if he hadn't been leaning into the backseat.

"What?" It came out as a squeak.

"Can you move? We need to get out of here."

A flailing of limbs behind Laurie's airbag. "I can't reach my seatbelt," he said.

Nicola groped around in the darkness for the buckle of her own seatbelt. Got it unfastened, reached over, undid Laurie's as well. She found her door handle by touch, because the airbag kept getting in the way of everything and she couldn't see a damn thing, and yanked it up. Her door swung open. "We're going to go out my side, Laurie, okay? Just hang on to me."

She slipped her right arm around Laurie's tiny waist and grabbed hold of him by his hip. With a silent prayer that he had no injuries that would be exacerbated by movement, she tugged him sideways toward her.

Laurie slithered out from beneath his airbag. When he was finally out of his seat and over the gear shift, Nicola wriggled around beneath her own airbag. Thanks to the tilt of the car, she had to slide up to get out, which was disorienting, especially in the darkness. She reached in with both arms, shoved the airbag out of the way as much as she could, and helped Laurie slip up and out.

The night air in the desert was crisp and still. Hard to believe the day had been so sweltering. Way too open here, protected only by the shallow ditch and the tilted car. If anyone was shooting at them, they'd make a hell of an easy target. "Keep down. We're going to stay in this ditch and sprint toward the overpass, okay?"

They moved, Nicola with her arm around Laurie's waist, half-pulling him along with her. She saw headlights leaving the overpass, a car driving down the curved ramp that merged with the road. It could be their attacker, coming down to finish the job.

The street lights shone down on them, glinting off of Laurie's pale satin shirt, and that wouldn't do at all. As soon as they were beneath the protection of the overpass, Nicola pulled him to the ground. "Lie flat," she told him.

Laurie obeyed without complaint, lying on his stomach in the dirt and gravel and cigarette butts and fast-food wrappers in the ditch. Nicola wore a black long-sleeved shirt and jeans, and in the dark she'd be damn near invisible. She crawled on top of him and covered him with her body. "Stay still," she whispered.

Beneath her, Laurie was frozen. She heard him breathing, fast and raspy with fear, felt his heart hammering hard enough to shake his entire body. Headlights swept the road and illuminated the concrete wall of the overpass beside them. The headlights passed on, followed by another set of headlights, then another.

Traffic moved as it should. No one was going to shoot them. Nicola rolled off of Laurie. Neck felt stiff, chest felt like she'd taken several strong punches to the ribs.

"Are you hurt?" she asked Laurie.

Laurie looked up at her. In the harsh light of the streetlights, he looked sick and stricken, like he was trying hard not to cry. He shook his head.

"You sure?" she asked. She took a quick visual inventory. His shirt was dirty, and he had a nasty welt across the side of his neck from his shoulder strap, but he seemed okay. No blood.

She groped around her jeans pockets. Somewhere between their car and the overpass, she'd lost her phone. "Do you have your phone on you?" she asked.

Laurie stared at her, his expression vacant and stupid, as though he didn't understand what she was asking. Then he shook himself out of the fog. He reached inside his pants pocket and handed her his phone.

Nicola took it from him and dialed 911.

CHAPTER TWENTY-THREE

THE SHERIFF'S STATION was located in a white one-story strip mall, wedged in between the DMV and a 7-Eleven. Shortly after Nicola called 911, a deputy had arrived on the scene, lights swirling atop her patrol car. The deputy, a stout blonde woman with an air of grim competence, made a brief but thorough examination of their crashed car. Nicola had seen the small round bullet hole embedded in Laurie's seat back. She'd felt like throwing up.

And now they were here, in this clean, aggressively bright space, with the blindingly white walls and the fluorescent lights overhead.

Acting Sheriff Sandy Cowell had light brown curls and pale blue eyes. He sat at a table in the conference room, with Nicola and Laurie across from him, and grilled them on the evening's excitement.

The shades were up. The windows faced the parking lot and the street beyond it. In the bright, bright room, Nicola couldn't see anything in the darkness outside.

"Can we close those blinds?" she asked.

"I'll do it." Sheriff Cowell got to his feet and yanked down on the roller shades, blocking out the darkness. Nicola immediately felt better.

Cowell was in uniform, brown shirt and pants paired with a beige necktie. Even though it was just after eight, he looked fresh and crisp. Nicola and Laurie looked like hell. Back on the road, Laurie had appeared so battered and bedraggled the deputy had wanted to summon an ambulance. Only Laurie's forceful insistence that he was one hundred percent undamaged had dissuaded her.

"Do you usually work nights, or did you get called back in for this?" Nicola asked Cowell.

He smiled. Nice smile, seemed genuine. Dimples. Early forties maybe, plenty cute. "I was off duty. My deputy called, said there'd been an incident near the highway, thought I might find it interesting." He shrugged. "Sooner or later, I'd like to get the 'acting' stripped off of my title, and going the extra mile seems like one way to do it."

Nicola smiled back at him. It felt a bit wan, but that was probably okay. Someone had just tried to shoot her and Laurie. Nobody would expect her to be chatty and perky.

"We've got coffee if you need it, though it's probably the same stuff that was brewing when I left at five. I can fetch you some tea if you want something a little fresher."

"I'm okay," Nicola said. She glanced over at Laurie, who hadn't spoken much since the ambush. He stared down at the table. "Laurie?"

Without looking up, he shook his head. Cowell looked at him curiously, but didn't comment.

"I can tell you now that it looks like someone fired down on you from the overpass. We'll know more about the gun type when my guys dig the bullet out of your seat. A rifle would be my guess, something long-range." He leaned forward in his seat. "So I guess now the question is whether someone was shooting at you two in particular."

Nicola was quiet for a moment, organizing her thoughts. "Two possibilities, as near as I can tell," she said at last. "I don't really think it's this first one, but you should know about it anyway. When Laurie and I drove into town earlier today, three guys at the Texaco station gave us a hard time. One of them shoved Laurie."

"What were they giving you a hard time about?" Cowell asked.

Laurie looked up from the table. His expression was hard. "They called me a drag queen," he said.

Cowell nodded. "Can you describe them?"

Nicola thought. "Not in any great detail. Like I said, there were three of them. They looked college-aged, maybe a little older. They were white. The one who shoved Laurie was wearing a white t-shirt and shorts and a ball cap. No logo on the shirt, and I don't remember much about the cap, other than that it was blue."

"What were they driving?"

She shook her head. "I didn't see them arrive, and we left before they did."

"They pulled up in a white SUV," Laurie said. "I don't know what it was. Something big and ugly. The one who shoved me was driving."

Cowell nodded and jotted down the information on the steno pad in front of him. "Did they make any threats?"

"They said people like me would get beaten up in this town," Laurie said. He looked miserable. "They were total dicks, but it didn't seem like they'd try to *shoot* me."

"We'll check into it. The gas station has surveillance cameras out front. We can maybe pull a license number from that." Cowell looked at Nicola. "And the second possibility?"

"Yeah. This is going to sound confusing, so I apologize in advance if I explain it poorly." Nicola gestured to Laurie. "Laurie's a fashion designer. He's got a shop in New York, which is where we're from. He's, ah, also the star of a reality show on MTV. It's called *NYC Elite*."

Cowell frowned. He didn't seem dazzled at having a television star grace his town. He *did* seem like this information would make him more skeptical of their story. The phrase "reality show" seemed to trigger suspicion in people.

"Anyway, we came here because Laurie wanted to track down another designer, a woman named Joelle Sutton."

Here, Cowell's body language changed. He sat up straighter at the mention of Joelle, though he said nothing.

"We think Joelle Sutton might have designed some of the wardrobe for a television show that was on last year, *Holmby Hills*. Laurie wanted to talk to her about the those clothes. We were in Los Angeles last month, and we talked to Molly Gable, the woman who was in charge of the wardrobe on the show." Nicola inhaled. "She said she'd ask around, but she never got back to us. And I really don't know if or how this would be connected to us, but the day after she talked to us, she was shot to death while she was driving."

Cowell scribbled on his notepad. "Molly Gable. When was this?"

Nicola thought. "September seventeenth, I think. Molly tipped us off about Joelle, so Laurie and I came here hoping to find her. We talked to her former roommate, Cady."

"Cady Moss. Sure. I suppose Cady told you what happened to Joelle?"

"Yeah. A drug buy gone wrong. She said Joelle was just in the wrong place at the wrong time?"

Cowell ignored the question in her tone. Nicola continued. "So we were just driving back from Cady's house when someone fired through our windshield."

Cowell nodded. "Okay," he said. "But what's the connection? Why would someone try to shoot you just because you were asking about Joelle Sutton?"

"I don't know. I don't have any idea." She was exhausted. God, she was exhausted. "One other thing, though." She fished the cocktail napkin the bartender had given them out of her jeans pocket. She spread it out on the conference table. "We're staying at the Royal Yucca. The bartender in the restaurant there told us someone had been asking about Laurie three weeks ago. He gave her this number and offered to pay her if she spotted us."

Cowell picked up the napkin and looked at the number. "Los Angeles," he said. "You don't know who this was?"

"No idea. We haven't tried calling that number."

Cowell stared at them for a while. "Huh," he said at last. "Laurie, do you have anything to add to Nicola's story?"

Laurie shook his head and didn't say anything. Cowell leaned back in his chair. "Here's my concern. You've got someone out there who already took a shot at you once. I don't know if it has anything to do with this Molly Gable, but we'll coordinate with the LAPD and see if we can swap notes. For tonight, though, I'm going to have my deputy run you back to your hotel. Stay inside, that's my suggestion. She'll do a few passes during the night, just to make sure no one suspicious is hanging around."

"Do you need us to stick around town for anything?" Nicola asked. "I think Laurie and I would feel better if we returned to New York in the morning."

He shook his head. "Go ahead. I've got your info." He smiled. "We're going to be keeping your rental car for evidence, though, not that you'd be able to drive it as it is."

"Any place in town where we could get a car?"

"You can ask at one of the service stations, someone might have a loaner. Greyhound stops here twice a day on the way to Vegas, so that's another possibility. I were you, though, I'd just call your rental company and get them to send you a replacement. It might have to come from Vegas, so that could delay you a bit."

"Thanks," Nicola said. She rose from the table. Laurie looked confused, like he hadn't realized the interview was winding down, then stood as well.

Cowell stood up and extended a hand to her. Firm handshake, warm and solid. "You did a good job getting out of the car and staying down, by the way. That was real smart of you," he said.

"Would've been smarter if I'd managed not to crash in the first place," Nicola replied.

"Don't sell yourself short. Someone was shooting at you." Cowell smiled. Another flash of dimples. "You've got a good head on you. Might've kept you both alive."

It felt good to hear that, even though Nicola knew they were alive only because Laurie had been making a fuss about being hungry.

Laurie wasn't doing well. His nerves had been shattered by the attack, and by the time Cowell's deputy dropped them off at the hotel, his mental state had progressed from numb shock to panic.

"Let's leave now," he said. "Call Galen and see if he can get us a car. I don't want to stay here."

"We'll figure out how to leave in the morning. Right now, we're safer in the hotel than we are on the road." Nicola was in Laurie's hotel room, calming him down and getting him settled for the night. She did a covert sweep of the space while she was there, just to make sure no one was hiding in his shower or under the bed. "I'll be right next door. Sit tight, get some sleep, and I'll come get you in the morning. Okay?"

Laurie nodded. He looked so miserable—bruised and broken and jittery and freaked out—that it seemed wrong to leave him alone. "Do you need anything?" she asked. "If you're hungry, I can see if the lounge can deliver you a sandwich."

He shook his head. "My head hurts, I'm sore all over, and I feel terrible," he said. "Do you have any Tylenol or anything?"

"I'll ask at the registration desk," she said. "Be back in a minute."

The clerk at the desk directed her to the vending machine on the first level near the stairs, which stocked various necessities, including trial-sized packets of acetaminophen. Nicola picked some up for Laurie and snagged him a can of ginger ale to wash it down.

From behind her: "Hey."

She turned. Young guy. Wiry build, buzz-cut hair, jeans and a green t-shirt. It took her a second to place him, and then she had it.

The lobby of their hotel in Los Angeles, the guy who'd asked about Laurie.

He was empty-handed. That was good. She swallowed. "Hey," she said back. Her voice was a little shaky. So were her legs.

"You recognize me?" he asked.

She nodded. "From Los Angeles," she said. "Lobby of the Burton Hotel."

"Good memory." He smiled. "Hey, I just wanted to check with you about something real quick."

Laurie's room was up the stairs, maybe about twenty yards away. She'd have to get past this kid. She'd have to run for it. She shouldn't even bother talking to him. Maybe she should scream, as loudly as she could.

She could see the road behind him. Damn it, the deputy was supposed to be keeping an eye on this place. If she saw the patrol car drive by, maybe she could flag it down. "Go ahead," she said.

"He ducked, right?" He looked curious, like her answer was important to him. "The Sparks kid. He must've ducked right before I fired, because I have kick-ass aim. They should be cleaning the marshmallow fluff he calls brains off the upholstery of your car right now."

He blocked the stairs. While Nicola's brain searched for a course of action, her body decided to move. She tried to dart past him, but he grabbed her wrist and yanked her back. She jerked out of his grasp and stumbled against the metal handrail. She hit it full-on with her ribs, which were still bruised from where her shoulder strap had caught her during the crash. It *hurt*.

The pain helped her focus. Even as he grabbed for her again, she scurried up the stairs. He hooked her ankle and yanked her down. She hit the steps, concrete against her palms and knees.

A hand grabbed at the back waistband of her jeans. She scrambled forward on all fours up the short flight. When she reached the top, she ran. "Laurie!" she shouted.

She sprinted toward Laurie's room. Didn't know if the guy was behind her, no way she was going to turn around to check. "Laurie, open up!" She flung herself at Laurie's door and pounded on it with her scraped palms.

The bolt slipped back. Laurie opened the door. "Hey, what's—"

She shoved him back, no time for niceties. She slammed the door shut behind her, flipped the bolt, slid the hook-and-eye lock in place. "Get down. Away from the windows, on the floor."

Laurie obeyed immediately, which was gratifying and a little surprising, considering the fuss he usually kicked up over the simplest requests. He sat on the floor beside his bed. Nicola crouched beside him, facing the door. "What's going on?" he asked.

"He's out there. The guy from the hotel lobby in Los Angeles, he's the guy who tried to shoot you." She was shaking all over, and goddamn, she hurt from all her bruises and scrapes. She reached up and yanked the hotel phone off the bedside table. Did she need to dial a nine or something to get an outside line, or would just dialing 911 do the trick? She glanced at the little laminated instruction card taped to the top of the phone without comprehending it, then dialed 911.

It did, in fact, do the trick.

CHAPTER TWENTY-FOUR

AND THEN THEY were back in the sheriff's station, talking to Acting Sheriff Sandy Cowell for the second time in an hour. He listened to Nicola's incoherent story, asked a few clarifying questions about where she'd seen the guy before.

"He didn't have a gun on him?" he asked.

Nicola shook his head. "He didn't show one. He didn't have a bag or anything that I saw. I suppose he could've had a handgun hidden in his pants, but certainly not a rifle."

"Why did he talk to you? Why didn't he just shoot you?" Cowell asked. "For that matter, why did he talk to you in Los Angeles? Why didn't he just ignore you, if his target was Laurie?"

Laurie tensed a little at this, but said nothing. "No idea. All I can tell you is, he seemed off. Mentally unstable. He talked to me like he knew me, like I'd be totally cool with him trying to kill Laurie," Nicola said. "It was weird."

"Sounds like it." Cowell flashed her his nice smile. He seemed open and sympathetic, which was a relief, because if he thought she was lying, she'd probably burst into tears. "We'll circulate your description of him immediately. Maybe the bartender at the Royal Yucca can ID him as the guy who came in looking for Laurie three weeks ago."

Nicola held up her hand. "He grabbed my wrist. He might've left a fingerprint on my watch." She wore the tank watch Laurie gave her in Paris. It had dug into her wrist when the kid grabbed her on the stairs.

"May I? Hold your hand out, wrist up," Cowell said. He used the tip of his ballpoint pen to unhook the clasp. The watch slid off her wrist and dropped onto the conference table. "We'll dust it for prints."

"He seemed like he might be military." Nicola wrinkled her brow. "Like I said, he had a buzz cut, but even more than that, he reminded me of a soldier. His body type, maybe even his attitude. Maybe you could check his fingerprints against military records? Is that something you can do?"

"We can. Not a bad thought. You've got some good ideas." Cowell smiled. "We've called in our sketch artist, if you care to sit down with him."

Talking to the sketch artist took forever. It was all done via computer, a painstaking process of trial and error and minute adjustments. In the end, a sullen kid with a bad crew cut stared back at her from the sketch artist's monitor. Not a perfect likeness, but it captured his basic essence.

Cowell joined them as they were finishing up. "We got a nice thumbprint off your watch, so that might be a big help. We're keeping your watch for the time being, but I'll be sure to mail it back to you when we're done. Looks like it might be valuable."

"Probably. It's a gift from Laurie, and he tends to be a little extravagant," she said. She glanced over at the conference room where Laurie sat at the table by himself, his head resting in his hands, an untouched paper cup of tea in front of him.

Cowell followed her stare. "He going to be okay? Seems like this has spooked him pretty bad."

"I think so. I'd really like us to get out of this place, though, no offense to your town at all. Any problem with us leaving now?"

"No, none at all. Go right ahead." Cowell seemed a little disappointed. "You got your car situation all settled?"

"Working on it now," she said.

She rejoined Laurie in the conference room. "Let me borrow your phone. Mine's still lost in that ditch somewhere."

"About time you upgraded anyway," Laurie said, with a semblance of his usual flippancy. He passed it over.

She glanced at the clock on the wall. Ten o'clock here, which meant it was one in the morning in New York, which meant she'd probably wake Galen up from his beauty sleep. No one ever said being Laurie's assistant would be easy.

It rang four times before Galen answered, sleepy and lovey-dovey. "Hey, angel. Missing you," he said.

"Sorry. It's Nicola," she said. "I'm just using Laurie's phone."

"Oh. Wow. Nicola, I'm sorry. I thought—"

"We're in Decline," she said. Sounded almost poetic, and painfully apt. "I crashed the rental car, and we need another one as soon as possible. Can you work your magic and get one sent to the county sheriff's station here immediately?"

"Sheriff's station?" He sounded sleepy and dreamy, like he was having trouble following the conversation. "You crashed? Is Laurie okay?"

She glanced at Laurie, who looked ragged and peaked. "He's fine. Someone shot through our windshield earlier this evening, though. I think we were set up. Someone's trying to kill him."

"That's ridiculous." Galen's voice went cold. Defensive and resentful, like Nicola had just accused him personally of shooting Laurie, and all of a sudden things clicked into place. For a long moment, she couldn't answer.

She took a deep breath. "Galen, just get us a car as soon as possible, please. Within the hour, if you can manage it."

"Okay, sure." Galen swiftly recovered on his end. "Of course, no problem. Wow, that's really weird and scary. The sheriff's station?"

Nicola gave him the street address. "Soon as you can, right?"

"Are you heading to Las Vegas tonight? Do you need me to book you on a flight home?"

"We'll handle it on our end. We'll see you when we get back to New York." She hung up, glad she was able to make it through the call without calling Galen out for being a lying little snake.

For whatever else Galen might be, he was a damn good assistant. Within the hour, a rental car arrived in front of the sheriff's station, via a dealership in nearby Pioche. Nicola filled out the necessary paperwork and collected the keys, then retrieved Laurie from the conference room.

They headed back to their motel, a patrol car shadowing them for the entire short trip. It seemed like a waste to leave town without the boxes of Joelle Sutton's possessions, but they'd call Cady later and see if she'd received permission from the brother to send them. Right now, they needed to get out of this place.

After Nicola finished packing her bags, she went next door to Laurie's room and stuffed his belongings back into his suitcases. Under usual circumstances, Laurie would protest this graceless treatment of his expensive, outlandish outfits, but there was no fight in him. He sat on the edge of the bed and stared at the carpet. It scared her, this passivity, as though fear had rendered him catatonic.

Finally on their way. The open road once more, after what had been only a handful of unexpectedly grueling hours in Decline. The patrol car shadowed them to the state highway, then gave a honk and flipped a U-turn. And then they were on their own.

Nicola started out at the speed limit, then edged it up until they were flying down the road. Not much traffic around this late at night. She kept an eye on the rearview mirror, just to make sure, but no one was tailing them.

She glanced at her dismal passenger. "We're on our way, kiddo," she said. "We'll check into a nice hotel when we reach Vegas, okay? Soft beds and room service. Sounds good, right?"

"Will it be safe, though?" Laurie asked. His voice was hushed. "That guy found us in Decline. What if he's tracing my credit cards or something? What if he finds us in Vegas?"

"He's not tracing your credit cards, Laurie. It's no big mystery how he found us. He'd been expecting us to show up there, remember?"

"He's from Los Angeles. Unless he's been staying in Decline for the past three weeks waiting for us to arrive, it would take at least, what, six hours to get here from Los Angeles? We'd only been in town a couple hours before he started shooting at us."

It was easy to forget Laurie was sharper than he looked. "Yeah, I know. I thought of that too," she said.

"So he's tracking us somehow, that's the only solution. Either he's bugged us, or he's keeping tabs on my credit cards, or—"

"It's Galen," she said. "Galen tipped him off. Or more likely he tipped someone else off, whoever that guy who shot at us is working for. Since we're talking about Galen, my money is on Kip Caprini."

Laurie stared at her. "Are you kidding?"

"When I told Galen someone tried to shoot you, he immediately got defensive. Like I was accusing him specifically. He'd just woken up and he wasn't thinking straight, but his first reaction was to deny everything."

"So what?" Laurie said. "It doesn't mean he's working for someone."

"Think about how we met Galen, okay? Kip Caprini's show. He got us into Caprini's show, and then into Caprini's after-party. He just happened to be there, and he was so very helpful, right when you really needed a new assistant, right after we got back from Los Angeles. I bet you anything Caprini sent him to get close to you. He probably wanted to find out what we knew about Joelle Sutton."

Laurie shook his head and didn't say anything. Nicola felt her stomach tighten. "How much did you tell Galen about what we were up to? Did you tell him how you thought Caprini faked his collection?"

"Not exactly." Laurie's voice was small and miserable. "But he probably could have figured it out in Paris. I wasn't all that careful about keeping secrets." He inhaled, deep and ragged. "But he was so *nice* to me."

"I know. I know you were involved with him. He called me 'angel' on your phone when he thought I was you." Nicola glanced over at him. "You could have told me the truth about that, you know."

"I thought you'd disapprove. Because I didn't really know him, and I hired him, and I know you thought that was a stupid thing to do." His voice was thick. Nicola kept her eyes on the road. "And I thought you'd think it was kind of sleazy, him being my assistant, especially with Jonathan before him, but it wasn't like that. It was nice."

He was crying in earnest now and making no attempt to hide it. "I've been so unhappy since Jonathan left, and I thought Galen *liked* me."

"I know. Oh, Laurie. I'm sorry he turned out to be a snake."

They drove. Fast, the dark desert zipping by, nothing much to see but dirt and sagebrush anyway. Laurie didn't say much until they were surrounded by the glitz and sparkle of the Strip, and that was only to shoot down Nicola's first few hotel suggestions. "I want something nice," he said. *Nice* to Laurie meant the Wynn, the gleaming bronze structure that rose above the Strip like a trophy.

While crossing through the opulent lobby, which glimmered with soft gold from every angle, Nicola made the mistake of catching a glimpse of her reflection in a mirror. She and Laurie looked like refugees, scraggly and battered and red-eyed with exhaustion. This was Vegas, though, and the implacable uniformed gentleman at the registration counter had clearly seen worse.

Laurie turned back to her, in the process of surrendering his platinum card. "Is it okay if we share a room?" he asked. "It'll be a suite."

It struck her then how frightened Laurie still was. Her own terror had ebbed as soon as they left Decline. Here, surrounded by all this luxury, the events of the evening seemed unreal, improbable. Laurie, however, still worried their mysterious attacker would find them, would maybe gun them down under the high, windowed ceiling in this gorgeous lobby.

"No problem," she told him. Laurie seemed to uncoil with relief.

A sumptuous suite, high up in the tower with a panoramic view of the Strip, the surrounding casinos pulsing and glittering like alien spacecraft. Two identical bedrooms, king beds blanketed in gold. Laurie looked ready to collapse, and he was trembling on his feet, so Nicola steered him toward the bathroom. "Take a soak," she said. "Get warmed up. I'll order us something to eat."

"Get champagne, too," Laurie said. "I need it."

While Laurie settled himself in the tub, Nicola familiarized herself with the room service menu. By the time he emerged, pink and scrubbed and swaddled in a plush robe, the round marble dining table was already covered with silver dome-topped trays of food. Along with Laurie's champagne—Krug, presented in a silver bucket that came on its own stand—she'd ordered gigantic chicken pot pies with flaky brown crusts, a platter of chocolate-chip cookies, a pot of chamomile tea. Food for sick people, food for people who'd had their nerves shattered and were in dire need of comfort.

Laurie poured the champagne. After the first glass, a little animation returned to his expression, and he started in on the food. Once he began eating, the floodgates opened, and he kept eating and eating, making a significant dent in his pot pie. More champagne, more tea, more cookies. Nicola ate some and drank some, but mostly watched, fascinated and cheered by the sight of Laurie returning to life.

"I don't remember the details of what happened on that road," he said at last. He settled back in his chair and held his champagne flute between two fingers. He looked so much like the old Laurie, even with his hair wet and plastered down and his face scrubbed bare, that Nicola felt a strange tension unwind inside her. "When we crashed, I remember the shoulder strap hurting a whole lot." He touched the angry raw welt on his neck. "But I don't remember getting out of the car, or anything until we were in that ditch. You pulled me out, didn't you?"

"Yeah. You were conscious, though. Your door was blocked by the ditch, so we went out my side."

"Thanks." He looked at her, eyes pale and intense. "If that guy had come down after us, he would have just shot me if you hadn't pulled me out of there."

"He didn't come down after us. There were too many cars around. I think he just drove off after he realized he missed. You would have been fine without me."

"Still," he said. He let out a deep breath. "You're so good at things like that. Emergencies, I mean."

She smiled. "Why don't you get some sleep?" she said. "Things'll look better tomorrow."

He nodded. "Thanks, Nicola," he said.

With Laurie off in his own room, Nicola showered. She availed herself of copious handfuls of the amenities, clementine-scented bath gel and lavender-scented shampoo and tea-scented body lotion, and dried herself off with a huge, fluffy towel. She changed into the sweatpants and t-shirt she wore as pajamas and crawled beneath crisp white sheets.

She was too wound up to sleep, and she'd finished the book she'd packed on the flight from New York, so she channel-surfed, reclining on a mountain of pillows while watching old sitcoms from her childhood on one of the classic cable networks. She kept the sound low and her door closed so she wouldn't disturb Laurie, but even so, there soon came a soft knock on the door. A pajama-clad Laurie entered.

"Hi," he said. He seemed sheepish. "I was hoping you'd still be up."

"Can't sleep?"

He shook his head. "Would it be okay if . . . I mean, you can say no, but I was wondering . . ."

Nicola patted the other side of the bed. "Climb in," she said.

Instant relief suffused his small body. "Thanks," he said. He slithered under the covers and pulled the comforter up to his armpits. "I don't take up much space, you know. And I don't snore."

"Good. I might. I've heard varying reports."

Laurie snuggled back on the pillows. He turned onto his side, curled his body into a small bundle, and stared at Nicola. "I can't stop being scared. I know it's stupid, but I can't help it."

"It's not stupid. Someone did try to shoot you. But you're safe here."

"I know." Laurie smiled. "Anyone wanting to get to me would have to get past you first. And you're the toughest person I know."

"Might want to broaden your circle of acquaintances in that case." Nicola shifted to her side so she was facing him. She snorted as a thought struck her.

"What is it?" Laurie asked.

She shook her head. "I think I'd probably kill someone to protect you, Laurie," she said. "And I'll be damned if I know why."

"It's because I'm so lovable," Laurie said. He yawned. "Are you going to be watching TV much longer? I'd like to get some sleep."

Nicola stared at him, then gave a resigned sigh and switched off the television and the bedside lamp. "Good night, Laurie," she said.

No response. Remarkable as it seemed, Laurie was already asleep.

CHAPTER TWENTY-FIVE

GALEN WAS SURPRISED to find Nicola in Laurie's beautiful, immaculate kitchen on a Saturday. Surprised, and maybe a little alarmed. He covered it well. He poured himself a mug of coffee, dumped skim milk in it, looked nonchalant. "Good morning, Nicola," he said. "Laurie's not making you work weekends, is he?"

"I had some loose ends to wrap up," she said. She sat at the breakfast nook, a small windowed alcove with a stellar view of Central Park, and sipped her own coffee.

"Is Laurie around?" Galen asked. "He texted me last night to stop by this morning. I wasn't even certain you were back in town." The tone was faintly accusing. "You should have called me. I would've sent a driver to meet your flight."

"We managed on our own." She motioned to the chair across from her. "Laurie's not up yet. Have a seat. We should talk."

Galen sat down obligingly. His face was open and honest. God-damn, he was attractive. Graceful and beautiful and elegant. Not hard to see why Laurie fell for him. "Yes. Tell me all about what happened. You said someone tried to shoot Laurie?" Appropriate horror and skepticism and concern in his voice.

"Yep." Nicola held out her hand. "Can I see your phone?"

A tiny smile on supple lips, a wrinkle of concern on that smooth brow. "I suppose. Why?"

"Because I want to check your call history to see if you've been in touch with Kip Caprini."

Galen stared at her. "What on earth are you talking about?" he asked. Still that tiny smile, like he was trying to play along with a game he didn't quite understand. He was good, very good.

"I'm talking about Kip Caprini asking you to keep tabs on Laurie. I figure your phone will prove that." She shrugged. "If you don't want to show it to me, it doesn't matter. We've already talked to the police in Nevada. Sooner or later, somebody's going to start investigating the part you've played in this."

He stared at her. Finally, he shook his head. "You don't need to see it," he said. "If I tell you what I know, will you keep me out of it with the police?"

"Probably not. Someone's trying to kill Laurie and, incidentally or not, me. You're in on it, and I don't think you should get a free pass for that."

"But I'm not," Galen said. "I'm not in on anything. I assure you, I'm only very peripherally involved in this."

He took a sip of his coffee. Nicola waited.

"I did some work in Kip Caprini's business office earlier this year. I've mentioned that before. It was just a temporary position, only for three months or so, but I became somewhat friendly with him. He contacted me at the start of Fashion Week and said he'd heard rumors Laurie Sparks was trying to sabotage him. That Laurie was making claims he'd copied some designs, that sort of thing. He asked me to try to get close to Laurie. So I trailed him around Fashion Week, looking for an excuse to introduce myself." Another drink of his coffee. "Kip only wanted to know if Laurie was saying anything slanderous about him, that's all. Just in case it later became necessary, he asked me to see if there was something he could use against Laurie. Leverage."

"And this struck you as okay?"

"At first? Absolutely." Galen fixed his gaze on her. He seemed earnest. "After a while, it occurred to me that Kip probably was, in fact, guilty of whatever Laurie had said about him. I honestly don't know the details. Neither Kip nor Laurie ever told me anything specific. All Kip wanted, really, was potential blackmail material."

"How nice," Nicola said.

"I know that's awful, I do. But it was sort of fun, too, playing at being a spy, and Kip's always been good to me."

"And he was paying you, I suppose."

"Yes, he was." Galen looked earnest. "But nothing about the arrangement seemed hurtful. I like Laurie. I wouldn't do anything to harm him."

"I'd have an easier time believing that if you hadn't been sleeping with him," Nicola said. Her voice was hard and cold. Galen looked like he was going to object, then reconsidered and kept silent. "You told Caprini that Laurie and I were going to Nevada?"

"I did, yes."

"Wonderful," Nicola said. "There was a hitman there waiting for us. You almost got Laurie killed."

"I didn't have anything to do with that, I swear." Galen exhaled. "Let me talk to him."

"Nope. If Laurie wants to talk to you, he will," Nicola said. "Between you and me, I don't think he will."

Galen nodded. "Will you tell him I didn't mean to hurt him?"

"Nope," she said.

Another nod. He seemed resigned. Before Nicola could ask for it, he fished a key ring out of his pocket and slipped off Laurie's key. He slid it across the table to Nicola. "I didn't make copies. Tell him to change the locks if you don't believe me," he said.

She did believe him. She believed he'd behaved with mischief instead of malice, believed he was horrified by the result. Not that it made things much better.

She escorted Galen out and locked the door behind him. She turned to find Laurie sitting on his stairs, watching her. "You were right?" he asked.

Nicola nodded. "He wants to talk to you so he can explain."

"Gee. No thanks," Laurie said. His tone was brittle. "You have any plans for the day?"

"Getting a new phone. Want to help me pick one out? I'll treat for lunch afterward."

He shook his head. "I'm going to stay inside. I could use some quality recovery time," he said.

"I was also thinking we should maybe call Cady today, see if she's talked to Joelle's brother yet about giving us those boxes."

"Let's hold off. I don't want to think about it right now," he said.

Nicola examined him. "How are you bearing up?" she asked. He looked good. Eyes lined in smudged violet, lips painted scarlet, clad in tight maroon velvet pants and a black t-shirt with an iridescent gold image of King Tut pouting enigmatically on the front. It was somehow very much like Laurie to get fully dressed up, makeup and all, for a lazy day at home.

"I'm fine," he said. "It just seems like maybe I should focus more on my collection right now, that's all. We might have gone as far as we can on the other thing for the moment."

Huh. A strangely nonchalant response, considering how much of Laurie's time and energy had been occupied by this for the past few weeks. Maybe Laurie just burned through obsessions quickly. More likely he was still spooked by the threat that had reared up in Nevada and tried to smash him out of existence. Whatever the reason for his new apathy, it made Nicola uneasy.

"Something else you should consider," she said. "I don't want to put you on edge, but have you given any thought to personal protection? If someone's after you . . ."

Laurie nodded. "Way ahead of you. I talked to Maurice, our doorman, this morning. He's got a nephew, Spiro, who works in the bodyguard business. Licensed and everything. Spiro can watch over me whenever I need to go anywhere."

"Well, good. I'm glad you're on top of things," she said. She hesitated. "Is there anything else I can do for you?"

"Nope, thanks. I'm good. See you Monday?" It was a dismissal. Laurie seemed fine. He seemed like he was coping pretty well, everything considered.

Still, Nicola wondered.

CHAPTER TWENTY-SIX

AS LAURIE SEEMED reluctant to pursue the matter of Joelle Sutton much further, Nicola mulled over the possibility of contacting Cady herself. She didn't want to step on Laurie's toes, but she hated leaving things dangling.

Before she could decide what to do, Joel Sutton called her.

"I understand you and Laurie Sparks have some interest in my sister's clothing," he said. "Cady Moss asked me for permission to pass some of Joelle's belongings on to you. At my request, she mailed them to me first." There was a pause on the line. Joel Sutton sounded courteous, but wary about their intentions. "I don't see any harm in giving them to you, but I'd like to meet with you and Mr. Sparks first. I gather you're in New York? I'm at my residence in the city today, if you're free to stop by."

"That'd be great. Thank you. I'd have to check Laurie's schedule, but I think we're free." It was Sunday morning. Laurie was probably still in bed, probably didn't have plans beyond placing a delivery order of Belgian waffles slathered in strawberries and far too much Nutella from his favorite local brunch spot.

He hadn't been getting out much since their return from Nevada over a week ago. Hadn't made it into his studio at all. He was still in the brainstorming stages of his new collection, which he could do just as well at home, but still . . .

"Would two o'clock work for you? I'm on Park, just north of 70th." He gave her the street address, which she jotted down on Donya's shoe-embellished notepad.

"I'll call Laurie right now. We really appreciate this," she said.

Laurie sounded cautious but intrigued when she filled him in. "Joelle's twin, huh? What did he sound like?"

"Friendly enough. Rich. He lives on Park Avenue. You'll probably get along like gangbusters."

"Doubt it. What is he, a lawyer? A *property* lawyer?"

"No sense being snobby, my dear. He should be able to answer some of our questions about Joelle. Aren't you interested in that?"

"I suppose."

"Cheer up. It sounds like he's planning on giving us the boxes. All of Joelle's designs, isn't that what you wanted?"

"Yeah. Sure. Two o'clock, right? You want to come here first? We can go over together."

Laurie's new bodyguard came with them. Spiro was hulking and grim, a burly young behemoth in a black windbreaker and jeans. They caught a cab to Joel's, the three of them wedged in the backseat. Cozy. Spiro kept his jacket partially unzipped; when Nicola glanced over at him, she caught a glimpse of the butt of his revolver in his shoulder holster.

Joel Sutton lived on the penthouse level. He answered the door himself, dressed casually for the weekend in khaki slacks and a cashmere v-necked sweater. Handsome and fiftyish, a gracefully aging preppie with a thick head of well-maintained blond hair. A flash of a gold Rolex on a tanned arm, a flash of even white teeth when he invited them inside and ushered them into his living room.

It was manly. Black lacquered walls, armchairs upholstered in oxblood leather, black leather sofa, chrome coffee table. It looked like the apartment of a coke dealer in a film about eighties decadence. Nicola kind of dug it, though it probably wasn't at all to Laurie's taste.

"My wife and my children are at our weekend home, so we'll have some privacy," Joel said. "I stayed in the city because I needed to go in to the office yesterday, but I'm all yours this afternoon."

Wife and kids. Nicola wouldn't have predicted that. This place looked like the consummate bachelor pad. "We appreciate you meeting us like this," she said. "I'm Nicola, and this is Laurie Sparks. And that's Laurie's bodyguard, Spiro."

Handshakes all around, a nod and a grunt from Spiro.

"Ah, bodyguards. A strange necessity of modern life." Joel smiled. "I'm in possession of one of those myself." He gestured for Nicola and Laurie to sit. He tapped once on a small black cube placed on an end table. It emitted a muted electronic buzz. Within seconds, a dark-suited man hovered respectfully in the doorway.

Joel gestured toward him. "This is Glen. Glen has worked for my family for years." Glen didn't move or acknowledge the introduction in any way. He was taller than Spiro, though not nearly as burly. Lean and wiry, almost gaunt, with sunken cheeks and humorless eyes. Next to him, Spiro seemed downright approachable. "Glen, why don't you take Spiro here to the den? I think we'll all be able to get through a conversation without it erupting into violence."

Spiro glanced at Laurie, who nodded at him. Glen and Spiro withdrew.

Joel moved to a sideboard and held up a bottle. "I'm having Scotch and soda. Quarter-century Glenmorangie. Can I fix you one?"

"If you don't mind squandering it on my underdeveloped palate, sure. Thank you," Nicola said.

Joel grinned and fixed the drinks in cut-crystal glasses. "The only way to develop a proper Scotch palate is through experience. Try this and see what you think."

The Scotch numbed her tongue, burned down her throat, consumed her stomach in its fiery wrath. It tasted like mahogany and magma and wealth. Laurie gave his an experimental sniff, sipped cautiously, swallowed, flinched. Joel watched them, amused. "Good stuff, eh?"

"Strong," Laurie said. "Strong."

Joel smiled and sat down on an armchair across from them. He observed Laurie in open fascination while he sipped his Scotch, amused at having a magical fairy creature gracing his sofa. "Laurie Sparks," he said at last. "You may not know this, but you and I are connected."

Laurie shifted in his chair under the weight of Joel's scrutiny. "Oh?"

"I've met your mother dozens of times. My father was Christopher Sutton." At Laurie's blank look, he continued. "Connecticut's senior US Senator, from 1980 to his death eight years ago. I interned in his office in Washington the year after I graduated from Yale. This would have been before you were born, of course, but I became well acquainted with your mother."

"Oh, wow. I guess I should have known who you were. Much to my mother's dismay, I don't keep up with politics much."

"No reason you should know. Old history." Joel smiled at him again. "Mind you, your mother and my father were . . . well, 'bitter enemies' might be a tad dramatic, but it's certainly fair to call them adversaries. They were worlds apart in terms of policy and beliefs. Still, I'm sure he respected her, even if he may not have ever liked her. Your mother was a hell of a woman."

"She still is." Laurie raised his chin. He took another sip of his Scotch. Nicola could see him shudder, just a little, as he swallowed.

"May I ask what your interest is in Joelle?" Joel sat forward in his chair, his forearms propped on his knees, his glass held between both hands. "It seems bizarre to me that your paths would cross in any way."

"I've been interested in her designs for a long time," Laurie said. "Except until very recently, I didn't know they were her designs at all. Did you know your sister designed Kip Caprini's 1984 collection?"

Nicola winced. Joel, however, just looked thoughtful. "Did she? No, I didn't, but I don't know that it surprises me. Do you mean Kip Caprini stole her designs, or did he pay her for them?"

"I don't have any idea," Laurie said. "I should probably point out that this is all speculation on my part. Nicola's glaring at me right now because she hates it when I toss around accusations like that, but I know for sure Caprini didn't design those clothes. And after seeing Joelle's designs for *Holmby Hills*, I'm equally sure she was the one who did."

Joel's smile turned brittle and wistful. "I think you know more about my sister than I do," he said. "*Holmby Hills*? What was that?"

"A short-lived television show. Joelle designed the wardrobe for the lead actress, Gina Davenport. Gina used to model for Caprini, and I think they're probably still friends. We suspect Caprini got Joelle the job, maybe to pay her back for what she did for him back in 1984."

"Or maybe to keep her quiet? Hush money?" Joel's mouth twisted a little. "Do you think Joelle was blackmailing him?"

"We couldn't say," Nicola said. "Honestly, we don't know anything about the kind of person your sister was."

"That goes for me, too," Joel said. "The last time I saw Joelle was close to thirty years ago, and believe me, that wasn't through lack of trying. We were so close, so exquisitely close as children, and then . . ." He exhaled. "She changed."

He sat up in his chair. "I suppose Cady told you how she died? Killed while purchasing drugs?"

"That's what we heard, yeah," Nicola said.

He nodded. "Then you already know a great deal about Joelle. So much promise, squandered through all her addictions and her bad lifestyle choices."

"Lifestyle choices like being gay?" Laurie asked. His eyes glinted, and there was an undercurrent of acid in his tone.

Joel stared at him in surprise. "Well, no," he said at last. "I meant specifically the drugs, though I will say she entangled herself in some downright unfortunate relationships as well."

"Do you mean Sabina Petrescu?" Nicola asked.

Joel raised his brows. "You know about that? You really have taken an interest in Joelle's life, haven't you?" He exhaled, weary. "I never knew Sabina, never even heard of her until after her murder, poor girl. Even back then, Joelle kept her secrets from me."

"Everyone we've talked to about Joelle has described her as not just messed up, but sad as well. Do you know why? Was it because of Sabina, or something more?" Nicola asked.

Joel sipped at his Scotch and considered this. "I don't know that I can answer that," he said. "Our father was not an easy man at times. I'm sure your mother, Laurie, could confirm that. He disapproved, often vehemently, of many of Joelle's choices. I'm sure it caused her some pain."

"What about you?" Laurie asked. There was a hint of a challenge in it. "How'd you handle her being gay?"

"She wasn't." The answer was startling in its sharpness. "Not by any means. Most of Joelle's relationships were with men. She engaged in some experimentation, I know, perhaps as a form of rebellion, but none of it seemed to mean much to her. But in answer to your question, no, I didn't always handle it well, and yes, that probably contributed to the distance between us. It was a different time, you understand, and times do change."

Laurie still looked prickly. Joel shifted the subject with the ease of someone well-trained in navigating conversational minefields.

"Cady mentioned you two had some trouble during your visit to Nevada. The sheriff came to talk with her after you'd already left town. Somebody shot at you? Did I understand that correctly?"

"Someone shot out my front windshield while I was driving. Sheer luck that it didn't hit Laurie," Nicola said. On the couch beside her, Laurie tensed.

Joel nodded. "They still haven't found Joelle's killer, you know. I call that sheriff often for updates, Sheriff Cowell. He never tells me much, but I know he doesn't think it was just a drug deal gone awry."

Laurie and Nicola exchanged glances. "What makes you say that?" Nicola asked.

"It's a tiny town, isn't it? If the killer were someone within the community, the sheriff would surely have some leads by now. The manner of her death was atypical as well."

Nicola frowned. "She was shot, wasn't she?"

"She was." Joel's mouth was a flat line. "She and that idiot teenager from whom she was purchasing methamphetamines. Both were shot from a nearby bluff with a long-range rifle."

Laurie gave a short gasp at this. Nicola stared at Joel. "Are you serious?"

"I am." Joel raised his brows. "In light of the attack on you two, here's my question, and believe me, I'm not trying to create a conspiracy where none exists. Do you think this business you've been looking into with Kip Caprini is related to her death?"

"We don't know," Nicola said. "It seems like there has to be a connection, but it could turn out to be unrelated."

"It's not," Laurie said. Both Nicola and Joel turned to look at him. "Of course it's not unrelated. Caprini's trying to kill me. And he probably killed your sister, too. We can't prove it, but that doesn't mean it's not true."

Joel settled back in his chair, his drink forgotten in his hands. He looked like his thoughts were somewhere far away. "I loved my sister, truly and deeply. I don't know that she always loved me in the same way, but for her entire life, there's nothing I wouldn't have done for her," he said. "Even now, if there's anything I can still do,

I will. If you can tell me, unequivocally, that Kip Caprini was responsible for her death, I will find justice for Joelle."

Nicola looked at that cold, handsome face, an avenging angel mourning a lost part of himself, and felt chilled. "If we find anything out, of course we'll take it straight to the police," she said.

Joel seemed to relax a little. He smiled. "Of course. Good," he said. "In the meantime, if there's anything I can do for you, please do let me know. I have resources."

"Thank you," Nicola said. "We appreciate that."

Joel rose from his armchair. "Would you like to see a picture of Joelle?" he asked. He pulled a leather photo album down from a high shelf on a floor-to-ceiling bookcase. His movements were sure and graceful. He'd kept fit into middle age. Tennis and golf on the weekends at his country home, probably. Racquetball, maybe. Did high-powered businessmen still play racquetball, or had that gone out of style decades ago? Was it all Pilates and capoeira lessons these days?

He leafed through the album. He found the correct page, flipped the book around, and passed it to Nicola and Laurie. "Here we were, in better days."

Joel and Joelle. Beautiful blond twins, maybe eighteen or nineteen here. Joel had been a full-fledged preppie then, complete with the polo shirt with the little alligator on the chest and Top-Sider loafers. Side-parted hair with a feathered swoop of blond bangs. He and Joelle sat side by side on the stone steps in front of the Met.

Joelle was punk and gorgeous. Danielle had described her as a pretty girl, and Nicola had pictured her as one of the popular girls at her high school in Modesto a quarter-century ago, girls with big blonde perms and large chests and round, pretty faces. Joelle, however, was high-fashion skinny, though she was much too small to be a model. Short peroxide-white hair sticking out in all directions, eyes lined with too much black goop, an oversized leather jacket hanging off her tiny body. Ripped black tights, heavy combat boots, no pants. Joelle was Goth before Goth had broken through to mainstream culture. Her expression was gloomy and haughty. She looked terribly unhealthy, and she was beautiful.

"She looks like you, Laurie," she said. The eyes were the wrong color, dark brown instead of pale green, but 1980s Joelle and present-day Laurie could've passed as twins.

"I thought the same thing," Joel said. Nicola looked at Joelle's real-life twin, who was staring at Laurie and smiling. Laurie glanced up and blushed at the intensity of Joel's scrutiny.

Joel cleared his throat. "I have those boxes from Cady Moss," he said. "There's not much to them, apart from her clothing and a few books. Her sketchbooks are there as well, which Laurie might find interesting. You're welcome to it all."

"That's very kind of you. Thank you," Nicola said.

"I'll have Glen carry them downstairs for you," Joel said. He rose from the couch and held out his hand to Laurie. Laurie got up and shook it. "It was nice talking to both of you. Laurie, I'm glad we got this chance to meet."

"Me, too. I'll tell my mother about seeing you," Laurie said.

"Please give her my best," Joel said. He turned his attention to Nicola. "Thank you for this," he said. "For taking an interest in Joelle. I'm sorry it's put you both in danger, but it makes me happy knowing someone else cares about her."

A pang of guilt at that, because until now Nicola hadn't given much thought to Joelle, the miserable girl and troubled adult who, in death, was creating so many problems for them. Laurie, she imagined, had given Joelle even less consideration. It'd be pointless and cruel to tell Joel this, however, so she and Laurie murmured meaningless pleasantries and made their farewells.

CHAPTER TWENTY-SEVEN

THERE WERE FIVE boxes in all. Nicola and Laurie lugged them from the taxi and into the tiny gated elevator in Laurie's building. Spiro refused to schlep boxes on the extremely valid grounds that a) it wasn't what he was hired to do, and b) if his arms were filled with bulky objects, he couldn't reach his gun in a hurry if some miscreant were to attack Laurie. Laurie tried to refuse as well, on the grounds that a) his silk shirt was far too expensive to ruin by sweating in it, and b) he didn't want to, but Nicola was having none of it.

Once the boxes were stacked on the floor in Nicola's makeshift office, and once Spiro had been dismissed for the day, and once Laurie had taken a lingering soak in a warm tub to soothe his muscles from his uncharacteristic burst of heavy lifting, Nicola and Laurie tore into them.

They mostly contained Joelle's personal wardrobe, a pile of un-washed t-shirts and skinny leggings. The clothes were saturated with a stench of body odor and old cigarette smoke. Nicola bagged them up in garbage sacks and stuck them by the door to lug to the trash later.

There were only three pieces of clothing that Laurie identified as Joelle's own handiwork. A lightweight black coat lined in ivory silk, a pair of wide-legged black silk pants, an unfinished ruby red satin dress with the sleeves pinned in place and the bodice loosely basted to the skirt. Laurie tapped the dress with a finger. "This was for

Holmby Hills. It looks like the stuff she designed for Gina Davenport. The show probably got canceled before she finished it."

They went through the rest of the boxes. Pattern books, fashion magazines, a couple of paperbacks. Sketch books, like Joel had said. Laurie perked up at these.

"Oh, cool," he said. He gathered the stack of sketch books together and plopped down in an armchair. He propped the books on his legs and flipped through the pages, looking at Joelle's hand-drawn designs, lost in his own world.

Nicola grinned at the sight of him curled up with Joelle's sketches, like a child with a treasured picture book. "Good stuff, Laurie?"

"Mm-hmm. Or maybe not good, but interesting. It's all pretty dark and avant-garde," he said. "Not at all like her *Holmby Hills* clothes." He held up a page to show her what he meant. It featured a spidery pen-and-ink sketch of a headless woman in what looked like a black catsuit made out of a woven tangle of straps. The loose ends of the straps draped down to the floor, tail-like. Flashes of skin, scribbled in with a peach colored pencil, were visible through the straps; a huge neckpiece of straps rose like insect wings from the back. Creepy.

"Did Joelle think someone could actually wear that?" she asked.

Laurie gave her a look of withering scorn. "Of course not. I said it was avant-garde."

"Sheesh. Sorry," Nicola said. She returned to her task. Laurie continued flipping through the sketches.

He giggled. "Oh, Joelle," he said.

Nicola glanced back at him. "What's up?"

He handed her a slim, square envelope, yellowed with age. "Naughty photos."

Inside were two Polaroids, faded and cracked. Both photos were of a dark-haired young woman. In the first, she was in bed, shoulders bare, white sheets pulled up to her armpits. Her hair tumbled into her eyes, which were tilted up, staring at the camera in flirtatious mischief. In the second, she was lying on top of the sheets on her stomach, legs in the air, crossed at the ankles, her chin propped on her hands. Same coquettish look in her eyes, and here she was unmistakably nude.

"Naughty photos," Nicola said. "Very tame naughty photos, by the way. She looks like a model. Do you suppose that's Sabina Petrescu?"

"Could be," Laurie said. He leaned over Nicola's shoulder and looked at the photos. "Is that writing there at the bottom?"

Faint spidery script, faded to a pale yellow, almost illegible. Nicola brought the Polaroid closer to her eyes and squinted. "*All my love* . . . I can't read the signature. Does it say Alan?"

"Does she look like an Alan?" Laurie took the photos from her. "Alana, maybe. I can't tell."

Nicola frowned. "Hey, Laurie? When we were talking to Danielle Marcin, do you remember the name of the first model who got strangled, the one before Sabina? It wasn't Alana, I don't think, but it was something like that, wasn't it?"

"I don't remember. Didn't Danielle say the boyfriend did it?"

"The husband. She said he was suspected but not charged, and that he had an alibi for Sabina's death."

Laurie stared at her. "Yeah, but she wasn't connected to Joelle, was she? There's no way both murdered models were Joelle's lovers. That's too much to believe."

"I know, but let's rule it out, okay?" She went to Laurie's computer.

It took a bit of Google finesse, but she found what she was looking for in a *Times* article from 1983. Alina Lowe, who also modeled under her maiden name, Alina Galoyan. An Armenian immigrant who came to New York to become a model. Married to investment banker Mark Lowe, who reported her missing from their Greenwich home in August of 1983.

Found washed up on Great Captain Island three days later, raped and strangled.

The only photo of Alina Lowe she could find online was a scan from an editorial spread in *Cosmopolitan*, circa 1981. Dark-haired, flirty, pretty. Nicola squinted at the photo. "Hey, Laurie?" She beckoned him over to the monitor. "Is that the woman in Joelle's photos?"

Laurie held the Polaroids up close to the screen to compare. Eventually, he nodded. "Yeah," he said. "Yeah, it is. Same jaw, same nose." He looked at Nicola. "I'm sure it's her."

Nicola mulled this over. "So Joelle has intimate photos of a model who was murdered in 1983. And a year later, Joelle's girlfriend, another model, is murdered in the same way."

"Yeah." Laurie chewed on his lower lip. "What do we do about this?"

"Danielle said she was in contact with someone in the police department about the investigation into Sabina's murder," Nicola said. "She said Greenwich, right? Wasn't Sabina's body found there?"

"I don't remember. I wasn't paying much attention to that part of the conversation," Laurie said.

"Greenwich is close, isn't it? Commuting distance?" Nicola asked. "We could take a train up there and talk to the police. They need to know about this."

She stared at the Polaroids, at flirty, mischievous, dead Alina Lowe.

Laurie's voice cut through her thoughts. "This doesn't have anything to do with Kip Caprini, does it? Alina and Sabina, I mean. If we think he killed Joelle . . ." He trailed off.

"Could he have killed the other women, you mean? I don't know. Maybe Joelle knew something about what he did, maybe that's why he had her killed." Nicola considered, shook her head. "Scratch that. I'm talking nonsense. The only connection that we know of between Caprini and the murdered models is Joelle. Maybe he and Joelle were sleeping together, and he got jealous of her girlfriends? Her brother did say that Joelle dated men."

"He said that. I don't know how convincing he was. Sounded to me like he didn't want to believe his sister liked girls."

She glanced over at him. "You got a little prickly with Joel, you know. Everything okay?"

Laurie shrugged. "Yeah, it's fine. He's probably an okay guy. Just that he seemed pretty judgmental about Joelle."

"It's not like anyone we've met thus far has had much good to say about her, kiddo. And she was his sister, after all. If anyone should know about the kind of person she was, he should."

"A sister who didn't make any effort to contact him for thirty years. Real close family ties there. And was it me, or was he suggesting he could have Caprini whacked?" Laurie wrinkled his nose. "Creepy."

"That wasn't quite the way he put it," Nicola said. "But I'll agree that it was a little on the creepy side. Maybe he was just being overly dramatic. His sister was murdered, after all."

"Yeah. Her and Alina and Sabina." Laurie exhaled heavily. "Add Molly Gable to that list, too. Seems like we've been hearing about far too many murdered women lately."

He sounded glum. Nicola knew how he felt.

IN THE END, Nicola took a short and comfortable trip on a Metro North train to Greenwich by herself. Laurie claimed he was too busy thinking about his new collection to go with her. On the spectrum of Laurie's excuses, it was pretty weak, but there was nothing to be gained by calling him on it.

This would be more fun with Laurie along. She'd never been to Greenwich before, and it was lovely. Bucolic suburban living, purchased with plenty of old money. Stately Colonial mansions set far back on wide green lawns, well-maintained parks, dozens of adorable cafes and boutiques along tree-lined Greenwich Avenue, all of it so different from the frenetic hustle of nearby Manhattan.

She'd emailed Danielle Marcin in Paris for the name of the detective investigating Sabina Petrescu's death, then called the department to set up this interview.

Detective Tally looked young for a detective. She also looked like she might bite the head off of anyone who suggested that. Early thirties, dark-skinned, unfussy in a navy pantsuit and sensible loafers, hair knotted back into a no-nonsense chignon. She stood to greet Nicola and shook hands without smiling, then pointed for her to sit in the chair across from her desk.

No office, just a bare-bones cubicle. Propped on the corner of her immaculate desk were framed photos of two toddler girls, all frizzy hair and cute gap-toothed smiles.

"You said on the phone you knew something about the murders of Sabina Petrescu and Alina Lowe?" Tally asked without preamble.

"I'm not sure what I know, actually," Nicola said. "I got your name from Danielle Marcin in Paris. She said she checks with you every year to see if there's progress in the case?"

"Uh-huh."

"Sabina Petrescu's girlfriend was a seamstress named Joelle Sutton, right?" Tally didn't bother with a response to that, just stared at her coldly, so Nicola plunged ahead. "I've been doing some work for a fashion designer, Laurie Sparks, and he's interested in some clothes Joelle Sutton designed. Joelle died recently, I don't know if you know that, so Laurie and I were looking through some of her old sketchbooks, and . . . we found this."

She took the Polaroids out of her messenger bag and handed them over. Tally examined them, holding one in each hand. She was quiet for a long, long time. Nicola cleared her throat.

"That's Alina Lowe, isn't it?"

"Uh-huh." Tally kept staring at the photos, not saying a word.

The silence became uncomfortable. Nicola shifted in her chair.

Finally, Tally looked up at her. Same humorless expression. "I'm going to need you to start from the beginning. Who you are, what your interest in Joelle Sutton is, everything you know."

Nicola spilled her guts. It was a rambling story, and Tally had little patience for it. She interrupted constantly, she grilled her on minute details, she was blunt and snappish. Nicola usually held up okay under pressure, but she grew flustered and annoyed. All the while, Tally jotted down notes. Her handwriting was old-fashioned and flowery, the penmanship of a gracious Southern grande dame instead of a curt, charmless detective.

After she'd yanked and tugged and extracted the entire messy story out of Nicola, Tally sat back in her chair and stared at her. "So you don't have anything at all to link Sutton's death to the deaths of those two girls, do you?"

"No. But Joelle Sutton is linked to both women—"

"Yeah, I got that. That's not what I'm asking."

"Then no, I don't. But it all centers around the fashion world in New York in the early 1980s. If you can find any connection between Kip Caprini and Sabina and Alina—"

"I don't need suggestions how to do my job." Tally gave her an icy stare, eyebrows raised in challenge. "I'm better at it than you are."

"I'm sure you are. Didn't mean to suggest otherwise," Nicola said. It sounded chilly and snotty.

Tally drummed her pen against her notepad in a percussive beat. "You think Kip Caprini was behind the deaths of Sutton and that wardrobe girl in Los Angeles, okay. From your story, sounds like you could be right. But it also sounds like you've got a hard-on for the idea of Caprini as the killer of those girls, and you've got shit to back it up. The Sutton murder, your business with Caprini, that's none of my concern unless there's a link to my dead girls. And you can't give me that."

"Sorry if I've wasted your time," Nicola said. Her voice was stiff.

"Don't get shirty with me." Tally almost smiled. "You gave me those photos, those photos are good. Now I know Joelle Sutton was connected to both girls, and that's a mighty nice clue. So thanks for that."

"You're welcome." Nicola got to her feet. "Are we done here?"

"Uh-huh. We're done." As Nicola started to walk off, Tally's voice stopped her. "Too bad Laurie Sparks didn't come with you today. Kid annoys the crap out of me on that idiot show of his. I'd be curious to see if he's as obnoxious in person."

Nicola turned around. "Good thing he didn't come. You'd've eaten him for breakfast."

Tally laughed. It seemed genuine. "Probably. It's happened before." She nodded at her. "Thanks for stopping by, Strozyk. And don't worry, I'm going to take a look at Caprini. But I'm not going to railroad him just because he was a dick to you and the Sparks kid."

"Yeah, I understand that," Nicola said.

Tally glanced around. "Between you and me, if I started arresting people for being dicks, that'd take care of the entire damn population of Greenwich." She waggled her ballpoint pen at Nicola. "And I'm plenty busy as it is."

CHAPTER TWENTY-EIGHT

"WHAT DO YOU think?" Laurie asked.

Nicola scrutinized her reflection in a floor-length mirror in his studio. She wore a short jacket made from thin pieces of gold-tinted aluminum stitched together with copper wire over a distressed bronze leather base, paired with a thigh-length bronze skirt. She was shirtless under the jacket—Laurie had insisted on this to ensure the best fit—and she felt exposed and ridiculous under his scrutiny.

She was filling in for the afternoon for a fit model with food poisoning. Tedious work, modeling.

"I look like a disco gladiator," she said.

Laurie nodded. "But in a good way, right?" Without waiting for a response, he stepped forward and tweaked the collar of the jacket. "How does it feel?"

"Comfortable. Heavy, but it's surprisingly flexible. Pretty tight across the shoulders, though," she said.

"Yeah, I'm not worried about that. You're burlier than my usual fit models. The skirt pulls too much across your gut, too."

"'Abdomen' is a kinder word than 'gut,' Laurie. In the interest of heading off any eating disorders your models might develop in the future, I suggest you learn to use it."

"Duly noted." Laurie grinned. "So what's your verdict?"

"It's fabulous. Very post-apocalyptic chic. I can see this catching on, provided no one who wears this ever needs to go through airport security."

"Excellent. That's what I want to hear." Laurie stepped back. "Thanks for coming down here on short notice."

"No problem." She held still while Laurie scrutinized her. "So, hey. I finished the whole research project this morning. Everything's done. You should be good to go."

"Great, fantastic." Laurie wasn't paying attention to her words. He'd probably never even look at his piles of research materials again, now that she'd organized and arranged all of it in the most Laurie-friendly way possible. He was already going great blazes on his new collection.

"So that's probably it for our arrangement," she said. "If you just pay me through today, we'll be all good."

Laurie stared at her. He looked confused for a moment. Then he nodded slowly. "Yeah, okay. Stop by whenever I'm home and I'll write you a check."

"Cool deal." And no, she did not have a lump in her throat over the end of what had been an unexpectedly dramatic freelance gig. "Can I change back into my clothes?"

Before Laurie could answer, his receptionist hurried up to them, out of breath from taking the stairs at a fast clip. "Hi, Laurie, sorry to bug you, but Kip Caprini's in the building. They just called from the security desk downstairs. I said to go ahead and let him up. Was that okay? I know we're screening all visitors these days, but I thought it'd be fine. I mean, it's Kip Caprini."

For a moment, Laurie looked panicked. Then he relaxed and smiled at her. "Of course. Send him up when he gets here, would you, Erica?"

Erica nodded and went back down to her perch at the reception desk. Laurie looked at Nicola. "This could be interesting."

"I'll be right here, Laurie," she said.

He shook his head impatiently. "There's lots of people around. He's not going to try anything."

He was right, of course. Still, it would be nice to have the bulky and implacable Spiro on hand, just to be on the safe side. Spiro escorted Laurie to and from his studio as needed, but there was enough of a security presence in the building that it had seemed unnecessary to have him hang around all day while Laurie worked. Now, though . . .

Caprini charged up the stairs two at a time. He looked sleek and strong and suffused with an almost noble vigor. He strode over to them. Nicola wedged herself in front of Laurie, but Caprini raised an arm and shoved her to the side with a single forceful push.

He struck Laurie once on the cheek, hard. Laurie recoiled back and raised his hands to protect his face. "Hey!"

"You chickenshit bastard," Caprini said. His breath came in jagged gasps. He balled up both his fists at his sides, ready to swing at Laurie again at any moment. "First you go spreading lies about me stealing my designs, now you've got the cops talking to me about a couple of dead models? Saying I *raped* them?"

His voice boomed in the vast room. Everyone around them, Laurie's entire design staff, froze in place and watched the spectacle unfold.

Laurie's hand was plastered across his reddening cheek, his mouth slack with shock. "I didn't—"

"What are you thinking, you vapid little whore?" Caprini asked. He dropped his voice to a hiss. "I get all the tail I want. World-class beauties in droves. I'm married to a goddamned supermodel, for Christ's sake. I don't have to rape anybody." He seized Laurie by his shoulders and slammed him back against the wall.

"Don't touch him. Get away from him," Nicola said. She yanked on Caprini's arm and tried to tear him away from Laurie.

Caprini didn't even look at her. He released one hand from Laurie, placed it against her face, and pushed her away. She stumbled back. Couldn't move in the tight skirt, couldn't catch her balance, fell on her ass.

He slammed Laurie against the wall once more and let go. Laurie crumpled to the floor, legs collapsing under him. He stared up at Caprini, shock on his face.

"Stay the fuck away from me, or I'll bash that pretty face of yours into pulp." Caprini gave Laurie a kick for good measure, then turned and strode off.

Nicola crawled over to Laurie. The receptionist, Erica, hurried up the stairs to investigate the commotion; Caprini brushed past her without breaking his stride. "Call the police," Nicola called over to her.

"No, don't bother." Laurie got to his feet. He prodded his bruised cheek gently with two fingers, assessing the damage. "Don't call anyone. It's fine."

He looked around at all the concerned faces. "It's fine," he said again.

Nicola stood up. "We should talk to the cops. That was assault and battery. They could arrest him for that. At the least, we should file a restraining order."

"No." Laurie's face was red. "We're not going to do that. I don't want anything more to do with this." He motioned toward the stairs, in the direction of Caprini's exit. "You went to the police in Connecticut, and that's what happened because of it." He looked embarrassed and angry. The anger seemed to be directed— misdirected, surely—mostly at her.

"This isn't exactly my fault, kiddo. You know that, right?"

"I wish we'd never gotten involved with this," Laurie said. His voice was hollow and miserable. "I just want it all to go away."

"Ignoring it isn't going to help anything."

"Then what do we do?" He looked scared and exhausted.

She thought about it. "I'll have to get back to you on that."

IT WAS GOOD just sitting with Donya on their sofa, feet up on the coffee table, drinking wine and getting caught up. Donya had returned that afternoon from another trek to Los Angeles, where she'd been taping another *PM Magazine* segment. Two whirlwinds, Nicola and Donya, spiraling wildly in opposite directions for the past month, intersecting at last.

The story got easier to tell with repetition. Donya had no trouble following her narrative, even after a couple glasses of the excellent Beaujolais Nicola had brought back from Paris. She'd intended to save it for a special occasion. This qualified.

At the account of Caprini's assault on Laurie, Donya raised her eyebrows in surprise. "And Laurie won't go to the police?"

"Nope. Ever since Nevada, he's been closing his eyes and sticking his fingers in his ears and hoping this all goes away. Not that I blame him that much, but it's not helpful right now."

"Too much has been set in motion in too many directions," Donya said. "You've got the LAPD investigating Molly Gable's death, you've got your sexy sheriff in Nevada investigating Joelle's death and the attempt to kill Laurie, you've got the cops in Greenwich looking into those two murdered women. And Laurie's involved in all of that, whether he wants to be or not."

"I know. He's pretty deeply spooked, and I need some way to take some of the pressure off of him. Which is where you come in. You know any hard-hitting investigative journalists?"

"Well, me. Or am I a little fluffier than what you're looking for?"

"You're an unstoppable force of awesomeness. Clearly. What I really need, though, is someone with a print background."

"You should talk to my girl Cerise. Cerise Cherry. I used to work with her at the E! network, but she's all about print these days. She writes for the *Observer*, and she's pretty kick-ass. What are you thinking about? An article on this?"

"Makes sense, doesn't it? Like you said, we've got too many crimes in too many places, and we need someone to link them all together. I'm thinking a good journalist could do exactly that," Nicola said. "We get this out in the open, and it takes the heat off of

Laurie. No sense in trying to kill him if everyone knows as much as he does."

"Both of you. Not just him." At Nicola's look of confusion, Donya clarified. "It takes the heat off of both of you. Someone tried to kill you, too. You keep ignoring that."

"The target was Laurie. I don't think Kip Caprini or Gina Davenport are sufficiently aware of my existence to consider killing me. Which is maybe a little insulting, but I'm not going to complain." Nicola shrugged. "You'll call your friend? What's her name, Cerise?"

"Cerise, yeah. I'll put her in touch with you." Donya looked at Nicola over the rim of her wineglass. "You're finished with this project with Laurie, right? Might be for the best if you get some distance from him for a while. Laurie's a barrel of drunken monkeys, and I know you like the kid, but I'm not sure he's been all that good for you."

Nicola raised her glass and took a sip. "Hey, at least I got to go to Paris because of him, right?"

It sounded forlorn and weak, even to her ears.

CHAPTER TWENTY-NINE

CERISE CHERRY WAS in her early thirties. She had long, pale hair held off her face with a wide red leather headband. Pleated wool skirt, baggy cardigan over a white button-down shirt, enormous black motorcycle boots. No makeup, no jewelry, save for a slim gold ring through her right eyebrow. She carried a canvas backpack, Army surplus, in which she rooted around before producing a digital recorder and a notepad. She plunked both items down on the table in Laurie's breakfast nook.

"I've already heard Nicola's side of the story," she said to Laurie. She gave a nod in Nicola's direction. "I just wanted to take you through this as well."

"Sure thing." Laurie had been pretty agreeable about all this. There'd been a chance he'd shoot down the whole idea, but then again, Laurie liked publicity. Talking to the police might not be his idea of fun, but getting his name in the newspaper was something he could get behind.

He looked extra-sparkly today in a gold-and-black patterned silk shirt and black leather pants. He'd recently dyed his hair a reddish-gold, and the overhead light made the top of his head look like it was on fire.

"Any questions before we get started?" Cerise asked.

"Is 'Cerise Cherry' your real name?" Laurie asked.

Her lips twitched. "Sadly, yes. Thanks, mom and dad."

She made an adjustment to the placement of her recorder. "We're on the record now, Laurie, if you're ready to begin."

Nicola's phone buzzed in her pocket. She moved into the living room to take the call. 775 area code. Nevada. Could be Cady Moss. "Hello?"

"Nicola Strozyk?" A male voice. "This is Sandy Cowell, Lincoln County Sheriff's Department?"

"Sheriff Cowell, of course. Hi. How are you?"

"Just wanted to fill you in on developments here. I got off of a very interesting call with the LAPD just now. That fingerprint we lifted from your watch? We got a match. Military records, you were right, Jerry Palamara, a private in the US Army. Completed sniper school at Fort Benning, served in Afghanistan, general discharge earlier this year for what's been categorized as a personality disorder. Police picked him up at his apartment in Baldwin Hills yesterday afternoon." He sounded downright cheerful. "Had a prepaid phone on him that matched the number given to the bartender at the Royal Yucca. They found a rifle stashed in an air vent. Ballistics matched the bullet that killed Molly Gable, plus the bullet that was embedded in the front seat of your rental car. And because every once in a while at my job I get to have a really, really good day, it was a match for Joelle Sutton and Ricky Sanchez, too."

"Wow. Wow. That's good news. Has he confessed to anything?"

"Nope. LAPD says he's clearly got mental health issues, probably some PTSD. Not sure I followed the entire conversation, but I know the phrase 'diminished capacity' came up once or twice. In any case, he's all lawyered up now. Hasn't said a word, probably isn't ever going to. So that's less than ideal, but here's one more interesting thing."

"Yeah?"

"His mother, Kim Palamara? Is Gina Davenport's sister. The kid's her nephew."

Nicola's brain spun in circles around this information. "Wow. That's . . . wow. Has Gina been arrested?"

"No reason to arrest her, yet. You can bet the cops will be having a long chat with her soon about her nephew's hobbies. It's all very interesting, don't you think? You and Laurie Sparks might breathe a little easier now."

"I'll let Laurie know. He'll be glad to hear it. Joelle Sutton's brother will probably be happy to get the news, too. Thank you so much for calling."

"No problem. You were a big help to me, and I sure do appreciate it." A pause on the line. "Hey, look, there's every chance you'll be contacted by the DA's office in Los Angeles about your encounters with Palamara. They might fly you out to talk with them. Just giving you a head's up."

"That's fine. Whatever I can do to help."

A nervous chuckle on the other end. "And if they do, maybe I could talk you into making a side trip to Vegas? I probably couldn't coax you all the way out to Decline again, but I'd like to treat you to a nice dinner sometime. Just to say thanks and all that."

"Thank you. I'd like that." Her face felt warm. Cheeks were probably red. If Laurie were in the room, he'd tease her about that. She ended the call, feeling like things were starting to look up.

CHAPTER THIRTY

MARTINIS AND THICK, manly, meaty steaks dominated the menu at the Cook Club on East 95th. Nicola had never developed a taste for martinis, but she loved a good steak. She and Maggie Sparks both had the porterhouse, served with sides of roasted fingerling potatoes and broiled asparagus. Laurie nibbled on a lobster salad.

It was the first Maggie had heard of their escapades in Nevada. She demonstrated appropriate maternal horror at the idea of anyone trying to kill her son. "Are you sure you're not being hasty in dismissing your bodyguard?" she asked.

Laurie shrugged. "The guy who tried to kill me is in jail in Los Angeles. I figure there's no more need for Spiro to hang around."

"I hope you're right." Maggie took a dainty bite of an asparagus spear. "I want to thank you, Nicola, for taking such good care of my boy here. If there's anything I can ever do for you, you have only to ask."

"Thank you. Laurie and I had a pretty good time together."

"Except for the part where we were lying in ditches with people shooting at us," Laurie said. He seemed flippant and nonchalant about their ordeal. Good. With the arrest of Jerry Palamara, some of the fear that had gripped him since Nevada appeared to have ebbed away.

"Right, except for that," Nicola said.

"What are your plans now?" Maggie asked her.

Nicola considered. "I'll go back to looking for work, I suppose. Again."

"I'll make some calls. Perhaps I can find you some leads. This is a beast of a time to be unemployed. Laurie, don't you have anything available in your studio for Nicola?"

Laurie shook his head. "Not unless you're a secret whiz with a sewing machine. Sorry. I'd hire you as my new assistant, but I suspect it'd work out poorly for us both."

Nicola smiled and took a drink of her wine. "Not enough money in the world for that, kiddo."

"Laurie Sparks! And Nicola, too. What a nice surprise."

Nicola looked up. Joel Sutton hovered beside their table. He looked business-appropriate in a well-tailored three-piece suit. Another flash of very white teeth. "I thought that was you over here. Sometimes New York seems like the world's smallest city."

He extended a hand to Maggie. "Senator Sparks, Joel Sutton. I don't know if you remember me—"

"Joel, of course. How nice to see you again after all these years. Nicola and Laurie just finished telling me about how their paths have recently crossed with yours." Maggie took Joel's hand and tilted her head up. He leaned down to receive her peck on the cheek. "I'm so sorry to hear about your sister."

"Thank you," he said. He nodded at Nicola. "Nicola called last week to tell me about the new progress in the investigation. Thank you for that," he said to her. "Looks like thus far Caprini has avoided having any of the stink land on him, but having the bastard who pulled the trigger rotting in jail is a step in the right direction."

"No problem. At the very least, it's a good break in the case," Nicola said. She examined Joel carefully. He seemed eminently sane and civilized. Despite Laurie's earlier concerns, it seemed unlikely he was plotting any dark vengeance against Kip Caprini.

"Will you join us?" Maggie asked.

He shook his head. "I'm meeting a client. I just popped over to say hello." He turned to Laurie. "It's fortunate I ran into you, Laurie. I've been mulling over an idea, and I could use your input. What would you think of an exhibit of clothing based on the designs in Joelle's sketch books? I'd fund it, of course, but you'd have a much better idea of how to go about implementing something like this. I thought it'd be a nice tribute to her. Perhaps the proceeds could be donated to a charitable cause." He gave an ironic smile. "Under the circumstances, a drug treatment center might not be an inappropriate choice."

Laurie looked surprised. His brow creased in thought. "That's actually a cool idea," he said. "Her designs in her sketchbooks are really weird, I'm not going to lie, but they're powerful, too. She deserves some recognition for them."

"Fantastic." Joel glanced back in the direction of the bar. "We'll have to discuss this later, but I just wanted to give you something to think about. I'll talk to you soon to see if we can set something up." A nod to Nicola, another handshake with Maggie. "I'll let you all dine in peace. Nicola, Senator, good seeing you again."

Maggie looked after him, her expression strange. When he was out of earshot, she turned to Laurie. "Will you indulge me in listening to a piece of motherly advice?"

"I always do, don't I?" Laurie looked amused.

"Don't work on that project with Joel Sutton. It's best if you give him a wide berth."

Laurie stared at her. "Why not? What's wrong with Joel?"

"Keep your voice down, darling," Maggie said. She took a quick glance around the restaurant. "There's not much to be gained by dredging up old rumors, but please, just humor me."

Nicola frowned. "When we first met Joel, he suggested you had an adversarial relationship with his father," she said.

Maggie smiled. "And you suspect I'm judging the son on the sins of the father? There may be something to that, if I'm honest. But no, that's not what concerns me." She sipped her wine. She appeared to consider how much to tell them, then shook her head.

"There were some . . . difficulties with Joel when he was interning at the Capitol. A rumor reached my office that he'd attacked a young female intern. I made discreet enquiries, but found nothing to substantiate it. Whether that was because the rumor was groundless, or because his father had wielded his considerable influence on his behalf, I couldn't say." She glanced from Laurie to Nicola. "I do not, as a rule, spread gossip. Joel was always nothing but charming to me. The story could be entirely spurious. But you are my child, Laurie, and I love you more than anything in the world, and thus I want you to stay far away from him."

Laurie glanced once at Nicola, his brows raised. He nodded at his mother. "Sure. I mean, I'm busy with my own collection anyway. It's not like I'd even have time to work on anything else right now."

"Good." Maggie relaxed. She smiled. "Enough of that. Now we can devote our attention to trying to think of a new job for our Nicola."

Conversation and the consumption of excellent food resumed normally, and the topic of Joel Sutton's murky past was abandoned.

CHAPTER THIRTY-ONE

IT TOOK FIVE weeks for Cerise Cherry to finish her article about Kip Caprini and Joelle Sutton. Nicola read it online. It was fourteen click-though pages long, it was dry and factual, and it was devastating.

Straightforward journalism, no sensationalism or unwarranted speculation creeping into it anywhere. Cerise ferreted out bits of information and reached well-supported conclusions in such an organized, meticulous way that it made Nicola feel embarrassed by the manner in which she and Laurie had blundered through their own investigation.

The opening: A succinct and factual appraisal of Kip Caprini's pull and prominence in the design world, his success and fame, his talent and influence. A neat segue into Laurie Sparks, rising design star, who'd had reservations about the legitimacy of the fashions Caprini debuted in his 1984 fall runway show.

Another segue: The coat from the *Holmby Hills* wardrobe fell into Laurie's possession, and Laurie believed it to be the work of the same designer responsible for the 1984 collection. Laurie's search for the designer led him to Molly Gable in the *Holmby Hills* wardrobe department, and at this point in the article, Cerise revealed pieces of the puzzle Nicola and Laurie hadn't been able to fit into place on their own.

Cerise talked to police officers, she'd pulled phone and financial records, she'd interviewed everyone she could find with any tie to the investigation. In short, she'd done some damn good journalism.

After Molly had met with Laurie and Nicola, she'd placed a call to Kris Hofferman, the executive producer of *Holmby Hills*, to ask how she could get in touch with Gina Davenport. Hofferman referred her to Gina's agent, Tom Ewes. Ewes refused to speak on the record to Cerise, but his personal assistant had emailed her a copy of the message Molly Gable had left, which Ewes had forwarded to Gina: "I need to talk to you about Joelle in Nevada."

Per Gina Davenport's phone records, upon receipt of this message, Gina called Kip Caprini in New York. Next, she'd called her nephew, Jerry Palamara, a veteran with a history of mental disorders. She'd transferred two thousand dollars into Jerry's checking account, and by the next morning Molly Gable was dead, shot with the rifle later found in Palamara's apartment.

At this point in the article, Cerise delved into the mysteries surrounding Joelle Sutton. The accounting department of *Holmby Hills'* production company gave Cerise copies of generous checks paid to Joelle for what was classified as "miscellaneous wardrobe." Five months before Molly's murder, two weeks after the announcement of the show's cancellation, Gina Davenport had made an initial payment of two thousand dollars to her nephew. A few days after this payment, Joelle Sutton was dead, murdered along with hapless local teen Ricky Sanchez in what was initially assumed to be a drug deal gone wrong.

Cerise didn't speculate as to a motive, though she did reveal that, since 1984, Caprini's company had made a number of mysterious payments to Joelle Sutton. Could've been blackmail, could have been some kind of mutually agreed-upon arrangement that Caprini no longer felt like honoring.

The attack on Laurie and Nicola in Decline was covered in detail. Nicola was described in the article only as Laurie's research assistant, which, while factually accurate, made her feel a little inconsequential.

Caprini and Gina Davenport had not been charged with any crimes at the time of publication. Jerry Palamara had, on the advice of his counsel, refused to comment.

Alina Lowe and Sabina Petrescu went unmentioned. Cerise had unearthed nothing to link Caprini to their murders.

While reading the article on Donya's laptop, Nicola first felt invigorated, then deflated, as though she'd surrendered her role in this adventure to Cerise, or as though her part hadn't been important in the first place.

The day after the article broke, Laurie sat down for an interview on CNN. Nicola sprawled on Donya's plush amethyst sofa and watched him, beautiful and sparkly and charming, as he fielded questions about his role in all this. Her name wasn't mentioned.

She called him after the interview and left a chatty voicemail, asking if he'd be up for meeting for champagne to celebrate. He didn't call her back. A text the following day went unanswered. Ditto for an artfully casual tweet.

Word broke on the gossip blogs that MTV had, as expected, renewed *NYC Elite*. Laurie signed up for another season, with a rumored huge bump in pay.

Good for Laurie. Nobody was trying to kill him now, and he was even more famous than before. And Nicola couldn't help thinking that Donya had been right, and maybe knowing Laurie hadn't been all that good for her.

CHAPTER THIRTY-TWO

IN THE FIRST week of December, Nash called Nicola to ask her for a favor. A very similar favor to the one she'd asked back in August.

"Our boy Laurie Sparks," she said. "He's the man of the hour these days, isn't he? I called his publicist to see about lining up another interview, but she said no dice. He's booked on all the big-name talk shows, and I guess she didn't think my little website was worth his time. So I was wondering, since you two have been pretty tight lately . . ."

"If I'd ask him for you?" Nicola asked.

"Exactly. My thought, if you wanted, was to have you conduct the interview yourself, like the first time you guys met. That'd be cool, right?" Nash sounded gleeful. "Aren't you glad I talked you into meeting him? If you look at it the right way, it sort of seems like you owe me one."

Nicola snorted. "I'm not sure of your logic there." She considered. "All I can do is ask him. No promises. Ever since that article came out, he's sort of been blowing me off."

"Fame went to that pretty little head of his, huh?" Nash said. "Hey, have you given any more thought to Davey's friend Mike?"

"Not a single flickering, fleeting whisper of a thought. Sorry."

"Too bad. You're missing out. Seriously, Nick, it might do you some good to put stinky old Alex in the past forever."

"Already done, trust me. There might even be someone new on the horizon."

"Oh? Do tell."

"Nothing to tell yet. Besides, it'd have to be a long-distance sort of thing, and I don't get out to Nevada any too often. I'm not sure it's worth pursuing."

"Nevada, huh? All right, keep your mysteries." Nash sounded agreeable. "You'll talk to Laurie?"

"I'll call him right now. I repeat, no promises."

She ended the call. Considered for a moment, then dialed Laurie. Again.

Voicemail. At the tone, she said, "Mr. Sparks? This is Nicola Strozyk, from *HyperReality*? I was wondering if you'd be interested in sitting down for an interview with one of the internet's preeminent purveyors of reality-show news and gossip. I'll buy the champagne." She paused, then continued. "Seriously, Laurie, call me, will you? I hate getting blown off."

He returned the call within the hour. "Sorry I missed you. I was in the bathtub. You're really weird sometimes, you know."

"Well aware. The interview request is sincere, though. It's for my friend Nash again. Want to try to recreate the magic of our first meeting?"

Laurie giggled. "Oh, why not? You want to come here?"

"Right now?"

"Sure. It's Saturday, and I'm doing exactly nothing for the entire day. Come on over. Better leave me in charge of picking up the champagne, though. My taste is better than yours." He was quiet for a moment. "Sorry if I've been blowing you off."

"I know you're busy."

"I miss you," he said. "I wish you were still working with me. I've been feeling . . . weird or something. About Cerise's article." He laughed weakly. "I sound really brave in it, and I wasn't. I was so scared the whole time, ever since Nevada, and I just wanted to hide in a hole and stop thinking about what was going on. And I probably would have done exactly that if you hadn't forced me to confront it. So now that everyone's making such a fuss about me, I feel kind of crappy. Like they should be fussing over you instead."

"Don't worry about it. Enjoy your moment. We're cool. I'll see you in about an hour, okay?"

"Awesome." Laurie paused. "You know you're my best friend, right?"

"Thanks, Laurie." She cleared her throat. "It's mutual."

Laurie laughed. "That sounded like it hurt you to say."

It had. A small hot pain burned in her chest, as though her affection for Laurie had concentrated itself into a tight ball of molten lava. It wasn't an unpleasant pain, though, which was good. She suspected it'd be with her for a while.

CHAPTER THIRTY-THREE

MANHATTAN-BOUND TRAINS from Queens could be scarce on the weekends. It took her almost an hour and a half to reach Laurie's building.

Maurice wasn't on duty at the front door. She was greeted by Felipe, a gangly kid who worked weekends to help pay his tuition at Columbia. He grinned at Nicola.

"You just missed him," he said.

Nicola stared at him. "Laurie went out? Really?"

Felipe shrugged. "Yeah, maybe an hour ago."

Oh, Laurie. "He say where he was going?"

"Couldn't tell you. He didn't have a car waiting or nothing, so I don't think he was going far. He was walking toward the park. Getting some exercise, maybe."

Hard to imagine Laurie deciding to take a spontaneous stroll in Central Park. "I've got my key, so I'm just going to go up and wait for him."

"Sure, of course. Maybe he'll be back soon," Felipe said. He looked sympathetic. "Mr. Sparks, he's maybe not the most reliable person ever, you know?"

Nicola did know.

Kind of weird, entering Laurie's dark apartment once more. She sent him a text message: *At your place. Are you going to be gone long?* As soon as she hit the send button, she heard a muted beep from a few yards away. He'd left his phone behind on the coffee table.

She checked the fridge, which was tragically devoid of champagne. Usually he'd just have it sent up, but she'd teased him a lot about his laziness. Maybe he'd gone to the liquor store downstairs. The shop entrance was east of the lobby door, in the direction of the park. Maybe that's where Felipe saw him heading.

Felipe said he'd left an hour ago, but it was possible, just possible, that Laurie could spend an hour deciding upon exactly the right champagne.

Bored with waiting for Laurie, she headed downstairs to see if she could hunt him down. The only customer in the liquor store was an elderly society matron in a yellow lace dress who was purchasing a fifth of Grey Goose. After she'd completed her transaction, Nicola approached the counter.

"Hi. You know Laurie Sparks? Lives in this building?"

The store owner, a heavyset man with a thick beard, nodded. "Sure, of course. Are you picking those up for him?" He gestured toward the far end of the counter, upon which rested two bottles of Perrier-Jouët.

"He was in here today?"

"Maybe an hour ago. Put those on the counter, I had a rush of other customers, and before I could ring him up, he'd left with his friends."

Nicola stared at him. "Who was he with?" she asked.

"Dunno. He came in by himself, they entered a couple minutes later. Obviously knew him, though. Went right up and started talking to him."

So Laurie had met someone he knew and had either forgotten about Nicola, or had blown her off. Huh. Even given his occasional bursts of rampant flakiness, this surprised her.

"Do you remember what they looked like?" she asked.

He shrugged. "I thought the one guy might be his dad or something. Looked the right age, looked rich as hell, had the same blond hair. Then again, who knows what the hell Laurie's hair color really is, am I right? He walked in here as a redhead today, I barely recognized him, except for all the makeup."

Blond hair . . . "What did the other guy look like?"

"Like a thug in a good suit. No, that's mean of me to say, and it's not like he was a big guy. Pretty lean, really. Tall and gaunt. Just kind of scary, you know?" He stopped and stared at her. "Hey, honey, you okay? You look like you're going to be sick."

"Sorry. I'm fine. Thank you." She turned to leave.

"You think he still wants the bubbly, or should I put it back on the shelf?" he called after her. Nicola barely heard him. Her heart hammered in her chest. Joel Sutton and his bodyguard. Glen, that was the bodyguard's name, scary Glen. They'd just happened to run into Laurie here, and Laurie had walked out with them, and now she couldn't find him.

Nothing to freak out about, surely. He'd only been gone an hour. Maybe Joel wanted to discuss Joelle's designs with him, maybe they stopped for a quick drink somewhere and Laurie had lost track of time. So why was she feeling this sudden wave of panic?

Maggie Sparks had explicitly asked Laurie to stay away from Joel. Laurie had ignored her warning, a warning fueled by hazy rumors. Something about violence against an intern . . .

Oh, she was stupid. She and Laurie both, they were idiots, or they'd been too convinced, based on the flimsiest of evidence, that Kip Caprini had killed those two poor models, Joelle Sutton's lovers. Sad, tragic Joelle Sutton, who'd left New York in 1984 and had gone into hiding. She'd let Kip Caprini know where she'd been—the payments his company had made to her in the years since then proved that—but she'd broken off all contact with her twin brother.

And Joel had been openly fascinated by Laurie, and he'd coincidentally shown up during their lunch at the Cook Club, and now here at the liquor store . . .

Too many coincidences. Oh, she was stupid.

She could call Joel, ask if he'd seen Laurie. No. That would tip him off that she was on to him. She'd show up at his apartment, and she'd talk her way in, and if there was any sign of trouble, any at all, she'd call the police immediately.

Upper West Side to Upper East Side. Ordinarily she'd go on foot, cutting through the park, but the shortest distance between two points was never through Central Park, and time was of the essence. She hailed a taxi.

"Park and 70th, please," she told the driver. "Please hurry."

She was thwarted by the doorman at Joel's building. "He's not even here, lady, Mrs. Sutton and the girls have the place this weekend. He's at their other home."

She stared at him. "He was just on the Upper West Side an hour ago," she said.

He shrugged. "Don't know about that, I just know he's not here now. If Mrs. Sutton's here, Mr. Sutton sure as hell isn't. That's the way they work. You want to talk to Mrs. Sutton?"

Did she? Lightning-fast consideration. "Please. My name's Nicola Strozyk. Tell her . . ." She thought. "Just tell her it's about her husband."

He gave her a strange look at that, like he suspected her of being Joel Sutton's scorned mistress or something, but he picked up the phone and dialed up to the Sutton apartment without comment.

"Mrs. Sutton, there's a lady here, Nicole Strodgit, wants to talk to you? Says it's about your husband?"

Nicola couldn't hear the reply. The doorman continued. "She looks okay. Not crazy or nothing. You want me to send her up?"

An agonizing pause, then he turned to her. "She says go ahead. You know where it is? Penthouse, right?"

"I know. Thank you."

A uniformed maid met her at the door and wordlessly ushered her into that aggressively masculine living room where she and Laurie had once sipped Scotch with Joel. Mrs. Sutton sat on the couch, her legs drawn up beneath her. She wore a camel-colored cowl-necked sweater and matching wool trousers. She was tiny and blonde. Very pretty. Fragile, and so thin she almost looked ill. Surprisingly young. Late twenties, probably. She looked up at Nicola. "I'm Natalie Sutton. I understand you know my husband?"

"My name's Nicola Strozyk. I'm a friend of Laurie Sparks. I don't know if your husband has mentioned Laurie . . ."

Natalie Sutton nodded. It was timid. "You mean that business with Joel's poor sister. I read about it in the paper."

"He didn't talk about it with you?"

"We don't talk much." A nervous confession. "My husband and I haven't been close lately."

"I'm sorry," Nicola said. She hesitated. "May I sit down?"

"I suppose." Natalie looked flustered, and frightened. She was picking up on Nicola's own anxiety and fear, probably. "Would you care for tea? Coffee?"

"No, thank you. I'll try not to take up much of your time." She perched on the edge of the oxblood armchair where Joel had sat while entertaining her and Laurie. It was like sitting on a throne made of raw meat. "Have you and Joel been married long?"

"Seven years," Natalie said.

"And you have children?"

A reflexive smile. "Two girls. Six and four. They're at the park with their nanny."

Nicola was stalling, feeling her way around the conversation, trying to figure out what to ask. Laurie wasn't here, that was obvious. "Has Joel been married before?" she asked.

It was an impertinent question, but Natalie didn't seem to take offense. She nodded. "I'm his fourth wife," she said. It came out almost as a whisper.

There was no way to ask, but Nicola thought she probably could guess. All of Joel's wives would be young and blonde and tiny. All of them would resemble Joelle. And all of the marriages would've ended badly.

Natalie stared at her. She looked ashen and unwell. She still hadn't asked for the purpose of Nicola's visit. Probably knew it was nothing good.

"The doorman told me your husband is at your other home right now?" Nicola asked.

"Yes. We live in Greenwich. The girls go to school there," Natalie said. "He said he needed to do some work in privacy this weekend, so he sent us here until Monday."

"Your husband was on the Upper West Side about an hour ago. His bodyguard Glen was with him. They were with Laurie Sparks." Nicola stared at Natalie. "I'm trying to find Laurie. It's very, very important I find him soon."

Natalie swallowed. She shook her head. "I don't know anything about that," she said.

Hard to pick the right words, hard to convey what she needed Natalie to know without saying too much and spooking her into silence. "I think Laurie's in trouble. Please help me find him."

Natalie stared at her. An eternity passed. She trembled all over. She crossed her arms in front of her body and clutched her stomach, protecting herself from unseen blows. She nodded.

"What can I do?" she asked. Her voice was almost a whisper.

"Give me the address of your place in Greenwich. Please."

"It's the Sutton Manor. On Pemberwick. It's Joel's childhood home." Natalie picked up a pen from the end table, looked around for something to write on. Nicola fished her notepad out of her bag and passed it to her. Natalie scrawled down the address. Her hand shook so much her writing was almost illegible.

"Thank you," Nicola said. "Thank you very much."

Natalie didn't say anything. She stayed as she was on the sofa as Nicola left, staring at nothing in particular, curled in around herself like a wounded animal.

236

CHAPTER THIRTY-FOUR

SAFE OUTSIDE ON the sidewalk, the cold December air calmed Nicola a little. She'd felt overheated to the point of near-panic inside the Sutton penthouse. Now, she was still keyed up and jittery, but she could focus.

Greenwich. That meant the brusque Detective Tally. It was a Saturday, and the odds of Tally being on duty were low.

She called. A bored-sounding male officer answered. "Greenwich Police Department. Detective Division."

She froze, unsure where to start. The officer on the line sounded impatient. "Hello? Anyone there?"

"Sorry. I'm trying to reach Detective Tally. Or any detective really, only she already knows what this is about, I've talked to her before and it's a terrible emergency, so it's really best if—"

"Just hang on." The officer sounded amused at her agitation, which was infuriating. She was put on hold for maybe ten seconds, then a curt female voice came on the line. "Tally."

"It's you. Thank God. Sorry. I didn't think you'd be at work today. This is Nicola Strozyk, we talked before about Sabina Petrescu—"

"Yep. What's up?"

"It's Joel Sutton, Joelle Sutton's twin brother, he's the one who killed those two women, and he's got Laurie Sparks right now, I think Joel Sutton grabbed him and took him to his home in Greenwich."

"Back up. Hold on. Do you think Joel Sutton killed the women, or do you know it?"

"I'm pretty sure, but I don't have proof. Right now it doesn't matter. He's got Laurie, we need to worry about Laurie right now. I can give you his home address, if you can check it out."

"I know where the Suttons live." Something dark and ironic in Tally's voice came through the phone line. "Believe me, we all know where the Suttons live. I can knock on his door right now, but if there's no obvious sign of anything amiss, that's not going to do any damn good. Can't search his place without a warrant, you know. I can get one, and I will if there's reason to think the Sparks kid is being held there against his will, but you've got to give me something."

Nicola thought fast. "The guy working the counter at Estate Liquor on West 75th in Manhattan, he saw Laurie with Joel Sutton a couple of hours ago. Have someone show him a photo of Joel, he can identify him for you. He might even have surveillance video from inside the store. And Joel's wife just told me he's at the Greenwich home, that he specifically told her he wanted privacy there this weekend." Her words fell over each other, her tongue unable to keep up with her thoughts.

"Deep breaths, Strozyk." Silence on the line, maddening under the circumstances. "I'm on it. Sit tight. You can call the front desk for updates."

"Please hurry. If he's got Laurie, he's probably going to kill him."

"I said I'm on it." The line disconnected abruptly.

Nicola gripped her phone so tightly her palm hurt. It was in Tally's hands now, nothing more she could do. Especially here in Manhattan.

The train ran to Greenwich on a frequent schedule, and it was a fast trip. Even on a Saturday, she probably wouldn't have a long wait.

No. She needed something faster. If she only had a car. If she were in Los Angeles, she could fly down the freeway, be there in no time.

Different city, different rules. She stepped to the curb, raised a hand, hailed a cab.

"I need to go to Greenwich. I mean Connecticut, not Greenwich Village," she told the driver. Middle-aged, female, Indian.

The cabbie nodded, eyes on the road. "You want Metro North. Grand Central or Penn Station. I take you there, you catch a very fast train."

"No, I need you to go all the way to Greenwich. Please," Nicola said.

The cabbie turned around to stare at her. She had dark hair cut very short and wore glasses with huge red plastic frames. Like Sally Jesse Raphael, back in the day. She frowned. "That is a very long trip, for a taxi. You take a train, it is very short."

"I know. It doesn't matter. I need to get there as fast as possible."

"This is very expensive for you, you see, and no good for me. At the end of the trip, I am in Greenwich. I cannot pick up fares in Greenwich."

"I'll double whatever's on the meter, I promise. Here, you can hold my credit card right now to make sure I don't skip out on the fare. You can hold my entire purse."

The cabbie shook her head. "No, no." Nicola had a panicky moment when she thought the woman was refusing to take her before she realized she was refusing payment up front. "I take you, it is fine, I take you. It is a waste of your money, though. The train here, it is very good."

"Thank you. I need to hurry. Please take the fastest way possible."

The ride took too long. They took the I-95, and traffic moved briskly on a lazy Saturday, but even so, Nicola had to resist the urge to tell the cabbie to break the speed limit. Getting a ticket wouldn't help matters.

Was she overreacting? Laurie could be flaky, that was undeniable. Could he have gone somewhere with Joel on his own volition and simply forgotten about his plans with her?

No. She was right, she knew it. Joel showing up at the liquor store was too big a coincidence. Joel had swooped out of nowhere and grabbed Laurie, and now he was gone.

She leaned forward and spoke through the sliding window separating her from the front seat. "Do you know Greenwich? I'm looking for a place on Pemberwick Road."

The cabbie nodded. "Sure, sure, yes. I have been here before, many times. Businessmen and businesswomen, they are impatient like you, they do not want to wait for trains." Her eyes, dark and worried, met Nicola's in the rearview mirror. "Everything is okay? You do not look well."

"Everything's fine," Nicola said. "Please, can you go a little bit faster?"

Another glance in the mirror. The cabbie nodded once and edged up the speed.

Forty-five minutes, and the taxi pulled to a stop outside the Sutton home. It was situated up on a grassy hill, separated from the road by a stonework fence. The manor was designed in the Queen Anne style and looked like a birthday cake, pale blue trimmed with white around the windows and turrets.

A black iron gate prevented access to the driveway. There was a little stone guard booth beside it, and that wasn't good news.

"Here we are," the cabbie said. "This is what you wanted, yes?"

"Yes. Thank you very much," Nicola said. She paid with her credit card, doubling the meter fare as promised.

"You want, I can wait here to take you back to the city, if you do not think you will be long," the driver said.

"No. Thank you. I'll take it from here."

The cabbie wanted to stay, was worried for her, and Nicola couldn't bear the weight of her concern any longer. She slid out of the backseat, closed the door, watched as the cab drove off.

Well, then. Here she was, by herself. She could see a dark blue BMW parked at the top of the circular drive by the entrance to the manor. Someone was home.

The guard booth was empty, but there was a surveillance camera on top of the stone fence where it joined the gate. This was crazy. There was too much security here to even think about breaking in.

No. There was no one at the gate, and that was significant. If Joel Sutton had taken Laurie here against his will, he wouldn't want anyone else around. Glen, maybe, but that'd be it. The camera would be unmonitored, surely. Maybe.

Nicola wandered along the perimeter of the fence. Not much traffic on the road. A few cars were parked on the street, but no one was in sight. Good. That meant there was no one to see her doing this. She grabbed hold of the ivy, the toes of her loafers digging into gaps between the stones, and pulled herself up the wall.

It was only about eight feet high, and this was easy. She had good upper-arm strength, always had. She was up, she was over, and she was in the front yard of the Sutton house.

She landed on loose bark in a small fruit orchard. It hadn't snowed yet this year, but the ground was frozen and cold, and the trees were bare and spindly. They didn't offer much protection. If anyone in the house looked outside right now, she might be in trouble.

Now she had to get closer to the house. Her plan from there wasn't clear. She'd get inside, if she could, or maybe she'd just peek through windows looking for any sign of Laurie. If she saw anything, she'd call Tally.

She stared at the house. The sunlight glinted off the leaded-glass windows in front. One of the diamond panes had a fist-sized hole through it. Huh.

A dull rustle behind her, the tread of heavy feet on bark.

She turned around. There was a blur of movement, and before her brain could process what she was seeing, her vision exploded into a supernova of brilliant red stars.

CHAPTER THIRTY-FIVE

SHE WAS DROPPED onto a parquet floor like useless baggage. The impact was enough to jolt her out of what had been something short of unconsciousness. More of a state of incomprehension, really. She'd been bonked on the head in the orchard, then dragged across the lawn, strong hands gripping her under her armpits. At some point, she'd been hoisted over someone's shoulder, then roughly deposited here.

Her head swam. She sat up. Everything shifted for a while, and then her vision settled. She was in the Sutton living room, Queen Anne furniture to match the Queen Anne exterior. Chairs with graceful curving legs and backs, seats upholstered in richly patterned fabrics, English landscape paintings hung high on the blue-and-ivory striped wallpaper.

Laurie sat in one of the chairs, and he looked terrified. His makeup was smeared, his satin shirt was torn, and there were purple bruises on his pale throat. A series of red burns on the back of his left hand, something blue knotted around his right wrist. A Yale necktie, of all the damn things. Alex had one, which he always refused to wear in public. This one must be Joel's.

Because of course Joel was there as well, in all his middle-aged preppie glory, polo shirt and khaki pants and tasseled loafers. He sat across from Laurie, his Scotch resting on the end table at his elbow, a lit cigar dangling between his thumb and forefinger. Glen stood just behind his chair, his face impassive. Glen held a gun at his side, something small and squat. Probably what he'd bonked her over the head with earlier. She should probably be glad he hadn't just shot her on sight.

She stood up, slowly. Ground swayed a little. No one moved.

Joel smiled at her. "Nicola, I'm sure there's a very interesting story as to how you ended up here." He gestured at the couch. "Why don't you take a seat?"

Her knees didn't feel like they could support her weight right now. She sat. "Hey, Laurie, you okay?"

"I'm fine," he said. His voice shook.

"The Greenwich police know we're here, kiddo. They know everything. I'm going to get you out of here."

"Seems unlikely." Joel settled back in his chair. He seemed nonchalant and vaguely bored. "The Sutton name is an old one in Greenwich. You'll find it on a high school, on a park, on a library. The police here would be very, very reluctant to so much as knock on my door without firm evidence of wrongdoing."

"How'd the window get broken?" she asked.

"I chucked an ashtray through it," Laurie said. The defiance in his voice almost made her smile.

"Good boy," she said.

"Stupid boy," Joel said. "I had Glen break his wrist for that."

Nicola ignored him. Focused her attention on Laurie. "They grabbed you in the liquor store?"

"Yeah," Laurie said. He threw a scared glance over at Glen. "He showed me the gun."

"The store owner identified them. There's surveillance camera footage." It could even be true. "They're going to get caught for this."

She swallowed hard. Felt shaky, and her head hurt so much it was hard to focus, but she was doing okay. She looked over at Joel. "Grabbing Laurie was a huge blunder, you know. Enormous. I'm surprised you took that kind of risk. He's a public figure. You can't just make him disappear without people kicking up a fuss."

"Why not? I've done it before." Joel's eyes glittered.

"Oh, I know. Sabina Petrescu and Alina Lowe. Why'd you kill them? Jealousy?"

"I killed them because they were whores," he said. Very calm. "Because they lured Joelle into unnatural acts. So I taught them what a man could do."

"How lovely," she said. "And what's your excuse for grabbing Laurie?"

Joel shrugged. That air of bonhomie, that eerie nonchalance. "Does it matter? He's *unnatural.* Let's say I was curious to discover whether he was a boy or a girl and leave it at that."

Jesus. Nicola took a deep breath. "Unnatural. As opposed to the healthy inter-sibling relationship you had with Joelle, right?" Keeping her voice light, keeping the conversation blithe, trying not to let any of the crazy tension building up inside creep out. "She knew it was you, didn't she? Maybe not when Alina was killed, but by the time Sabina's body washed up, she knew. And she fled all the way across the country to get far away from you."

Joel's face darkened. "Joelle loved me," he said. "She made mistakes, but she and I, we were perfect together. So whole and beautiful."

Nicola nodded slowly. "I'm taking Laurie out of here now," she said. "All the police have on you on thus far is kidnapping, and if you've got as much pull in this town as you seem to think, I'm sure your lawyers can get you out of that one. Sabina and Alina, that was all long ago, and it's going to be an uphill battle to prove anything at this point. You might win that fight in court. If Laurie and I disappear, though, you're screwed."

She stood up. Joel didn't move.

"Shoot her," Joel told Glen. So calm. Glen raised his gun.

An explosion of deafening noise. Two gunshots, a muzzle flash, the sound of breaking glass. Nicola was across the room before she'd realized she'd moved. She yanked Laurie out of the chair and pulled him with her behind the couch.

There followed a moment of stillness, which gave Nicola's brain enough time to catch up to the action. The first gunshot had come from the hallway. The bullet struck Glen in the forehead. He'd fired once, wildly, and it'd hit the window.

Laurie whimpered. Nicola wrapped her arms around him and pressed him to the ground, sheltered between the back of the sofa and the wall. She lifted her head, very carefully, and looked around the edge of the couch.

Detective Tally, a vision in a gray pantsuit and sensible shoes, stood in the entrance to the living room, gun pointed. "Nobody move. This is the Greenwich Police Department. Joel Sutton, get your hands in the air."

Nicola froze. Laurie clutched her, fingers digging into her arms so hard it hurt. She clutched him back every bit as tightly. From their position behind the couch, she couldn't see Joel, but Tally seemed to have the situation well in hand.

"On your knees. Hands behind your head." A series of thunks, a click of handcuffs. Nicola and Laurie still didn't move.

"Strozyk?" That was Tally. "How you doing there?"

It took Nicola too long to answer. "I think we're okay."

"Sit tight for a second. Is there anyone else in the house?"

Laurie had his face buried in her chest. Nicola gave him a gentle shake "Laurie, listen, is there anyone else in the house?"

He shook his head. "No. Just them," he said, his voice muffled against her sweatshirt.

"Stay where you are, you two. I'm going to check it out," Tally said.

Nicola remained in place, still clutching Laurie. He started crying, which naturally meant she started crying, too, and all she could do was cling to him, sobbing, until a cluster of uniformed police officers arrived, until Joel was taken away in a squad car, until a pair of very kind, gentle paramedics crouched beside them and coaxed her into letting go of him at last.

CHAPTER THIRTY-SIX

JONATHAN SAT ON the bench outside Laurie's room, head resting in his hands. Nicola knew he looked familiar, but in this strange context it took her too long to figure out who he was. He looked up and addressed her by name, and she stared at him blankly before putting it together.

"How are you?" he asked. "The nurse at the front desk said you'd been discharged."

She touched the gauze patch on the back of her head. They'd shaved off a small circle of hair around the cut on her scalp where Glen had whacked her with the gun, which probably looked wonderful. Didn't feel great, either.

"Yeah. I'm okay. Concussion, but just a little one."

"How's Laurie?" Jonathan asked. He looked sick with worry. Purple marks under his eyes beneath his glasses, face drawn and gray. Still beautiful, even in his misery.

"I haven't seen him since we were admitted. His doctor assured me he's fine." She'd tried to see him last night, tried to creep into his room, and had been escorted firmly but politely back to her own room. "How'd you hear about this? It hasn't made the news yet, has it?"

Jonathan shook his head. "His mom called me. We drove up together. She's in there with him now. I told her not to tell him I'm here."

"You're not going to see him?"

"Not yet. Not now." Jonathan exhaled. "I want to. More than anything in the world, I want to go in there and kiss him and tell him everything's going to be okay. But . . ." He looked weary, sick, dead on his feet. "Not under these circumstances. When he's ready to see me, he will."

The door to Laurie's room opened, and Maggie Sparks stepped out. She pulled the door closed behind her, then crossed over to Jonathan and hugged him. Jonathan murmured something into her hair that Nicola couldn't hear. Upon releasing him, Maggie pulled Nicola into her arms and patted her on the back, like she was burping a baby. "Dear girl," she said.

"How is he?" Nicola asked.

"He'll be fine." There was something terrible and cold in her expression. "If Joel Sutton wasn't in police custody right now, I believe I'd kill him myself."

Nicola nodded. "I know." She let out a deep shuddery breath. "Me, too."

Maggie motioned to the door. "He'll want to see you, Nicola." She shook her head. "I need to thank you properly, and I will, but right now . . ."

She didn't seem able to finish the sentiment. Nicola patted her on the arm and went into the room.

Laurie looked small against the pillows. No makeup, so she could see the bruises plainly on his face and neck. Gauze-wrapped burns on his hand from Joel's cigar, a fiberglass cast on his broken wrist replacing Joel's makeshift Yale-tie brace.

He smiled at her. "Hey," he said.

"Hey, yourself." She sat down on the edge of his bed. "I tried to sneak in to see you last night, and they booted me out."

"Too bad," Laurie said. "I was bored to death with bad television. I could have used the company."

She cleared her throat. "The doctor didn't give me much information about your condition," she said.

"I'm okay." His mouth was a grim twist. "I wasn't raped or anything, you know. He didn't get around to it. He had Glen rough me up when I broke the window, and he burned my hand. The broken wrist is the worst of it."

"Ah." Lump in her throat. "I guess that's one good thing."

"If the doctor gives the okay, I'm checking out this morning. I'm going to spend some time with my mom at the house in Philadelphia."

"That sounds like a good idea," she said.

"Thank you for saving my life," he said. It came out as kind of a gasp. "Thank you so much."

She shook her head. "I didn't do much other than get whacked over the head. Detective Tally did all the important stuff. You talk to her yet?"

Laurie nodded. "Last night. She scares me," he said.

"Yeah, she's good at that. She bawled me out pretty thoroughly for interfering with her investigation." Nicola smiled. "She was staking out the Sutton place before I even got there, just waiting on a search warrant. When she saw me go over the fence, she followed me in. She told me she figured arresting me for trespassing was as good an excuse as any to get into the house. So I guess I did probably help you a little, but it was mostly by accident."

"It's awful to say, but I was glad you were there. Even if they were just going to kill us both, I didn't want to die alone." His face scrunched up, and the last word came out as a sob.

She leaned over and pressed her lips against his forehead. "I'm glad I was there, too."

CHAPTER THIRTY-SEVEN

"SO WHAT DOES it mean, going into business with Laurie?" Donya asked.

"I haven't the foggiest idea," Nicola said. She looked around the living room for her messenger bag, then finally found it dangling off the back of a chair. "I imagine Laurie doesn't, either. He said something hazy about me handling the uncreative side of his company, which probably involves taking care of anything he doesn't feel like doing. Doesn't really matter. It just seems like a good idea."

"Uh-huh. Whatever makes you happy, I guess." Donya observed her. "So what did your sexy sheriff have to say? That was him on the phone, right?"

"That was him. Just wanted to let me know his contact in the LAPD told him Gina Davenport cracked. She's agreed to testify against Caprini in exchange for immunity. They'll be arresting him soon, if they haven't done it already."

"Good news. Hey, is Laurie doing okay?" Donya asked. "Now that the news has gotten hold of the story, he's going to have people pestering him about it all the time. That's got to be rough."

"He's tougher than he seems. He'll get through this. And in any case, I'll be there to protect him."

"You'll probably end up doing a lot of that," Donya said. She looked very old and very wise.

Nicola shrugged. "He's worth it."

LAURIE WANTED TO meet in his studio. He'd spent most of his time there since returning from his recuperative stay at his mother's home. Throwing himself into his work, devoting all his energy to his new collection. Probably the best possible thing for him.

"Try this on. I want to see how the lapel falls," he said. He handed her a coat. Long and belted, distressed gold suede. The interior was bright copper silk.

Nicola pulled off her sweatshirt, slipped the coat on, tied the belt. It fit like it was made for her. Come to think of it, it probably was.

Laurie fussed with the collar, which was constructed of short strips of gold metal arranged in an overlapping manner to look like tiny pleats. "Perfect," he said.

"You mentioned in your text that you're quitting the show," she said.

"Uh-huh. My management informed the producers this morning of my intention to break my contract," he said. He tugged at the back of the collar, flipping it up.

"How'd they take it?"

"They're threatening to sue me." He smiled wryly. "They won't. They're panicking a bit because they know another season with me would get huge ratings, but they'll come around. They know forcing me to stay on the show after everything's that happened would reflect very, very poorly on them."

Sun streamed through the windows behind him, giving him a white-bright aura. He looked like some kind of supernatural creature. A seraph, maybe, clad in a white velvet jacket with a huge feathered collar that framed his face. Matching white feathers at the cuffs, huge gold buttons down the front. Pink and gold eye shadow, rose-tinted lips, flawlessly-applied makeup covering the bruises. He looked grim and lovely.

"Yeah. That wouldn't look too good for them," Nicola said.

"And if they do sue me, I don't really care. I just want to be done with it."

"I'm with you one hundred percent, kiddo."

He stepped back and looked at her. "I'm going to get sappy now, probably because the painkillers I just took for my wrist are starting to kick in, but I love you, you know."

"I know. Same here."

He smiled then. "Hold your arms out to the side. I'm not happy with those sleeves."

Nicola lifted her arms, the belled sleeves of the coat dangling from her wrists. Laurie bent to his work, tugging and measuring and pinning, engaged in quiet industry. And all was well.

ACKNOWLEDGMENTS

First and foremost, *Bias Cut* would not have been possible without the constant support of my sister, Ingrid Richter. My sincere thanks also go to Morgan Dodge for his graphic design magic and artistic prowess, to Dan Liebke for his gonzo ideas and boundless knowledge, to Jason Gilman, Jenny Elliott and Jennifer Howell for advice and encouragement, to Cheryl Kraynak for the last-minute edits, and to Heather Stewart for always bringing a good wine.